IAN
BAKER'S
.45

IAN BAKER'S .45

Israel Allen

NEW PULP PRESS

Published by New Pulp Press, LLC, 926 Truman Avenue, Key West, Florida 33040, USA.

Ian Baker's .45 copyright © 2016 by Israel Allen. Electronic compilation/ paperback edition copyright © 2016 by New Pulp Press, LLC.

For information contact:
Publisher@NewPulpPress.com

Printed in the United States of America
Visit us on the web at www.newpulppress.com

ISBN-13: 978-0692660713 (New Pulp Press)
ISBN-10: 0692660712

For Jeff

CHAPTER 1

D r. William Baker's office intimidated students, other professors, and even the administration. Most of the faculty at Samuels University had state-issued furniture – false wood veneer on beige, sheet metal desks; pleather desk chairs for the professor; and one or two plastic, stackable chairs for visiting students. William's replica of the Resolute desk – complete with the university seal where the US president's would be – had been commissioned by his late mother when he took the position. After William earned tenure, his late father had replaced the state-issued seating with high-backed leather chairs – one with wheels for William and two without for students. Mrs. Baker had been a high school English teacher, and Mr. Baker had served twenty years in the Army before a second career as a locksmith. The furniture was more than they could really afford, and it clashed with William's workmanlike persona. He couldn't insult his parents by refusing the gifts, though, and he honored their memory by making the most of them each day.

He sat at his desk grading a paper from one of his American literature sections. The student who wrote the essay had no such honor for his parents' investment, William thought. He turned the pages with his left hand and made notes with the pen in his right. In spite of the use of several online essays as sources, some cited but most plagiarized, junior business major Matthew Gibbard was under the impression Edgar Allan Poe had written the short story "A&P." The paper even included a paragraph entirely devoted to speculation that the title grocery

1

store had been named for this author. To mistake an author that way was unforgivable in any class, but William had talked at length about Poe in the first weeks of the course. His doctoral dissertation had examined Poe's influence on twentieth century American perceptions of violence. He knew just about everything there was to know about Poe, and he dumped a great deal of that information on his students. In his second year as a professor, an obsequious student had presented him with a framed poster illustrating Poe's "The Raven." William liked the poster, but the blatant brown-nosing rubbed him the wrong way. He hung the poster, but he also cut out a picture of Baltimore linebacker Ray Lewis and taped it to the bottom, drawing a speech bubble around the final "Nevermore." Other posters followed, usually for novels or plays he taught, and he hung them too.

William drew an X over the offending paragraph. He couldn't muster the patience to elaborate. He required students to come during office hours at least twice during the semester, and he would grade a paper in front of the student, pausing to discuss errors of fact, logic, or grammar as he read. After fourteen years, he no longer had any faith that students would read the comments on their papers, especially when the essays were graded online. The university administration and the better students appreciated the extra one-on-one instruction. The worst students hated him for it. Gibbard had missed his original appointment and was now late for this one, so the grading was started without him.

William didn't look up when he heard a knock at the door. He expected to hear, "I'm sorry, Dr. Baker, but..." followed by a long and ill-conceived excuse, and he didn't want to listen to it. He wanted to finish grading the paper and never think of it again. If he tried to divide his attention, he would end up having to read at least some of the paper again, and it didn't contain a single sentence worthy of the first read, much less a second – not even in the plagiarized sections.

"Hey, Billy, how ya doin'?"

William stopped reading, but he didn't look up. He didn't need to. He knew that voice. There was a thick Southern drawl, even though the man speaking didn't move to the South until he was twelve years old. William had worked hard to drop his Southern accent. His older brother had made a point of developing one. William put the paper down and capped his pen, laying it on the paper. He took a deep breath and let it out slowly. Then he looked up.

"Jimmy, what are you doing here?"

"Four years, and I don't even get a hello? That's cold, little brother." Jimmy shivered and pulled his arms into his Hawaiian-style, jungle-print shirt.

"It's been four years for a reason. What do you want?"

Jimmy pulled his arms out and stepped through the doorway. He pulled back one of the chairs in front of William's desk – the chair Matthew Gibbard was supposed to be occupying – and sat down. "I need to talk to you about something," Jimmy said.

"You should have called."

"I was pretty sure you wouldn't answer."

"If I'd known it was you, I wouldn't have."

"That's why I'm here."

"You couldn't just leave a voicemail?"

"This ain't a voicemail kind of issue."

"If you're looking for money – "

"I know better than to ask you."

"That's right."

"I don't need money," Jimmy said. He leaned forward and pulled up his pants leg. He wore faded jeans and military surplus combat boots. He pulled a roll of cash from his left boot and waved it in front of William to illustrate his point. He returned the money, dropped his pant leg over the boot, and sat back.

William shook his head. Jimmy with a roll of cash usually meant someone had been robbed. William hated what his brother did, in part because it was illegal and immoral, but mostly because Jimmy was so often caught. It was embarrassing. It reflected poorly on their parents. Ian Baker had raised them to do honest work and to do it well. If Jimmy insisted on being a criminal, the least he could do was be good at it. William didn't like talking about his brother, but he found himself doing it all too often.

"What does your brother do?" a friend or colleague would ask.

"Time."

"What?"

"He's in prison."

"What did he do?" They always asked the question in a tone that made William feel like the expected answer was murder. Always murder.

"Breaking and entering," he would say.

William had learned not to use the word "thief" in these conversations. It gave people the wrong idea. Film and television had given the average person a specific image of the career thief: a man clad in black, using small tools to pick a lock, cut a hole in a window, or disable a security system. The thief slips in quietly and places small, valuable items in a soft, black bag or a stainless steel briefcase. The thief then disappears into the night with silent stealth.

Jimmy Baker was not a thief. William was pretty sure he had never executed a skillful heist, made a big score, or deceived a wily investigator. Jimmy Baker was a B&E conviction waiting to happen. He picked a home on the outskirts of a town, somewhere with as few neighbors as possible – no one who might see him and call the police. He arrived mid-morning when people are most likely to be at work, dressed in the uniform of his chosen profession: combat boots, jeans, a busy shirt, and an ostentatious hat. "Folks remember the outfit, not the face," Jimmy had said. William was never there for any of this, but he had heard the details more times than he could remember.

Jimmy made sure there were no vehicles before parking his own car in the driveway, his license plate covered with mud. He opened his trunk and walked to the front door. He rang the doorbell or knocked, waited, and knocked again. If someone answered, he asked for directions and left. If not, he looked around to make sure no one was passing by before he kicked in the door. Combat boots are perfect for this, Jimmy said. If the door didn't break down, though, he smashed a window with a flowerpot or a loose brick or whatever was to hand. Inside, he grabbed DVD players, game systems, flat screen TVs – any easily carried electronics – or jewelry, if it was available. These items went into the trunk in two or three trips – never more – and he was back on the road, scouting for the next house.

So far as William could tell, Jimmy was reasonably good at this part of the operation. He had never been caught in the act or shot by an angry homeowner. He was usually caught because someone saw something – a kid in a passing car, a retiree walking a dog – and called the police. They took a description of the car, radioed that to every officer, and Jimmy got pulled over with the stolen goods. Case closed. Sometimes, the problem came at the pawnshops where the stolen goods were sold. They kept records and used security cameras. Fake IDs put a layer of protection between Jimmy and the police, but it wasn't always enough. Jimmy might get away with the robberies for a few months at a time, even a few years at one point, but eventually someone saw him or matched a serial number, and then Jimmy went back to prison.

People often asked William why he hadn't turned out like his brother. He would look at the floor and shrug, wait a beat, then look the person in the eye. "I guess I always had goals, something to keep me focused." This was true, but it wasn't really an answer. He wondered if anyone ever suspected that he was thinking, "I don't get caught."

In the office that afternoon, William looked carefully at his brother's hair, thinning and blond-becoming-white. He could make out the line of a wide hatband. He pictured a top hat, a bowler, and a sombrero on Jimmy's head during a series of smash-and-grabs. The hats would have already been ditched, maybe even burned. William wondered where Jimmy got the hats, but he didn't ask. It was better he didn't know.

The brothers didn't look much alike. They could easily convince strangers they weren't related, and they sometimes had. Jimmy was built like a Greco-Roman wrestler – medium height and thick through the arms, shoulders, and chest. He had always been more of a grappler than a boxer, and his sleeper hold had been the stuff of legend at Osgood High. He had their mother's aquiline nose, blue eyes, fair hair, and pale complexion. William favored their father, lean and wiry, with dark hair, dark eyes, dark skin, and the rounded nose and chin of his Choctaw great-grandmother.

"How long have you been out, Jimmy?"

"Six months." This was a pretty good run for Jimmy.

"When are you going back?"

"Never."

William had given Jimmy the same speech about theft countless times. To make it a career, one must be perfect. One must never get caught. Any average below 1000 is unacceptable. He couldn't muster the energy for the full speech, so he just gave Jimmy the summary.

"Stealing ain't baseball."

"Fuck you, Billy."

"Stop calling me Billy. It's been William for twenty years."

Jimmy shrugged his shoulders. "What's the difference?"

William jerked his thumb toward the degrees on the wall behind him – a B.A. from Johns Hopkins with a double major of history and English and the M. A. and Ph.D. in English from Vanderbilt. "William Baker is an English professor. Billy Baker sounds like a kid who cooks snack cakes with a light bulb."

"All right, William," Jimmy said, throwing up his hands in a gesture of surrender. "I ain't trying to make you Little Debbie's bitch."

"What are you trying to do, Jimmy? Why are you here?"

Jimmy dropped his hands and leaned forward, looking William in the eye. "It's about Dad."

"What about him?"

"I found his gun."

"Where?"

"Pawn shop."

"You're sure it was his? They're not exactly rare."

"It was his. Somebody tried to file off the initials, but they're still there. And your scratches."

Billy had fired the gun for the first time when he was only seven. His father wanted to teach him gun safety, and he did, but the first shot didn't go well. The recoil so frightened Billy, he let the kick take the gun over his head and flung it behind himself with all his might. The gun ended up in Ian's pick-up bed, wedged between a steel tool case and the fender well. For punishment, Ian broke down the weapon and made Billy polish it for hours. Nothing could get out the two deep grooves cut by the corner of the tool case, one on the handle and one on the side of the hammer.

"Where did they get it? What did they say?"

"They didn't say anything," Jimmy said. "I had them get it out so I could get a good look and be sure, but when I asked where it came from, the guy just made a face. They know who I am. So I'm asking you."

"Asking me what?"

"Did you sell Dad's gun?"

"You know I didn't. I couldn't find it. I sent you a letter."

Jimmy nodded. "One letter in four years..."

"Don't start, Jimmy."

Matthew Gibbard interrupted. "Dr. Baker, I'm sorry I missed my appointment, but I – "

"Don't finish that sentence," William said. He pointed to a sign. "Omit needless words. – William Strunk, Jr." On his door and in the spaces between the degrees and posters, William had tacked a few dozen other quotes, things like: "The only obligation which I have a right to assume is to do at any time what I think right – Henry David Thoreau." "Obliqueness is the curse of the reading class – Stephen King." "A bullet in the neck is a very bad review – Margaret Atwood."

William uncapped his pen and drew a large circle on the bottom of Matthew's paper. "This is a zero. A third of it is plagiarized, and you don't seem to know who John Updike was." He held the paper out to Matthew who stepped inside to take it, ignoring Jimmy.

"John who?" Matthew asked.

"Updike," Jimmy said. "Guy that wrote 'A&P.' You know, that story about the kid who quits his job over some tail in a swimsuit."

"You mean Edgar Allan Poe?"

"Is he serious?" Jimmy asked.

"Sadly, yes."

"Teaching ain't baseball, either, is it?"

"Touché."

"You gave me a zero?"

"Matthew, you're dismissed."

"But..."

William gave a backhanded wave, an upward motion, like shewing a fly.

Jimmy turned to Matthew. "That means get out. You wouldn't believe how many times he's done that to me. You better get, though. You don't wanna see what happens next."

The young Billy had learned to read by the age of four, and by five he could be found at any hour of the day or night with an open book. When interrupted, he gave that dismissing gesture, even to his parents. Further interruptions were often met with a violent fit. Ian was big enough and strong enough to restrain Billy safely, but Jimmy learned a sleeper hold was usually the safest way to avoid a nasty fight. Because of the age difference, the outcome was never in doubt, but Billy always did damage. The adult William was more tolerant of interruption, but he still used that gesture.

Matthew left.

"I get one of those every semester."

"I thought this was supposed to be a good college."

"It is. That kid's not stupid, not really. He's just lazy and drunk all the time."

"Smelled like it."

"Which pawn shop?"

"Eagle," Jimmy said. He reached across the desk and picked up William's pen and a pad. "Here's my number," he said, scribbling as he spoke. "I want to know how they got it. I just can't believe Dad would've sold it. He wouldn't have given it to anybody but you."

"They really wouldn't tell you who sold it?"

"They know who I am. They're not gonna tell me anything."

"And you think they'll tell me?"

"Yeah," Jimmy said.

"Why?"

Jimmy pointed to the degrees on the wall. "Will you go down there and take a look?"

"I'll think about it."

"Billy – I mean William – this is important. Whoever sold that gun might know who killed Dad."

William shook his head. Jimmy had written about his suspicions, but William ignored the letters. He knew all he needed to. "It was an accident. A wreck. I put a copy of the police report in the letter."

Jimmy let out a scoffing sigh. "Police report. I'm just supposed to take some cop's word for it?"

"It's all we have."

"And whose fault is that, Miss Marple?"

Their mother had been a fan of Agatha Christie's mysteries, and she kept an extensive collection of the books in their home. When Billy began reading them, Jimmy added Miss Marple to the list of nicknames he used for his younger brother. Even as a child, he would have preferred to be called Dupin – the detective in Poe's mysteries – or failing that, Poirot, but he was pretty sure his preferences didn't enter into Jimmy's thinking.

"He was losing his memory, Jimmy. He had taken to driving around at night, just burning gas. He wasn't himself. He had a wreck. There's no mystery."

"I don't believe that."

"What you believe doesn't enter into it."

Jimmy shook his head. "That gun's important to me," he said. "It was important to Dad. Whatever happened to him, I wanna know where they got that gun. It didn't feel right, seeing it in that glass case. I'd like to have it, but they can't sell it to me. If I can't have it, it belongs with you. Dad would've wanted it that way. I know that."

William nodded. "I would like to know where it's been the last three years."

"Least we've got one thing in common," Jimmy said.

"I've got a faculty meeting."

"They don't close till nine o'clock. I expect to hear from you before then, Billy. I'm mean, William. I'm serious about this." Jimmy stared William in the face, his ice-blue eyes pleading.

"I'll take care of it."

"I know you will."

CHAPTER 2

William tried to enter the back of the auditorium quietly, but the thunk of the panic bar resetting itself echoed over the dean's voice. Fire safety laws meant never going in or out unnoticed. Two of William's closest friends on the faculty sat halfway down the back row, and he joined them there. The group rarely sat through an entire faculty meeting, always ducking out in ones and twos when the boredom became too much to bear, echoing exits notwithstanding.

"Is this a mandatory meeting, Will?" asked Danny Moore. No one on the faculty attended fewer meetings than William, not even among these back-row slackers.

"My brother turned up in my office," William said. "I needed an excuse to leave."

"Did he break out?" whispered Janet, Danny's wife. They were also English professors. Danny taught rhetoric and composition, and Janet taught British literature. Everyone called them Mr. Dr. Moore and Mrs. Dr. Moore to avoid confusion. William had even heard them introduce themselves that way.

"Parole, I guess," William said. "You know I don't keep track."

"What did he want?" Danny asked.

"Money," Janet said, a little too loudly.

"That's right," said the dean. "Money." Her name was Mary, but everyone called her Dean Dillon, as if the title were her first name.

William had caught enough of the presentation to know it had to do with the budget. It was subtle, but he knew they were being chastised. These meetings were harder on him than his classes were on his students. He was sure of that.

The back door thunked again, and Kelvin Ingraham, a chemistry professor, slid in next to William. "I didn't know this was a mandatory meeting," Kelvin said. "Did I miss anything worth hearing?"

"I have no idea."

"No wonder you're still single, Will," Kelvin said. "You've got to learn to *listen* to *women*."

William's lack of a wife had become a frequent topic of discussion over the years, among the faculty and the students. Other professors tried to fix him up with new faculty members or women from other universities. No one ever introduced him to a non-professor, and he had never asked why. It was better he didn't know. Janet had returned from nine consecutive conferences with prospects, each time calling him into her office to look at online profiles. He was never impressed. When asked, he had learned to say, "I can't bring myself to settle for anything less than the perfect woman, but the perfect woman can't bring herself to settle for me."

William didn't say this to Kelvin. Instead, he said, "Remind me again why *you're* still single?" Kelvin's looks were a subject of a lot of student discussion. William had once overheard one student say to another, "Dr. Ingraham is just too hot to be teaching chemistry. No one could concentrate that hard."

"I would like to tell you that there are too many variables," Kelvin said, "that it's one of those unsolvable problems the math boys whine about at faculty parties."

"But you aren't going to tell me that, are you?"

"No." Kelvin shook his head and looked down, an expression of weary sadness. "The truth is that I look like Denzel Washington and sound like James Earl Jones. I'm too much sexy for one woman to handle all by herself."

"Did you confirm that with the biology department?"

"Twice."

The dean gave them a withering stare.

"You two are so gonna have to stay after school," Danny said.

"You have something to add, Mr. Dr. Moore?" asked the dean.

"No, ma'am." Danny looked down, his expression much like Kelvin's had been a moment before. His sadness was genuine, though, rather than feigned for effect. Even at forty-five, he still sank when chastised by a superior, something William chose to ignore because he couldn't begin to understand it.

The door thunked once more and Heather Rodgers took the seat next to Kelvin. She was the only female history professor at Samuels, and her office was on the floor beneath the English department. According to Heather, her colleagues were "flabby old men who smell as musty as the documents they lust after." She escaped them by socializing with the English faculty. That afternoon, she leaned across Kelvin, placed a hand on William's knee, and addressed Janet at the end of the row. "Did I miss anything?"

Janet shook her head.

William looked at Kelvin, who grinned and shrugged. They were both accustomed to Heather's invasions of personal space and neither minded. She was a former college athlete, tall and toned, with naturally curly blond hair that fell to her shoulders. She never wore makeup or jewelry, accessorizing only with perfume. That day's scent struck William as almond-based, matching the color of her eyes, but the aroma didn't suit her as well as some of her other choices had. He wasn't sure he had caught the same scent on her twice.

When she settled back into her seat, Kelvin turned to her and whispered, "Will and I are about to get detention."

"It's about time," she said. "Just be sure to take Danny down with you. I want to see him cry."

Dean Dillon stopped her presentation, put her fists on her hips, and stared at the back row for a full thirty seconds. William and the others stopped their chatter and faced forward, Danny going so far as to sit up straight.

William closed his eyes and ignored the rest of the meeting, instead thinking about Jimmy's visit.

~ ~ ~

Mamie Baker had died from cancer in her lungs twelve years earlier. She had never smoked or even lived with a smoker. The cancer started on her heart sac. A mammogram caught the edge of the first tumor. She had surgery and treatment, but two years later, the cancer was in her lungs. Six months after that, she was gone.

William was only twenty-nine, much too young to lose his mother, he thought. When he had graduated high school, he went to Johns Hopkins, hoping to leave Osgood, South Carolina, for good. He enjoyed Baltimore, but the graduate programs at Vanderbilt had been too good to pass up. After six years, he had become at home in Nashville. He liked the Music City lifestyle. He liked the concerts, the beautiful women who wore dresses and heels to the grocery store. He liked pretending not to notice famous people in the cars next to him at West End red lights. He was supposed to be able to have his life and still have his mother visit him four or five times a year, still talk to her on the phone every week. He had known a perfect woman, and she had loved him very much and ruined him for every other woman in the world. He had finished coursework when she was diagnosed, so he took the job at Samuels and wrote his dissertation at the Resolute desk.

Ian Baker was ten years older than his wife, and he was furious and heartbroken to have outlived her. Ian's mother had died of Alzheimer's before William was born, so when his memory began to dull, William worried. The doctors said Ian wasn't sick. He was just old. When he was found dead, his truck upside down in a creek bed, William blamed himself for not keeping a closer eye on his father. The policeman who came to deliver the news said it looked like Mr. Baker had taken a curve too wide and slipped off a high shoulder. He wasn't going very fast, they thought, but the angle tipped the truck over, and it rolled at least twice. "He would have been killed instantly," the officer said. William knew that was just what the man was trained to say so the family members could sleep without nightmares about loved ones choking on their own fluids, upside down, hanging from a seat belt.

Jimmy was in prison then. As far as William was concerned, Jimmy might as well have been dead, too. The age difference meant they had never been close – more like uncle and nephew than brothers in the best of times, more like comic book nemeses in the worst. William often said nasty things about his brother, even in his classes. He used stories from his childhood to illustrate points, always introduced with, "My brother, the villain..." Jimmy liked the taste of formula and stole the infant Billy's bottle on a regular basis. Later, Jimmy stole cassette tapes, CD players, VCRs, cars, jewelry, and money – sometimes from family members. For a time, William had blamed Jimmy for their mother's death, the black growth on her heart the metastasizing grief over Jimmy's crimes. Jimmy was at her funeral, and William fantasized about shoving him in after the casket and burying him alive.

After Ian's death, William had packed up the things he wanted to save and disposed of his parents worldly possessions – along with some of Jimmy's – in an estate sale. William had noticed Ian's service pistol was missing. His father had always kept the weapon cleaned and ready, but it was stored in various places at various times. When Billy was small, it had been on a high shelf in his father's closet. At times, it was boxed and tucked under the seat of Ian's truck. Sometimes, it was kept in a bedside table. Billy was only three when his father retired from the Army and settled in Osgood, but he had learned enough about Army life to know what a Standard Operating Procedure was and to wonder why the gun's SOP was always changing.

When Billy asked, Ian said, "I keep the gun in the best place to keep my family safe. The gun shifts when circumstances shift." William had wondered where circumstances had left the weapon and hoped it wasn't at the bottom of the creek. He thought he would someday find it in one of the boxes he had sifted but never really sorted before the estate sale, boxes that went into his garage and were never opened again.

~ ~ ~

One by one, William's friends slipped out of the faculty meeting, each exit punctuated by the same thunk. When it finally ended, he moved quickly to the door, but not quickly enough.

"Glad you could make it, Dr. Baker," Dean Dillon said. William nodded. "And you even stayed to the end. Do you think you'll make a habit of it?"

"Not likely."

"Fair enough. If I had more professors like you, we wouldn't need so many meetings."

"Thanks," William said. "I think."

Another professor called to the dean, so William gave a curt goodbye nod and went back to his office. He packed a set of tests into his satchel and walked home.

CHAPTER 3

During his mother's illness, he had lived with his parents, helping in any way he could. After she died, he could barely stand the sight of the place. Osgood had once been a mill town, and its rolling upstate hills were dotted by mill villages. The small, brick houses came in only a few floor plans, the size and layout a mark of a man's position at the mill. As the mills sold the houses and shut down, the houses had been individualized a little at a time by new owners – new rooms, porches, and so on. William bought a three-bedroom place originally built to house some middle manager. It sat just two blocks from the Samuels campus. Brick arches spanned a small front porch, and William had hung a swing that faced the street. From there, he could see between the houses across the road, over Main Street and right into the central campus quad. Many of his neighbors were students, staff, and other faculty. William was friendly with them, but he didn't consider them friends.

In Osgood, winter shows on the calendar but not the thermometer, so after the hot, humid days of early fall came to an end, William would often sit on the swing to grade. He settled there without even going inside. Jimmy's visit made it difficult to concentrate. William couldn't stay focused long enough to read the essay responses on the tests. After a few minutes, he gave up trying to read and began marking the matching section – authors and their works, literary terms and their definitions. He always felt a little embarrassed about including these sections on a sophomore-level exam, but they gave the students an easy platform from which to springboard to the more abstract, analytical questions. They were also easy to grade. When he couldn't keep his eyes focused long enough to match a test to the answer key, he knew the effort was pointless. He put the tests away and went inside.

The previous owner had installed a dishwasher and updated the guest bathroom, but the rest of the house was 1920s original when William moved in. He and Ian had remodeled the master bathroom themselves. There had been no showerhead in the bathtub, which was an easy fix, in and of itself. Rather than open the wall and reroute the plumbing, they replaced the spigot with a modern fixture with a diverter for a hose attachment – the same kind used in many modern houses for an extra hand-held showerhead. That job took ten minutes. The previous owner had never done it because of the large window just above the tub. To make the shower waterproof, the walls had to be tiled, which meant removing the window and filling the hole. On the inside, that meant insulation, dry wall, and tile. The outside needed new brick to fill in the hole, which wouldn't match the rest of the house. William had purchased all the materials and set up a time with his dad to do the work before the answer came to him.

Early one morning, before anyone but the paperboy was out, William drove over to one of Osgood's old mills. It had been the first to open and the second to close – when manufacturing jobs began to go overseas, long before Americans learned to call it outsourcing. The building was condemned, and its walls had fallen down in places. William thought there had been a fire there when he was a boy, but he couldn't remember the circumstances. Every few years, someone threatened to tear it down and build a

store or an apartment building or whatever the city
council thought Osgood needed that year. He sifted
through the loose bricks, salvaging enough whole ones
for the job, each roughly the same age as the house.
He thought of Jimmy that morning, wondering what
level of larceny he was committing. Whatever the
crime, William felt it was justified. The actual owner
clearly didn't care about the property. And he knew he
would get away with it. The mill bricks weren't a
perfect match, but William and his father agreed a
person would have to be looking for the difference to
notice it.

William washed up in that master bathroom
before making his supper – a bowl of soup from a can.
Through the kitchen window, there had once been a
line of sight across the next block and south down
Wilson Street to the old mill. William had often sat
and watched the sun go down behind the decaying
brick structure. Then Preston Mitchell, an economics
professor, had parked a thirty-foot boat in his back
yard – something about docking fees going up out at
the lake. Instead of sitting in the kitchen, William
tried to watch the evening news while he ate, but it
didn't hold his interest. He rinsed his dishes and put
them in the washer before going out to the garage.

The mill houses didn't have attached garages;
most people didn't own cars when they were built.
Where the lot size allowed it, homeowners had added
them over the years. William used his as a storage
shed, leaving his Toyota Corolla in the driveway. He
rarely drove, preferring to walk to work or to the
store. The car was only used on long trips or when he
was planning to buy something too large to carry. Ian
had teased him about the car, thinking every grown
man should have a pickup. William had bought the

Corolla new when he started at Samuels, and it was still in mint condition.

In the garage, he shifted his own boxes — old teaching materials, his college notes and papers, books he didn't want to part with but didn't expect to read again. Then he started working his way through his parents' effects. His father's locksmithing tools were neatly organized in a custom-built case. A leather pouch with lock picks was tucked into a corner, held in place by an elastic strap. William dusted the familiar tools and moved on. One cardboard box held tax records dating back to the 1960s. Another, surely left by his mother, held baby clothes that must once have been worn by Jimmy or Billy or maybe even both. Ian never cared for his war medals, preferring to leave Vietnam behind. William found them among old souvenirs from national parks and theater ticket stubs. Evidently, Ian Baker had seen *Star Wars* on opening night. William couldn't imagine why. He'd never known his father to watch or read science fiction. Maybe that was something he kept to himself, like the medals and how they had been earned.

One box held an L-shaped cast Billy had worn on his left arm for six weeks when he was ten years old. He had climbed a tree in the woods behind the Bakers' home and then slipped, wedging that arm between a branch and the trunk, trying to keep himself from falling. It worked, but his body's weight and momentum snapped his ulna. The pain was blinding for a time, and he blacked out in a rage against the tree. When he came to his senses, he began thinking of a way to get down. Before he could execute his plan, his mother came looking for him. Jimmy was right behind her with a ladder. By the time the ladder was set, Billy had freed himself, so he went down the rungs and off to the emergency room.

"Thanks for finding me, Mom," Billy said while the doctor wrapped his arm in plaster.

"It wasn't me," she said. "Your brother came and got me. I didn't know where we were going until I saw you hanging in that tree. I nearly died of shock."

Jimmy had already been arrested several times by then, even spending six months in juvenile detention. Billy had trouble picturing his brother as the hero in any story.

"How did he know? He wasn't outside. I didn't even know he was home." Jimmy still technically lived with the family, but he wandered in and out – more out than in at that point.

"He wasn't," Mamie said. "He had a feeling something wasn't right, so he came looking for you."

"That doesn't sound like Jimmy."

"Your brother has his faults, but his instincts are good – better than mine or your father's. If he says something's wrong, I listen to him." It was information he didn't have many opportunities to put to use. In the years that followed, Jimmy was in prison more than he was out.

When the doctor finished, Billy and his mother found Jimmy in the waiting room. "Thanks," Billy said. He didn't know how to say what he was really thinking, how to ask the questions he had about his brother.

"No problem, little brother. Just keep your head on straight, all right?"

Billy nodded. Keeping his head on straight wasn't always easy for him.

Ian often said, "Billy was born without a flight response." No one in the family ever argued the point. Young Billy had been very dangerous; he tried to kill anything that made him genuinely scared, anything he thought might threaten his life or those of his family.

There were incidents.

At nine years old, Billy had nearly choked a neighborhood boy to death. The boy's twin brother had picked a fight with Billy and lost. Seeing his brother bruised and bloodied, the boy pulled a small knife from his boot, the sort of thing Ian Baker used to clean fish. The boy swiped twice at Billy's midsection before Billy caught the wrist in his left hand and seized the boy's throat with his right. He twisted the arm until the knife fell away, kicked the boy's knee, and fell with him to the ground. The shouts of the other children brought Jimmy out of the house. He had to pull Billy off the boy and give mouth to mouth to start his breathing again. Billy blacked out and only remembered the flash of the knife and the sight of Jimmy bringing the dead boy back to life – nothing in between.

A neighbor called the police. Because of the boys' age, no one was interested in formal charges, but the officer who came by the house suggested Billy see a psychologist. Mamie agreed, but Ian wouldn't allow it. He said Billy just needed to learn to control himself. Ian began teaching him hand-to-hand combat, putting Billy through essentially the same training he had received in the army. The training didn't do much to change Billy's nature, but it gave him tremendous confidence in his ability to fight, which meant he rarely felt himself in any real danger. That enabled him to keep his head on straight. He continued to discipline anyone he felt needed it, but he had only blacked out twice in the years since. As a freshman at Johns Hopkins, he started going by William and put all of these things behind him.

In the garage on the night of Jimmy's return, William went through every box carefully. Nostalgia and grief made it difficult to stay focused, and the job took much longer than it should have. There was no sign of Ian Baker's .45. William's watch said 8:30. He could still make it to the pawnshop.

CHAPTER 4

William's house sat near the west end of Harvie Road, a block behind Main Street and four blocks west of Osgood's town center. Harvie came to an end at the entrance to a city park, complete with playground equipment, picnic tables, and a gazebo. Decades earlier, there had been a small train station, a whistle stop on the route from Augusta to Greenville. In the late 90s, the city transformed the station area into Currie Park, and removed the derelict train tracks, converting the routes into a few miles of greenway – wide trails snaking through the middle of Osgood. One wound its way north, under Main Street and through the Samuels campus to the hospital on the north end of town; the other went west about a mile and a half, not quite parallel to Main and coming to an end at the Shirley's grocery store on Dickson Road. Dickson had been built as a sort of bypass – four lanes for traffic and a turning lane – curving around Osgood's west edge and giving travelers to and from Augusta and Greenville a chance to avoid the red lights in the town center. Like most bypasses, it had become a second main street, with fast food, box stores, and car dealers popping up shortly after the blacktop hardened. William often walked the greenway down to Dickson to shop or eat. The exercise justified the greasy burgers or syrup-soaked waffles in William's mind.

He could make it to Eagle Pawn on foot before it closed, but the time would be tight. The car hadn't been driven in more than two weeks, not since a trip to Charleston for a conference of American literature professors. On the road, he had been listening to

Harry Potter and the Half-Blood Prince on CD, and the seven-hour round trip left him with only three discs to go. The set had been part of a gift — all seven books in the series on home-burned CDs — from Nick Fuller, an English major who couldn't believe his freshman composition professor had never read those stories. That had been three years earlier, and William had made it through the first five pirated sets over the course of several drives to conferences, old friends' weddings, and Ravens games in Baltimore. He had no trouble picking up wherever he had left off, regardless of the weeks or months between trips. The night of Jimmy's return, though, he tapped the "Off" button at the first words from Professor Snape. William hadn't been able to concentrate on anything all evening, and he didn't think the boy wizard's problems would be an exception.

Because of the dead end at the park, he had to go east on Harvie, turn left onto Wilson, and turn left again onto Main before he could go west toward Dickson. He had been in the house almost twelve years, but the necessity of going the wrong way in order to go the right way annoyed him every time he made those two lefts. The trip to Eagle Pawn took almost ten minutes, six of those spent idling at red lights on Main.

When William pulled in, only two other vehicles sat in the Eagle parking lot. The rusted out Ford van belonged to Doug Fortune, a former student William knew worked there. The sight of it was disappointing. Doug was one of the most talented writers William had ever taught, funny and insightful, but he had dropped out of college after three semesters. Doug's younger sister had gotten pregnant, and their parents kicked her out of the house. When they found out Doug was letting her stay in his dorm room, they cut him off, too. Swell folks, William thought. Doug had gone from part time at the pawnshop to full time, so he could get an apartment for the two of them. William had hoped the setback was temporary. Two years later, it looked like it might be permanent.

The other car was a 1969 Dodge Charger, restored to near-mint condition in metallic, midnight blue. It looked like something Jimmy would drive, if he ever stayed out of prison long enough to steal the money. A car like that couldn't be stolen. Anything that rare and valuable would be tracked down in weeks, if not days or hours. A fence might put one on a container ship to some Arab sheik, but no one would be careless enough to drive a hot '69 Charger around upstate South Carolina. William locked the Corolla and went inside.

The front door had an electronic sensor that set off a chime, like an 80s era doorbell, and a voice like an old Speak & Spell. "Front door entry. Front door entry." William looked up to see where the voice came from and spotted a speaker mounted directly above the door. A red light blinked on the bottom of the casing, which included a shiny plastic rectangle that William took to be its "eye."

Doug stood at the far end of the counter, off to William's left, helping the only other customer in the shop. He didn't look over, so William took a quick look around. On either side of the door, shelves held flat screen TVs in every size William had ever seen and a few that were new to him. At the far end, across from Doug and the customer, were the smallest ones, smaller than the old black and white Billy had in his bedroom as a child.

The man Doug was helping seemed to be looking for an engagement ring. Doug was speaking quietly, but William heard "cut" and "clarity" too many times in his first thirty seconds for it to be anything else.

The man buying it looked to be well past sixty, with a smoke-yellowed fringe of hair around his red scalp. William wondered whom the man was marrying and what she would think about her engagement ring being bought in a pawnshop. Of course, if she were marrying that grizzled old guy, she couldn't be too concerned with appearances. Maybe the '69 Charger had been an influence.

On that end, between the wall of TVs and the main counter, were low shelves piled with CD and DVD players. To William's right, there was only one low shelf, packed with video game systems, some in boxes, some without, just a plastic shell wound by black cords. On the two end walls, hooks held guitars – acoustic, electric, and bass. William looked them over, wondering how they had gotten there. Each one looked like a story, something Fitzgerald might have written, full of lies and regret and other people's booze. He was pretty sure most of the stories involved booze. Or drugs. Someone's failure to hold it together, turn up at work each day, and pay the bills. Others would just be layoffs, mill closures, outsourcing, and the resulting booze – Raymond Carver's territory.

"I'll be with you in a minute," Doug called.

William nodded.

In the four corners of the shop, cameras looked down on the customers and merchandise, their little red lights on to tell everyone, "You are being recorded." William tracked their little black wires into the wall and guessed the recorder was in the back office. There as an entrance to that space behind where Doug stood. Jimmy and his ilk didn't stand much of a chance against that stuff, William thought. Even with a clown nose and a sombrero, they could pull a decent likeness from one of those feeds. Maybe make a composite, if it came to that.

The long back wall doubled as a gun rack, filled with dozens of shotguns and rifles, all secured with plastic-coated chains. William stepped up to the counter and started scanning the handguns under the glass. Eagle had just about everything William could imagine: derringers, five-shot pocket .22s, Saturday Night Specials, .32s with safety hammers, 9mms, .45s, a Desert Eagle, and on and on and on – three fifty-foot shelves with nothing but pistols. He found two other M1911A1s before he came to Ian Baker's .45. He was almost elbow-to-elbow with the old man when he spotted it. Just like Jimmy said, the initials had been filed down, but they were clear enough for a person who knew where to look. Whoever had worked on the initials had ignored the old toolbox scratches.

"Oh, Dr. Baker," Doug said, "I didn't realize that was you. Just a little bit longer, if that's okay."

William nodded.

"I can't seem to make up my mind," the old man said.

"Take your time."

William knelt and studied the .45. His father wouldn't have pawned that gun. Never. Vietnam was rarely discussed in Ian Baker's presence, but Mamie told the boys a few stories over the years. She said Ian had taken the .45 from the body of a dead soldier. He liked having a spare. Billy got the impression his father had done war up close and personal in Vietnamese jungles and villages. The closest Billy had ever come to asking about the war was to ask about the old gun. The military had stopped using them, and everyone from the Osgood police to big-screen bad guys had embraced the Glock 9mm.

"Dad, why don't you get a new gun?" Billy was eleven, and Ian had been teaching him to break the gun down and put it back together. By then, Billy had gotten over his fear and learned to handle a gun properly.

"Why would I want a new gun?" his father asked.

"The ones on TV are cooler."

"This one has sentimental value. And I know it works."

Billy was pretty sure his father didn't just mean that it would fire bullets. He had taught both his sons, "A pistol only has one real purpose: to kill a human being at close range."

"Then why do we shoot at targets?" Billy had asked.

"So when it matters, you'll be able to hit the person you need to kill and not hit anyone else."

Looking at the gun in the case made William sick to his stomach. It didn't belong there, and it shouldn't have been altered. Ian Baker wouldn't have sold that gun. He certainly wouldn't have pawned it. He had never been wealthy, but the house had been paid for and there had been money in the bank. After Ian and Mamie's house was sold, William's half of the inheritance had paid off his mortgage and left him more than enough to pay cash for a nice, new car when the time came to replace the Corolla. What Jimmy did with his half, William chose not to consider. He could only think of three possible explanations for the gun's presence at Eagle Pawn. His father often got calls to change locks after a divorce or a domestic violence incident. Ian Baker was old fashioned, especially about women, and he wouldn't have expected a lady to fend for herself against an angry husband. It was possible he loaned the gun to someone until she could buy a gun of her own. Possible, but not likely. With his failing memory, he could have forgotten the gun, left it behind somewhere and never come back for it. But his memory wasn't as bad as that, not that William had noticed, and he was a fanatic about gun safety. Again, it was possible, but highly unlikely. The only thing that made sense was for it to have been stolen. But if it had happened before Ian died, William would have heard about it. If it happened afterward, William should have seen signs of a break-in when he organized the estate sale. He wasn't ready to believe Ian had been murdered, but he and Jimmy agreed on one thing: something wasn't right.

"Are you looking for a gun, Dr. Baker?" Doug asked. "You didn't have a break-in, did you? I heard there had been a couple over near campus this summer. Lots of break-ins in Osgood lately, to tell the truth."

"No, I just wanted to check on you," William said. The lie came without any real thought. It was instinct.

When Billy was very small, not yet old enough for school, before even he could read, he had torn a few pages out of one of Mamie's books. She didn't address it, but Ian found the mangled paperback in the den when he came home. Billy lied when asked if he had done it. Ian knew better. He pulled his son into his lap.

"Billy," he said, "no one has to teach you to lie. It's as easy as breathing. Sometimes you have to do it to keep breathing. Are you really that scared?"

"No, sir."

"Then tell me the truth."

Billy did, and his punishment was simply to repair the book. Ian supervised the activity, making sure Billy's tiny hands painstakingly set the torn pages and taped them precisely, leaving the book perfectly readable, functionally as good as new. Young though he was, Billy never forgot his father's words. William needed a solid reason for lying, some justification, some sense of a greater good being served.

He didn't feel scared when he lied in the pawnshop, certainly not of Doug. If Jimmy was right, though, if there really was something wrong, William didn't want anyone to know he was looking into it. He let the words flow out, trusting his subconscious mind had justified the deception and would let him know about it in due time.

"I thought when you got on your feet," he said, "we'd see you back at Samuels, even if it was just part time. It's been two years. Don't you think it's time you got back on course?"

William had been so absorbed in the gun, he had forgotten about the old man. He was reminded when the Speak & Spell security voice said, "Front door exit. Front door exit." The thing could tell which way a person was going. Impressive, William thought.

"That was the plan," Doug said, ignoring the security voice. "But, you know, time gets away from you."

"Exactly."

Doug frowned and looked down at the guns.

"I know it's hard working and going to school," William said, "but you don't have to do it all at once. Just a couple of classes at a time. And almost everything can be done online now, so you don't have to worry about your work schedule."

"Why do you care?"

"About ten percent of my students are terrible. They don't care. They don't try. They're disrespectful. I hate them. I'm not supposed to admit that, but it's true. Eighty-five percent are just okay. They're checking boxes on their way to middle management. There's nothing wrong with that. It's the way of the world. I'm happy to help. But five percent – just five percent – are good. Smart kids who work hard and have the potential to do amazing things. I come to work every day for the five percent, for the good ones, Doug. You were one of the good ones."

Doug sniffed, holding back tears, William thought. It had been weeks since he'd made a student cry, and he hadn't expected it from Doug.

"Spring registration is next week," William said. "Get it done. Come by my office if you need help." With that, he turned and left. He didn't want to see Doug wiping tears.

"Front door exit. Front door exit."

Apart from the reason he came, everything William had said was true. He realized he should have had that conversation over the summer. He had thought about it often, looking out from the Shirley's exit and seeing Doug's van parked in the Eagle lot next door, but there was always something that seemed more pressing. The time had gotten away from him, too.

Jimmy sat on the Corolla's trunk lid.

"Get off my car. You'll scratch the paint."

"This car is fifteen years old," Jimmy said. "It could use a few scratches."

"You heard me."

"Yes, sir, Dr. Baker, sir." Jimmy put his hands down on the trunk lid and pushed himself up before swinging off the trunk lid. His combat boots hit the blacktop with a dull thud. The Hawaiian shirt had been replaced by a Darius Rucker concert T-shirt, and he wore a Gamecocks cap. "What did you find out?"

"Nothing. Get in. I don't want to talk here."

"Nothing?"

"Nothing. Now come on."

"I'll follow you."

William watched Jimmy pull keys from his pocket and walk over to the Charger. "You cannot be serious."

"What?"

"You stole a '69 Charger? You know how rare those are. They'll find you before breakfast."

"I didn't steal it. I bought it. Totally legit."

"Who'd you rob to get the money? Wait. Don't answer that. It's better I don't know." In that moment, William considered for the first time the possibility that Jimmy hadn't squandered his inheritance on ephemera, that he had actually put thought into the gift their father had given and used it for something that might last, something that might have even more value later than it did when he bought it. The idea was a little shocking.

William also wondered how the old man had gotten there, looked, and saw him walking through the Shirley's lot next door. The old man was taking his time. William got in and drove the Corolla north up Dickson, past Main Street, and pulled into the Waffle House parking lot. Jimmy came in right behind him and put the Charger in the space next to the Corolla. William walked to the door and waited for his brother.

"You know there's a Waffle House on the west side, don't you?" Jimmy asked. "Where we just were?"

"They know me there."

"You don't wanna be seen with me, huh?"

"Something like that." William couldn't justify what he was feeling, what had settled in his mind, heart, and stomach when he saw that gun in the case – not even to himself. He wasn't going to try to explain it to Jimmy.

Jimmy shook his head and followed William into the restaurant. William took the last booth, nearest to the bathroom. Osgood's two Waffle House franchises sat on opposite sides of the road, but the layout was exactly the same. This was William's usual spot at the west side location. Jimmy slid in across from his brother.

The waitress came over and introduced herself.

"A milk, a water, and two waffles," Jimmy said.

"That all?" she asked, looking to William.

William nodded.

"Don't look surprised, little brother. You're a creature of habit."

"Habits change."

"Some do. Some don't. And I know you. You may not know me, but I know you."

William let that pass, and the waitress brought the milk and the water. William pulled the water in front of himself.

When the waitress walked away, Jimmy asked, "What happened?"

"It was there. Dad's gun."

"I know that. That's why I sent you over there. What did he say?"

"I didn't ask."

"Why the hell not?"

William took a long drink of his water. "I think you're right. Something is off. Dad wouldn't sell that gun. He wouldn't give it away, and he wouldn't lose it. I don't know what happened in Vietnam, but that thing was a part of him, like an extra arm or something."

"I know."

"So that means it was stolen, right?"

"Had to be."

"But I don't see how. If someone broke into the house or his truck, he would have reported it. He would've told me."

Jimmy took a long drink of his milk. "What about after?"

39

"No signs of it. No broken windows. No busted doors."

"A good thief wouldn't leave signs."

"The TV was still there. Mom's jewelry."

Jimmy shook his head. "You don't steal the gun and leave the jewelry."

"Maybe the tow truck driver? After the wreck?"

"Maybe, but those guys usually play it straight. People hate them too much for towing them out of parking lots and side streets and stuff. If something came up missing, they'd never hear the end of it."

"So we've got nothing."

"That's why you were supposed to ask."

"They can't tell me. Privacy laws. You know that."

"They don't care about that. They report everything to the police, in case something's stolen. That's what they care about. You looked pretty friendly with that kid working tonight. You try again, I bet he bends the rules for you."

"Then what?"

"Then we talk to whoever sold it."

"He'll just lie."

"I'll make him talk. Or you will."

"I'm an English professor. I don't lean on people for information."

"Dr. William Baker might not, but I've seen Billy Baker set a few folks straight. And at least one dog."

"That was a long time ago."

The waitress brought the waffles and a container of syrup. They thanked her and ate several bites in silence. Finally, Jimmy said, "We need to know who pawned that gun. The simplest thing is for you to ask the kid. If he won't tell you, call the cops."

"I don't want to call the cops."

"Why not?" Jimmy asked.

"I don't know. I think I'm just paranoid."

Jimmy shook his head. "Mom said you had good instincts. 'If Billy says something's wrong, you listen to him,' she said."

"She said the same thing to me about you."

"Well, she's was either trying to make us be nice to each other, or she knew something we didn't. I say let's trust her. Tell me what's wrong, so I can listen to it."

William thought about this for a few more bites. He couldn't place what bothered him so much about asking for information on the gun. He just knew he wanted to keep things private. He didn't want to be on anyone's radar. And that wasn't the only thing bothering him. "What were you selling in there this afternoon, anyway? How long before the cops are looking for it? Looking for you?"

"I wasn't selling anything," Jimmy said.

"Then why the shirt?"

"Habit. If I think I'm going to a pawn shop, the loud shirts come out."

"If you weren't selling, what were you doing?"

"Buying."

"Buying what?"

"Engagement ring. I got a girl in Augusta. I'm finally doing it. Till death do us part. The whole thing."

"You're kidding."

"It's the truth."

"A girl?"

"Well, she's forty-three, but she's my girl. You know how it is."

"And you bought her ring in a pawn shop?"

"No," Jimmy said. "I didn't find what I was looking for. Eagle usually has good stuff, though. Lots of divorces in Osgood. Nothing to do, nowhere to go. People get bored. Bored people cheat. Cheaters get divorced. Divorced people hock their engagement rings."

"You're a regular Aristotle, you know that."

"Fuck you, Billy."

"William."

"Fuck you, William."

The brothers went back to their waffles and finished them before speaking again.

"Congratulations."

"Thanks," Jimmy said.

"What kind of ring are you looking for?"

"Diamond, of course, but Wendy likes sapphires. I'm looking for something with both. Diamond in the middle and sapphires on the sides."

"Nice."

"She likes rubies, too, so that could work."

William nodded and drank the last of his water. "I don't want to call the cops. I don't want anyone to know I'm looking into the gun. Like I said, maybe I'm just paranoid. It's just a gut feeling."

"What difference does it make?"

"You don't have to outsmart an enemy if he doesn't know you're out to get him."

"That sounds like one of those quotes," Jimmy said, "like on the wall in your office. Who said that?"

"I did. Just now."

Jimmy nodded. "It's good. I like it. But it don't help much. How do we find out who pawned the gun?"

"I'll think of something."

"You do that. I'm going down to Augusta tonight. See my Wendy. I'll be back in a few days. If you don't have a better idea by then, I'm going in there and raising a stink. Maybe twist an arm or two."

"All right."

"Goodnight, Billy. William."

"Goodnight, Jimmy."

Jimmy scooted to the edge of the booth and put his hand in his right boot. He pulled out a ten and left it on the table before walking out and driving away. William barely noticed. He was too busy thinking.

CHAPTER 5

William didn't get much sleep that night. He needed a plan, but nothing sensible came to mind. The worrying and plotting crept in even when he did sleep, and he dreamed about the pawnshop and his father's body in its casket and the gun and the truck upside down in the creek. By daylight, the only idea he had was so unreasonable, so foolish and irrational, he couldn't even allow himself to consider it for more than a few seconds before muttering his brother's name and shaking his head. The shaking didn't dislodge the idea.

He shaved and showered in cold water to wake himself. Samuels University had no specific dress code for professors, but William had developed a uniform for himself. He owned ten pairs of flat-front khakis, and he wore one of them every workday. He owned twenty light blue oxford cloth shirts, ten short-sleeved for warm weather months and ten long-sleeved for cold. During semesters, he did laundry every other Saturday. He owned three pairs of brown lace-up walking shoes, dressy enough for work but comfortable enough for the miles he walked. When any of these things wore out, he replaced it with an exact match or the nearest thing he could find. Kelvin said William was the dullest dresser on the planet. Not the worst, but the dullest. This suited William just fine. He owned jeans and T-shirts and sneakers and even a couple of suits, but those things were for his personal time. Ian Baker had worn the uniform of the United States Army for twenty years, and a light blue coverall for thirty-five more. The latter had "Baker Locksmithing" stitched on one side and "Ian" stitched on the other. If a uniform was good enough for his father, it was good enough for William.

By the time he was dressed, his automatic coffee maker had dispensed his daily sixteen ounces. He poured that into a stainless steel, insulated mug and took a NutriGrain bar from the cabinet. Breakfast. His leather satchel had a shoulder strap, which he used to keep his hands free. He ate on the walk to work.

Samuels was too small to have lecturers or graduate assistants, so each English professor taught one or two freshman composition courses each semester, regardless of the professor's rank or specialty. After fourteen years, William was the second most senior person in the department, so he got to pick his own schedule. He taught his composition section at eight o'clock on Mondays, Wednesdays, and Fridays, which meant fewer students and less grading. College students avoid eight o'clock classes for obvious reasons, and the Tuesday-Thursday section was slightly more popular because it meant one fewer early morning each week. William muddled through his discussion of process analysis and set the students to work, breaking down the specific steps in several common tasks: changing a tire, baking a cake, and the like.

He had his own task to break down.

The nine o'clock session required more focus. Studies in Major Authors was a senior-level course that focused on a single writer, chosen by the professor. William's best students were in the class, and he actually found the material interesting. He taught a section each fall, examining the works of Thoreau in even years and those of Poe in odd years. This was a Poe year. He began the course covering Poe's biography and lesser known nonfiction, mostly magazine articles on subjects so esoteric, so specific to the era in which they were written, that they were only of interest to historians and Poe scholars like William. They deserved to be covered, William thought, but he knew the material bored his students, so he moved through it quickly at the beginning of the term before other coursework had worn them down. In his years of teaching, students had often commented on how odd it was that someone as consistent and reliable as Dr. Baker should have devoted his education to the study of such a lazy ne'er-do-well. William adored Poe's fiction, but he had to admit he cared little for the man himself. Poe had been an arrogant, unreliable alcoholic, prone to abusing friends and enemies with equal fervor. "He was, quite frankly, an ass," William had told class after class, "but he sure could write." In even years, he said exactly the same thing about Thoreau, for very different reasons.

It was late October, and the class had covered all the poetry on the syllabus, as well as the Dupin mysteries, leaving the well-known horror and revenge tales for the last few weeks of the term. William had built the schedule this way to ease the end-of-semester strain on the students; most of them were already familiar with these stories. That Wednesday, they were discussing "The Fall of the House of Usher." William liked to start in simplest terms: first a review of the major characters and the basic plot, then a discussion of major themes. Literary theory discussions would come in a later class session. The character and plot review took the first twenty minutes of the class, leaving thirty for themes. Senior-level classes were always small – English was not a popular major at Samuels – but this section was unusually so, with only five students. William required them all to sit on the first and second rows of the room's three center columns of desks, forming a

tight little knot of students. William usually paced
back and forth from the board to the computer.
Things he planned to discuss were prepared on
PowerPoint slides and projected on a screen. Things
that came up during the discussion were written on
the white board next to the screen. Anything from
either medium was likely to be on an exam.

That morning, William stood by the board,
marker in hand and asked, "Major themes?"

"Insanity," Nick Fuller said. He had been in one of
William's classes each of his seven semesters at
Samuels, in spite of William's ignorance of Harry
Potter. Nick was what Ian Baker would have called a
"pretty boy," with light brown, floppy hair, always
carefully mussed, like a musician or an artist. William
had overheard female students – and a few males –
talk about Nick as if he were a member of a boy band:
stage whispers and high-pitched squeals. The kid
could be a little full of himself at times, but William
liked him. He was from a blue collar family – his
father delivered furniture for a local store and his
mother cut hair at the Osgood Walmart. Nick had
earned a full scholarship to Samuels, and he was
making the most of the opportunity. He never missed
a class and always came with an old microcassette
recorder, taping classes and making elaborate notes
based on the recordings. He was one of the five
percent.

"Come on," William said, "you're seniors. You
know better – "

"Be more specific," all five students said in chorus.
It was one of William's standard lines, a phrase he
used to encourage students to consider something
more subtle than the obvious. Any impression of him
included that line, along with "What's the next layer?"
and "Elaborate." The first time he heard a student

doing an impression, he considered changing his wordings, creating a list of phrases he could mix and match to avoid the frequent repetition. When he sat down to do the work, though, he thought about his own professors' catchphrases. The best ones had two or three, and the worst ones had none. He decided to keep his and to play them up, to use them as a shorthand rather than wasting precious class time trying to be cool.

"Paranoia," said Regina Seymour, the only black student in the class. Almost half the Samuels student body was African American, but only ten percent of the English majors were. This had always bothered William. He couldn't figure it out. As far as he could tell, no one on the department faculty was racist. They were all white, though, despite their best efforts to find new faculty of color. He hoped it was the reputation of South Carolina in general that kept qualified minorities from applying and not something they were doing at Samuels. He liked Regina and did everything he could to encourage her and the other minority English majors. He sometimes wondered if that were a form of racism, but he decided it was a form he was willing to live with.

"Yes," William said. He wrote "Paranoia" on the white board. "Give me an example."

"Do you want a list?" Regina asked. "From start to finish, that man is afraid something is coming for him – illness, weather, his dead sister."

"It's not really paranoia, is it?" John Kennedy asked. "I mean, some of it turns out to be true." Poor John was a persistent butt of jokes about assassination and conspiracy theories, from students and professors alike. Even William called him "Mr. President" most of the time. There was no relation, but William thought he looked a little like the young JFK.

"Can we talk about that?" asked Anna Perkins.

She was quiet, but smart and interesting and fated to drop dead of a heart attack before the age of forty, William was sure. She had been heavy when she started at Samuels – what Mamie Baker would have called "pear-shaped" – but Anna had gained significant weight each year. William estimated she had reached 300 pounds as a junior. Now a senior, she was having difficulty getting into the student desks. William genuinely worried for her health, thinking she either had an untreated thyroid condition or a serious eating disorder. He asked Janet Moore to speak to Anna, thinking it would be better coming from a woman. Janet couldn't bring herself to do it, but she was worried, too, so she and William sent alerts to the university health system. The alerts were intended to address depression, suicidal ideation, and substance abuse, but both professors thought they had to do something. William had also sent one about Matthew Gibbard. Because of privacy laws, they were only told the student had been contacted. Every time William saw Anna, he wondered if things would turn around in time.

"I wasn't sure how much Poe wanted readers to feel was actually about the man's mental illness and how much was about the sort of demonic power of the house," Anna said. "You know, like he's possessed by the spirit of the place."

"Oh, it's definitely both," Nick said.

"Elaborate," Charlotte Clements said. She rarely contributed to the discussion, but she was always listening and prodded things along occasionally, at times mimicking William. Her papers were interesting, William thought, and he wished she would express some of the ideas he read there for the other class members to hear.

The discussion made William think too much about his own family's home. He tried to imagine ways someone could have gotten in and taken the gun without leaving any signs, tried to imagine why someone would have taken the gun and left other valuables behind. He also wondered about his own paranoia, wondered what made him so sure he had to keep his questions about the gun to himself.

His father had once said, "Instinct is just your subconscious mind telling your conscious mind what to do about things it wouldn't understand. Your subconscious is smarter than your conscious." William wished it would be more specific, show him the next layer, and elaborate.

Nick elaborated on his point for several minutes, and William let him hold court for much longer than usual. An argument could be made that he was aiding Nick's education by allowing the student to experience a bit of what it was like to be the teacher, William thought, but the latitude was really rooted in his own distraction. When the discussion came to a lull, he nudged it along, but the rest of the session was really a dialogue between Nick and the other students.

On the way out, John said, "Dr. Baker, do you have a minute?"

"Sure."

John pulled a piece of paper out of a folder and handed it to William. "I'm applying to grad schools, and I was wondering if you would write a recommendation. That's the address and everything."

"Southern Methodist University," William read. "You want to go to grad school in Dallas? Is this a joke?"

"No, sir," John said. "I really like their program, and I have family there."

William shook his head. "Just promise me you'll stay out of convertibles."

"I'll try." John rolled his eyes, and William wondered how many times John had heard some version of that joke. Too many, he thought.

"What's the deadline?" William asked.

"It doesn't have to be in until mid-December. I didn't want to wait till the last minute."

"That's what I like about you, Mr. President. Come by the office next week, and we'll talk about your plans. I'll read up on their program, so we can make sure to hit the right notes in the letter."

"I'll be there." John walked away, and William went to his office.

He had often wondered if Jimmy's choices were rooted in stupidity or insanity or some strange mix of the two. Jimmy had been known to go on the occasional drinking binge, but he didn't seem to be an alcoholic, and William had never heard of him using drugs. He might have experimented, but he showed no signs of a habit. The only time Billy had actually asked his brother why he robbed houses, Jimmy said, "It's more fun than being a soldier or a locksmith."

"There's lots of other things you could be."

"Maybe," Jimmy said, "but I like stealing."

"But you're not very good at it."

Billy was sixteen. Jimmy was twenty-five. This was the first draft of the "Stealing ain't baseball" speech. It would go through many revisions, but the gist of the conversation was always the same. William had never wanted to be like his brother, but the idea nagging at him all night and through his morning classes made him wonder just how alike they really were.

William forced himself to work on grading the tests he had ignored the night before. He was able to wade through half the stack before the first student appointment. From then until lunch, he worked with three American literature students who, unlike Matthew Gibbard, showed up on time. William kept a stash of microwave soups in his desk, and he was about to take one of them to the break room when Kelvin knocked on his door.

"Dr. Baker, I'm a little lost. Could you help me?"

These had been Kelvin's first words to William the day he came to interview for the position at Samuels. The English department was housed in the Connell building, and the physics department was housed in the Cornell building, each having been named for major donors to the university. Dean Dillon's former assistant – former because of several chaos-inducing errors like this one – had put "Connell" in all the instructions she sent to Kelvin and the other applicants. Kelvin had quickly realized that Connell was not a science building, and William was the first person he found with an open door. William had walked him over to Cornell, and the friendship was born. Since then, Kelvin occasionally popped in and repeated those words.

"Dr. Ingraham, you don't belong here," William said. "This is a humanities building."

"Are you trying to tell me this university is segregated?"

"Yes, sir, by discipline, and scientists – like you – belong in the Cornell building."

"Did you just call me a scientist?"

"I did."

"Cool. You want some lunch?"

William held up the can of soup.

Kelvin shook his head. "You keep eating that stuff, you'll grow a Campbell's logo on your chest. Body art by Warhol."

Janet and Danny appeared behind Kelvin.

"Will, put down the can," Danny said, "and back away slowly from the soup."

"We're going to the caf," Janet said. "Come on."

William did as he was told.

~ ~ ~

To William, the Samuels University dining hall had always looked like an overgrown Shoney's. From the entrance, the section on the left had booths, and the section on the right had large, round tables. Beyond those were four buffet areas arranged in a semicircle: daily entrees and vegetables; burgers, hotdogs, and fries; salads; and desserts. Drink stations divided one buffet line from the next. The exit to the far left had a conveyor belt for dirty dishes and trays along one side. The place was decked out in the school colors – green and silver. Nick referred to it as "Slytherin House," but the colors were actually a celebration of the university's biggest benefactor. Arthur Samuels had founded the school with money inherited from Joseph Green, his mother's brother, who had struck a massive silver vein in Nevada. The Samuels mascot was a miner. The mascot's image was presented in larger-than-life size on three of the cafeteria walls – a sort of raven-haired Yosemite Sam in green overalls and wielding a pick as long as he was tall.

The four professors scanned their IDs and split up to get their preferred lunch. Five years earlier, a new president had instituted a program offering one free lunch per week to professors. She believed it fostered rapport between faculty and students if they ate together. In practice, the professors clumped at the round tables, and the students sat in the booths. William got his burger, fries, and soda before joining his friends and a few other professors at a round table. Heather Rodgers and two French professors had already finished eating when Kelvin and the English professors sat down. Everyone said hello, and the French professors got up to leave.

"That's just like the French," Danny said. "Always too snobby to visit with the ugly Americans." Both the professors rolled their eyes as they walked away.

"There's only one ugly American at this table, Danny," Kelvin said. Danny took a quick look at the group. "There's a reason *you* don't see him."

"Kelvin," Janet said, "was that an appropriate remark?"

"No, Mrs. Dr. Moore."

"What have I told you about insulting my husband?"

"Make sure it's true and *very* funny."

"Now, why didn't that qualify?"

"It wasn't funny enough."

"Exactly. Now, don't let it happen again."

"Yes, Mrs. Dr. Moore."

"Danny," Heather said, "why do you let your wife fight your battles for you?"

"Because she wins," Danny said.

"You can't argue with that logic," William said.

"I could," Heather said, "but I don't think it would have much of an effect."

Danny opened his mouth to respond, but he stopped before any sound came out.

Dean Dillon was sitting down at their table.

They had been eating as a group at least once a week for several years, and she had never done that before. The whole group went quiet and looked in her direction. William wondered if they were about to be chastised for talking during the faculty meeting the day before. The group had often joked about feeling like kids in the principal's office when talking to Dean Dillon. For Danny, it wasn't a joke.

Kelvin was the first to recover. "Good afternoon, Dean Dillon."

"At lunch, I'm just Mary," she said.

"Good afternoon, Dean Mary."

"Good afternoon, Dr. Kelvin," Mary said.

"How's Fred?" William asked. Fred Dillon and Ian Baker had been friends for as long as William could remember. He wasn't sure just how they met, but it had to have been right after the Bakers moved to Osgood.

"He's doing well. Retirement suits him. He's off deer hunting with the grandkids this week."

The grandkids. William always felt a little pang when Mary Dillon used that plural. She only had one surviving grandchild. She and Fred had two sons, but the younger one was a confirmed bachelor like William. The elder Dillon boy had two boys of his own, but his older son died when his truck rolled over an IED outside Tikrit. The younger boy wasn't old enough for college yet, and that generation of Dillons were homeschooled. Evidently, the curriculum included deer hunting.

"How old is Cody now?"

"Fifteen."

"And he's going to be wandering around in the woods with firearms?" Danny asked. He was originally from Orange County California, and he couldn't seem to get used to Southern attitudes about guns and hunting. He had also lost his best friend to a stray bullet during an L.A. drive-by while he was still in high school.

Everyone at the table had lost someone, William thought. Heather had lost a child. Janet's father had died the year before. Kelvin's sister. William wondered if the tragedies were really what bonded them all. He suspected the cynicism and sarcasm that characterized their banter was rooted in a resignation born of pain. He wouldn't let himself think about it very much.

"Cody has been well trained," Mary said. "He won't shoot anything with less than four legs."

"I'm counting on it," William said. He wasn't much of a cook. He could scramble eggs, fry sausage, and bake Bisquick biscuits, but his real specialty was a venison stew that had been passed down from Ian. William hadn't been hunting in years, since before his father's death, but Fred had brought a couple of pounds of meat to William each season since then. William always tried to pay him, and Fred always refused.

"Me, too," Mary said. "Cody is a crack shot, and he's ninja-silent. The kid scares me sometimes. I know you're not supposed to say that about your grandchildren, but it's true. He'll either become an army sniper or end up in prison."

Everyone else at the table looked at William on hearing the word "prison." He shrugged his shoulders, more concerned about Mary's casual discussion of war than the oblique reference to his brother's life.

"Oh," Mary said. "I wasn't thinking."

"It's fine," William said. "It's never been a secret."

"I guess not," she said. "So how is the villain these days?"

"Roaming free. Lock your doors and windows."

"He's in town, then?"

"Augusta."

"How long?"

"Six months."

"That's good. Maybe it'll take this time."

"We'll see." This was all William ever said about his brother's chances of staying out of prison.

"Anyhow," Mary said, "you'll be eating venison stew this time next week. I guarantee it."

"I'm looking forward to it."

"It'll be a lot healthier than that burger you're eating," Janet said. "We bring you down here to get a decent meal in you, and you go straight for the burger and fries."

William raised his arms. "Do I look like I have a diet issue?" he asked.

"Looking good, bro," Danny said.

"You still can't pull off 'bro,'" Kelvin said.

"I'm working on it."

"It's not the outside I'm worried about," Janet said. "Imagine what your arteries look like."

William grinned. "My arteries are also slim and sexy."

"That's right, bro," Kelvin said. He turned to Danny. "Did you hear that? Can you hear the difference?"

"I heard it," Danny said. "I'll keep working on it."

William had always been a fast eater – a necessity with Jimmy in the house – and he finished his lunch before the others were halfway there. One of Danny's students walked over with questions about an upcoming test. By the time the boy was gone, everyone but Danny had caught up to William.

"Well, I hate to eat and run," William said, "but Jimmy's visit has me a little behind. I've got a set of tests I'd like to start on before my next appointment." He stood and picked up his tray.

"You didn't give him any money, did you?" Danny asked.

"No."

"I can't believe he came by your office," Janet said. "He's never done that before, has he?"

"No."

"Jimmy was here?" Mary asked. "On campus?"

"Yesterday."

"That's not good," Mary said. "I know it puts you in an awkward position, but if he comes back, let me know. I'll have security escort him off campus. I know he's your brother, but he's also stolen a lot of electronics over the years. I can't have him wandering around where there are so many projectors and smart boards. I'm sorry."

"I understand."

"I really am sorry, Will," she said. "I know you can't pick your family. You deserve better."

"Thanks." William nodded and walked away, putting his tray on the conveyor belt on his way out.

He went back to his office and tried to grade, but the thought he'd been pushing back all day kept rising to the surface. He gave in and entertained it for ten minutes. It was lunacy, but it could be pulled off, he thought. With some planning and the right equipment, he could do it. He decided to look into it, to do the legwork. That much resolved, he was able to focus and make his way through the second set of American literature tests before Stacy Burton showed up to have her paper graded.

CHAPTER 6

After the last appointment, William grabbed his satchel and walked home. He was caught up on his grading, so the bag only held his coffee mug. Leaving the bag by the front door, he put the mug in the dishwasher before making his way to the front bedroom closet. His hunting rifle had been stored there when he moved in, and his father's rifle and equipment had eventually gone there, too. William knew his father would have been sorely disappointed to see how poorly he had cared for these weapons. Hunting had always been a father-son activity for William, and after the wreck, he had no interest. He didn't want to look at the rifles or any of the things that went with them. The weapons needed to be cleaned and oiled, but that would have to wait a while longer. He wasn't sure it mattered. He wasn't sure he would ever use them again.

Instead, he opened the trunk on the closet floor. Inside were a couple of orange coveralls, orange vests, a folding deer stand, and one hi-tech trail camera. Ian Baker didn't believe in such things, but Fred had gotten two as gifts the Christmas before Ian died – one from Cody and another from Mary. He gave the extra to Ian, and it ended up in the trunk with his other gear, still in the packaging. William opened it and read the instructions. It came with batteries, but he didn't trust them after so long in storage. He replaced them from a stash he kept in the kitchen before loading the camera, a bottle of water, and a bag of potato chips into the old backpack he used for shopping. He slung on the pack, locked the house, and walked to the greenway.

At William's usual pace, he could walk the mile and a half to Eagle Pawn in about twenty minutes. He moved more cautiously that afternoon, though, checking the various sightlines along the way. Trees lined both sides of the trail from the park all the way to Dickson Road, but some were evergreen and others were not. The view of the trail from the homes and businesses on the other side of the trees changed with the seasons. In spring and summer, William might encounter a dozen other people along the trail. In late October, he might see one or two, but only every few trips. By winter, no one else would be using it. The night after Jimmy's return, William saw just one other person – Micah Berry.

Mr. Berry lived at Osgood Arms, a senior center by the hospital. He could still walk, but his balance and stamina had left him after a mild stroke. Since then, he used a motorized wheelchair to get around. The trail was wide and smooth, and William often encountered Mr. Berry buzzing along, going to or coming from Shirley's. There were other grocery stores much closer to his home, and their prices were lower, but Mr. Berry was a loyal customer.

"Afternoon, William," Mr. Berry said.

"Afternoon, Mr. Berry."

"Yogurt's on special at Shirley's."

"Thanks for the tip."

"Anytime."

William walked on, listening to the fading hum of Mr. Berry's chair, but not looking back. The trail bent south about halfway along its length, taking it a bit farther from Main Street. It wrapped around the rim of a small basin where the Osgood Oaks apartment complex had been built. Samuels freshmen and sophomores were required to live on campus, unless they commuted from home, but many of the upperclassmen lived in that complex. The leaves turn late in upstate South Carolina, and they kept William from seeing down into the parking lot. In two or three more weeks, the view would be clear. William had waved to Charlotte Clements and Regina Seymour from the trail several times the previous winter. Evidently, their apartments were on that end of the complex. He didn't ask.

The path turned north just beyond the complex, before straightening out again. Eventually, the route took it right behind Eagle Pawn. William slowed until he felt Mr. Berry could have walked beside him. He scanned every angle through the trees behind the shop, then passed it and came out in the Shirley's parking lot. No one was coming toward the trail from the grocery store. He turned back, jogged up the trail, and pulled open the branches of a pine tree, slipping inside. William hadn't climbed a tree since he was in college, and he had never been fond of climbing pines. The loose bark made getting a grip difficult, and the sap left his hands and clothes dirty – giving him away to Mrs. Baker. She didn't want a second broken arm and had forbidden further climbing. Like any reasonable boy, young Billy had made sure she never found out.

The pine tree was the best cover behind Eagle, though, so it would have to do. Close to the trunk, the branches were almost bare, and the limbs were as close together as rungs on a ladder. Like a swirl of ladders, William thought. He twisted and ducked as he went. About fifteen feet up, he found a nice spot to sit and watch. From there, he could see the back door of the shop where employees would come and go, he assumed. The door had two locks – the handle and a dead bolt. Neither would present much difficulty.

His hands were smeared with sap, so he rubbed them together until they felt clean enough to handle the camera. It was designed to sense movement and take time-stamped pictures or video so hunters would know when and where to expect deer.

William wanted to use it to plan a break-in.

Unlike his older brother, William had never stolen anything for profit. Aside from the bricks, he had never even stolen anything for his own use. From time to time, however, Billy had recovered items he felt were in the wrong hands. In junior high, he reclaimed a classmate's diary from the locker of her jealous boyfriend. In high school, he liberated a friend's Walkman and a few other items from the principal's office. Each of these things had been carefully placed where their rightful owners would find them, making sure no one knew of Billy's involvement.

That Wednesday afternoon, William didn't think he would actually break into Eagle Pawn, but he wanted to find out if it could be done. If he could get in and out undetected, he could copy their records and find out who had stolen his father's gun. He hadn't allowed himself to think through what he would do with that information. When the camera had been programmed, he attached it to the tree. He wasn't sure the angle would be right to get a view inside that back door or if the resolution would be high enough to see anything useful. He wasn't entirely sure he had programmed the camera correctly to get the video he wanted. This was just a test run, in any case, so he left the camera, climbed down, and walked home.

It was still daylight, not quite five o'clock, and he was covered in pinesap. He was thankful he didn't run into anyone on the trail on the way back. He could have come up with an explanation, but he didn't want to have to maintain any more fiction than absolutely necessary. If he actually did break into Eagle Pawn, he'd be keeping that to himself for the rest of his life. Safely inside his own house, he stripped down and hung the stained clothes over the shower rod. He would have to put them back on to get the camera later, and he didn't want to get sap on the furniture in the meantime. The sap might not come out in the wash, and he didn't want to risk more than one uniform on the project.

He ate supper – more soup – and tried to watch the news. He kept thinking about the pawnshop. Getting in would be easy, but there had to be an alarm. If he set it off, he would only have a few minutes to get what he needed and get out. It wouldn't be enough time. He needed a way to get the code. The step after that could be even harder. Eagle's records had to be electronic. By law, they had to report each day's transactions to law enforcement. He had learned that much from Jimmy's failures. Surely that information went into a database. There was just too much of it for any other method. If there were a database, there would also be a login and password, and he didn't think he would get that from a deer camera.

He reread Tim O'Brien's short story "The Things They Carried" in preparation for his American literature sections the next day. The course textbook was still in his office, but almost every anthology he owned contained it. He had read the story dozens of times over the years, and he found some new subtlety in it almost every time. This time his focus was divided, and he took twice as long to read it as he normally would. He found no new insight.

The soup didn't taste very good, either. He was just killing time until ten, when he thought it would be safe to retrieve the camera and see what it had recorded. He got online and researched how to remove pinesap from clothing. The research took two minutes. Evidently, it could be done with rubbing alcohol.

William enjoyed football, in person and on TV, but he only had two serious hobbies: reading and walking. During semesters, his class preparations and grading kept him busy most of each day. He spent his down time reading news articles or novels. He had earned a doctorate in American literature, but he was constantly amazed by how much he hadn't read. A colleague would ask his opinion on something, and he would be embarrassed to admit he had never heard of it. His studies had focused primarily on nineteenth century literature, but he had read widely during his graduate studies. He was well prepared to do his job, but it left him woefully ignorant of things normal people read: thrillers, sci-fi, romance, teen fiction, and the like. If Jimmy hadn't returned, William would have spent the evening knocking out one or two novels by Maureen Johnson, someone several of his students seemed to be appalled he hadn't read. He had bought a tablet reader so he could get through more books without having to fill the house with shelves, but he could only read news on the thing. He found he needed paper. He also found Goodwill needed used books, so it worked out in the end.

Concentrating on the books would be impossible, so he decided to put on some sweats and go out to the garage instead. He went back through the box with his father's medals and pulled all of them out. They needed polishing, he thought, so he did that. Then he decided to build a display case for them. He didn't know where he would put it when it was finished, but there were several pieces of wood in the garage left over from other projects. William wasn't much of a carpenter, but when he bought the house he had promised himself he would learn to be handy as the need arose. He had the right tools for this simple job – a saw, a hammer, and a tape measure. He even found sandpaper, steel wool, and a can of stain. The project filled the hours until the pawnshop closed and its employees went home. The mindless repetition of the sanding gave him a chance to think things through.

At ten, he put the sap-stained clothes back on and walked down to the park. He often took late walks, and he almost never ran into anyone on that leg of the greenway at night. The other leg, running from the park to the hospital, included the underside of two bridges. They were sometimes shelter for a drifting homeless person or, more often, a hangout for teens to drink or smoke pot or have sex or whatever else kids wanted to do away from adult eyes. The lack of hiding places kept the west leg clear. William could hear people, though, some chatting on back porches near the trail, others driving along Main Street.

The temperature dropped quickly after sundown this time of year, and he almost wished he had a jacket during that first half mile, until his pace warmed him up. He found himself jogging instead of walking, resisting the urge to break into a full run. When he got to the pine tree behind Eagle Pawn, he didn't hesitate, just pulled back the branches and went right up the tree. There was no one around. The rustle of the leaves in the light October breeze was the only sound William could hear. He took the camera and climbed down.

He didn't try to fight his urge to run on the way back, but stretched out in long, sprinting strides. It had been years since he pushed himself this way, probably since high school football practice. It felt good to have his lungs fill all the way to the bottom, to put his head down and bull his way through the wind and gravity. He couldn't find a word for what he was feeling, but he liked it. He arrived at his porch panting, his legs and sides burning, his throat as rough as the sandpaper he had used in the garage. Inside, he forced himself to strip off the stained clothes and remove the sap before dealing with anything else. The rubbing alcohol worked, and he put the clothes into the washing machine by themselves to finish the job, ignoring the inefficiency for once. By then, his breathing had slowed to normal, and he fixed a glass of water before sitting down at the computer with the memory card from the deer camera.

The first video showed someone William didn't recognize, one of Doug's coworkers, it seemed. The man was maybe fifty years old, with thick salt and pepper hair and a beer gut the size of a medicine ball. He stood outside the door smoking until the camera's timer cut off the video. The next file showed Doug coming in to work, William thought. The back door wasn't locked, and Doug opened it and walked right in. William backed up the video and paused it while the door was open. The angle was poor for seeing into the shop, but he could tell the wall to the left of the door was clear, except for a light switch or an alarm panel. He couldn't be sure because Doug's body blocked most of the view. The door had an automatic return arm that pulled it closed slowly, but the camera angle was blocked early in the arc. The third video showed the first man leaving, and the fourth showed a heavyset woman leaving as well. She had to be sixty or older, and she was clad in a housedress Mamie would have been ashamed to wear in public. She must have been the one minding the store during the first man's smoke break. The last video showed Doug coming out, locking the door and leaving. William watched the video several times, backing up and pausing, trying to see beyond Doug's shoulder and into the shop. The thing on the wall was a security panel. He could make out the little red light glowing there in the last video, after Doug had shut off all the lights inside. William was going to need the code or some way to disable the alarm system.

He deleted everything from the memory card and muttered at himself for washing the clothes so quickly. He was going to have to get back in the tree. Instead of dirtying another uniform, he put on the sweats again, took the camera, and jogged back down to Eagle. The pine tree gave the best straight-on view of the back door, but a dogwood next to the pine would allow for an angled shot of the inside, giving him a view of the area to the right of the door. The tree's branches were low enough, but the leaves were a bit thin. The camera might be seen. William considered this for a moment before deciding to risk it. If someone saw it or even took it, he was pretty sure it couldn't be traced back to him. He attached it to the tree and went home.

That night, he got less sleep than he had the night before, and his dreams were even more disturbing.

CHAPTER 7

In the morning, he went to work as usual and muddled through his two American literature sections. He had lectured on "The Things They Carried" every semester of his teaching career, so he was able to do it on autopilot. He microwaved a soup for lunch and ate it in his office with the door closed. He wanted to go collect the camera, and he thought he had time, but he decided to risk leaving it the rest of the day. The more information he could collect, the better. He was exhausted, so he pushed his chair back, put his feet on the Resolute desk, and shut his eyes. He was able to fall asleep quickly and peacefully, for the first time since Jimmy's return. An hour later, he was awakened by a knock at his office door. MacKenzie Cline had come to have her paper graded.

He made his way through all the afternoon appointments without falling asleep at his desk again, although two of the papers put him dangerously close to it. Student work could be painfully pedestrian. He filled the time between work and the close of Eagle Pawn working on the display case, researching his father's medals and creating labels for them. He ate another bowl of soup in front of the computer and then re-sanded the case and added a coat of polyurethane.

When ten o'clock came, he jogged down the trail and recovered the camera. He made himself jog back this time, stifling the urge to sprint again. There were several new videos on the memory card. The first showed Doug walking up, unlocking the door, and going inside. He faced the wall with the security panel while the door closed after him. The angle didn't show that wall at all, but William was sure Doug was entering a code. Stopping and starting the video for the second or two the door was open, William was able to see a row of shelves along the wall behind Doug. The top shelf had a metal grid over it, making it look like a cage. The shelves were full of random boxes and cases, but the shot wasn't clear enough for William to be sure what they were. The second video showed the woman coming in. She stopped to unlock the door, then realized it was open and went in. The third showed the woman coming out for a smoke break. There was no audio, but she must have been talking to Doug or a customer, because she stood just outside the doorway for several seconds, looking back inside and blowing smoke over her shoulder toward the pine tree.

With no one blocking the shot, William could see the shelves clearly. The top one was a sort of cage, with a lock on its doors. The bottom two were open but full. He couldn't be sure, but his best guess was that the cage held items that had been pawned and were waiting to be redeemed. The lower shelves could be old, useless things or just things that weren't valuable enough to lock up. The rest of the videos showed Doug and his coworkers entering, leaving, or smoking. William didn't learn anything more from the files. He thought about putting the camera back in the dogwood tree, but he was pretty sure he'd gotten all he could from that angle. He wiped the memory card and went to bed, thinking and dreaming about his next move.

~ ~ ~

Friday morning, William continued the discussion of process analysis with his written composition students, examining the structure of example essays from their textbook. He wondered if there were "How to disable a security system" essays online. He felt certain there would be, but he also thought the NSA or someone like that might be monitoring those sites. He would have to figure it out on his own.

In his Major Authors section, they discussed a feminist reading of "The Fall of the House of Usher," its blatant failure of the Bechdel test, and whether the work should be considered overtly misogynistic. William didn't have a great deal of personal interest in these questions, but he believed a university education meant considering as many viewpoints as possible. The fiery debate between Regina and Nick made the class interesting enough to distract William from his impending felonies for a while.

After class, he settled in his office and considered the problem one more time. If his day and a half of surveillance were typical, only one person worked the evening shift at Eagle. It might be Doug or the other man, but the woman seemed to be on the day shift. Of course, a day and a half was hardly enough to be sure of any patterns. He needed more information. He decided to set up the camera again after work. He could put it in the pine tree again, so it wouldn't be seen and get three or four days' worth of entries and exits before he made any decisions. He needed his plan to be perfect and for everything to go exactly according to plan. He waded through his emails, responding as needed for the next half hour or so.

William was thinking about walking up the north greenway to Four Brothers, a local pizza place, for lunch, when Jimmy walked into the office. He didn't bother to knock, just pulled back a chair and sat.

"You wanna hear something unbelievable?" Jimmy asked.

"Probably not."

"I just used the faculty bathroom down the hall."

"I have no trouble believing that."

"There are two commodes and two urinals in there, and not a one of them had been flushed. Place smelled like a horse trailer." William shrugged. He had seen the bathroom in that condition many times. "I just couldn't believe it," Jimmy said. "Grown-ass men with graduate degrees can't flush the damn toilet. I know inmates more contentious."

"Did you just say contentious?"

"I did."

"All right."

Jimmy folded his hands in his lap and sat back in the tall leather chair. He looked comfortable, like he might put his feet up and have a nap, just as William had the day before. "So have you been thinking?" he asked.

"I have."

"What did you think of?"

There was a knock, and William looked up to see Danny at the door. "I'm going down to Dean Dillon's office. Anything you'd like me to mention?"

"No, thanks," William said. "I'll catch up with her later."

Danny nodded and walked away, heading back toward his own office.

"That one's not very good at coded messages, is he?" Jimmy asked.

"Not really. Mary Dillon heard you were here the other day. She told me to call her if you came back. She wants security to escort you off campus."

"Well, she always was a sweetheart. How's Fred, anyway?"

"Retired. Deer hunting this week."

"Venison stew would be nice. I haven't had any since the last time I was out."

"Let's walk and talk. If I know Danny, he's already called security."

Jimmy stood, and William followed him out, pausing to close and lock the office door before going down the hall and through the lobby. From the top of the stairs, William saw security on their way up. "Meet me at Four Brothers in fifteen minutes."

Jimmy nodded and walked down to the landing to meet them. "Good morning, gentlemen," he said.

"Are you James Baker?" asked one of the two uniformed men. William had spoken to the man two or three times over the years, but he couldn't come up with a name. The other man was a complete stranger.

"I am," Jimmy said. "Let's all go for a walk. I'd love to show you my car."

"That sounds great," the first man said. "We'll follow you."

Jimmy looked up at William and winked.

William went back through the lobby and down the west hall, avoiding Danny's office and taking the service stairs, leaving the building on the side nearest the north greenway. He waved and spoke to several students along the path, which saw much heavier traffic than the west greenway. He got to Four Brothers before Jimmy and took the booth closest to the door.

"Dr. Baker," the waitress said, "you're not in your usual spot."

"I'm expecting someone."

"You got a hot date?"

"It's just my brother."

Michaela had been in his freshman composition class several years earlier, but he hadn't remembered her when she started working at Four Brothers. She remembered the C she got in his class, which was better than she had expected. She was grateful for the gift, she had said. William wasn't in the habit of passing students out of kindness, so he felt certain she had earned the C. Michaela had learned William's order after two meals, and she didn't even ask if he wanted the usual anymore. He liked that in a waitress. "I'll have your food right out," she said, "unless you want me to wait."

"Don't wait. I'm not even sure he'll eat."

Michaela nodded and walked away, but Jimmy came in and sat before she had made it back to the counter. She turned and came back. "Can I get your order?" she asked.

"I'll have what he's having," Jimmy said.

"Are you sure?"

"I'm sure," Jimmy said. "I would also like a small pizza with ham and Italian sausage and Coca-Cola to drink."

"Coming right up," Michaela said and walked away.

"You were about to tell me what you've come up with," Jimmy said. "Before I was so politely escorted off campus."

"What took you so long? I walked here."

"Reggie and Scott just had to see under the hood of my car. I thought they might have me arrested just so they could take it for a spin while I was in lock-up."

"Seriously?"

"Seriously. They also let me know any future visits will result in prosecution for trespassing. I hate to speak ill of your employer, but that university is severely lacking in southern hospitality."

"I'll mention that at the next faculty meeting."

Michaela sat two glasses of Coke on the table and walked away without interrupting. William liked that in a waitress, too.

"So what's your plan?" Jimmy asked.

"I'm still working on it. I'll need a few more days. Maybe a week."

"I'm not waiting that long," Jimmy said. He shook his head and rubbed his hands on his jeans. "I guess I'll have to handle it myself."

"What's your hurry?"

"I'll be traveling for a few days. I don't want this gnawing at me on the road."

"Travelling?"

"For work."

"Are you planning to rob houses in all fifty states?"

"I don't do that anymore."

"Really? What do you do now?" William had trouble believing his brother would take a legitimate job, even if he could get one.

"It's better you don't know."

William had no trouble believing that. "I'll have it sorted out by the time you get back. Just trust me."

Jimmy huffed. "Three days is a long time with something eating at your insides, little brother. I want to deal with this. I'm leaving Sunday, so this has to be sorted out by tomorrow. I still don't understand why you don't just call the cops."

"And tell them what? That the gun our dad pulled off a dead soldier turned up in someone else's hands? I don't have a serial number, and we don't even know what the initials stood for."

"They don't need that to look into it. Between the initials and the scratches, you can identify the property. They have to open a file, and that file is public record. It'll tell me what I want to know. Now, just pull your little phone out of your pocket and make the call."

"No."

"Why the hell not?"

"Because when I find out who stole it, I'm going to break all his fingers, and I don't want cops getting in my way."

"It's good to see you, Billy."

William took a deep breath and tried to bring his temperature down. He hadn't felt the outburst coming, but it left his heart pumping as hard as the run two nights earlier. He hadn't let the idea reach his conscious mind, but he realized this was what his subconscious was working toward since he saw the gun in the glass case at Eagle Pawn. He wasn't just planning a break-in. He was planning revenge. Someone had stolen the only object Ian Baker had ever really cared about, and that person was going to be taught a lesson he would never forget. After that, William would go right on teaching his classes and living his life without any police intervention. That was the plan brewing inside his subconscious. Everything else was just tactics. With that settled in his own mind, he was finally able to get down to business.

"I'm going to need your help."

"You've got it," Jimmy said.

The restaurant had been dead when William arrived, with just one other booth occupied. Since Jimmy sat down, the lunch crowd had begun to arrive. William tilted his head toward the other booths, and Jimmy nodded. The brothers sat silently, sipping their Cokes occasionally, until the pizza came.

"I forgot how good this was," Jimmy said after his first bite. William nodded. "You don't get good pizza in prison."

"I'm not surprised."

"It's as good a reason to stay out as any."

"Any reason is a good reason."

"Almost."

They ate the rest of the pizza without talking. Michaela stopped by with the ticket, and Jimmy pulled money out of his boot again. "I'll get this one," he said. "I'm sure I still owe you for one thing or another." William nodded. They got up and walked out, Jimmy following William through the parking lot to the greenway entrance.

"I've got students coming. Meet me in Currie Park at three-thirty, and I'll tell you everything." Jimmy nodded and walked toward his Charger. William walked the greenway back to campus and graded papers with his students all afternoon.

CHAPTER 8

At three-thirty, William found Jimmy sitting on a bench in Currie Park. He was eating a candy bar William didn't recognize and drinking another Coke.

"They didn't have these the last time I was out. Have you tried this?"

William shook his head, and Jimmy held the bar out to him. William took it and tore off the bottom, as far away from Jimmy's teeth marks as possible. He handed Jimmy the rest of the bar and popped the piece into his mouth. It was good, some mix of caramel and vanilla cream. French vanilla, according to the label. William nodded, still chewing.

"You're welcome," Jimmy said. He offered William the bottle of Coke, but William shook his head. "I ain't diseased, you know."

"I'm not taking the chance."

Jimmy laughed.

William started walking down the trail, and Jimmy caught up after a few paces. "Where's this go?" he asked.

"Dickson Road. It comes out at Shirley's."

"Right next to Eagle."

William nodded. He kept an eye out for other people on the trail and explained what he had already learned, speaking in a low voice. By the time they reached the Osgood Oaks apartment complex, he had covered everything he knew, so he went on to tell Jimmy the next phase of the plan. They had passed Eagle and stopped at the edge of the Shirley's parking lot.

"How are you going to get in?" Jimmy asked.

"Pick the lock."

"Really?"

"Dad was a locksmith for thirty-five years. You don't think he taught me to open a door?"

"He didn't teach me."

William shrugged.

"You know what you'd say to me if I came up with an idea as crazy as this?" Jimmy asked.

"I'm sure it would be a stinging critique."

"That's a nice way of putting it."

"But it'll work."

"Parts one and two are pretty solid, if you're right about their schedule," Jimmy said, "but part three is a full-on crap shoot, and if that don't work, we've wasted a whole lot of time."

"True."

"It's your call, little brother, but I'm not sold on it."

"It'll work. Just do your bit."

"All right."

They walked back to the park and parted ways there. His plan in place and his mind made up, William was able to get a little sleep. He set an alarm for seven-thirty and lay down. He slept sound, dreamless sleep and woke up fifteen minutes earlier than he needed to. He dressed in black jeans and an old Ravens sweatshirt, black with dingy white lettering. It wasn't a proper thief's attire, but it was the closest thing he had. He wasn't planning to steal anything, in any case. He went out to the garage and checked the lock picks in the leather pouch. Satisfied, he tucked them and an old pair of work gloves in his back pocket, took the deer camera, and walked down the greenway to Eagle. He pulled back the pine's branches and hid inside to wait for Jimmy's text. There should only be one employee inside, unless Friday scheduling was different from Wednesday and

Thursday. William had no idea if pawnshops got busier on weekend nights like other businesses. Even Jimmy hadn't known for sure. He usually did his business on a weekday afternoon. William silenced his phone and held it in front of him so he could see a message coming in. He breathed slowly, keeping himself focused and calm.

The last time he could remember committing a crime had been stealing the bricks. He didn't even speed. Before that, it had been when he was a sophomore at Hopkins. He overheard a couple of guys saying they had copied the answer key for their American history final. They were throwing a party at their apartment that night instead of studying. William was offended for Dr. Cline, whom he really liked, and for all the students who had actually done the work. He picked the apartment lock that afternoon while the guys were in another final and spiked all their food and drinks with liquid laxatives. Fully half the class was at the party, and they all missed the test because of stomach issues. They had to take a make-up with a different answer key, and William never told a soul.

Jimmy's first text came in at seven fifty-five, exactly as planned. The message was simply "1." There was only one employee in the store. William slipped out of the tree and stood by Eagle's back door, waiting for the second text. He was a bit exposed there – anyone on the trail might see him, and it was possible someone in the Shirley's parking lot might glance from just the right angle to get a view. The odds were against it, though, and he wanted to save the precious seconds it would take to cross from the tree to the door. He slipped on his gloves and tested the knob. He expected it to be unlocked during business hours, but he needed to be sure. It turned, so he waited, his right hand on the door handle, his left hand holding the phone, the camera tucked under his left arm.

Jimmy's other job was to call the employee over to the game shelf and ask questions. That would put the employee the farthest possible distance from the back door. The second text came in at seven fifty-eight – the letter "G" for "Go."

William went. He dropped the phone into his left pocket and pulled the handle. The door turned silently on its hinges, and he stepped through, leaving it to swing closed on its own.

"Rear door entry. Rear door entry."

He ignored the Speak & Spell, letting the camera slip down his arm and into his left hand. Two strides took him across the space to the storage shelves. He set the camera on the second shelf, behind an instrument case. The word "saxophone" flashed in William's mind as he positioned the camera to face the control panel on the wall. He turned his body to gauge the sightline. It looked good, so he stepped back to the door, catching it before its return arm brought it closed. He looked back at the shelf to be sure the camera wouldn't be seen. If you were looking directly at it, maybe, he thought. Close enough. He stepped outside and pushed the door closed as quietly as possible.

"Rear door exit. Rear door exit."

The sound was muffled by the door, but he heard it as he darted around the pine tree and hid inside its trailside branches. He was breathing hard, so he forced himself to breathe through his nose and as slowly as possible. He crouched inside the pine branches and leaned one direction, then another until he had a sliver of a view to the door. It took much longer than he thought it would. He started to count seconds, but realized it was pointless.

Finally, the door opened, and Doug came out, looking in both directions and walking around the building toward the parking lot. "Rear door exit. Rear door exit." William had to adjust his position to keep watching. He wasn't sure the pine branches were as thick on the sides as they were on the front and back. He worried Doug would see him when he turned around, which Doug did just at that moment. He stopped and looked right at the tree. If he saw William, he didn't show it. He turned his head slowly, as if trying to catch a sound, like the twist of an old AM dial, William thought. Doug was probably too young to have ever listened to AM radio. He gave up after a few seconds and ran around to the other side of the building.

William couldn't get a view of that side, so he waited, turning his own head slowly to listen for Doug's footsteps. After a few seconds, he heard them. Then he saw Doug come back into view. Doug opened the back door and went inside.

"Rear door entry. Rear door entry."

There was nothing more William could do until after Doug closed up shop, so he slipped out of the tree and walked back to his house. He sat on the porch swing, enjoying the night air and waiting for Jimmy. A few minutes later, the Charger's headlights came into view on Wilson Street. The car turned down Harvie Road and passed William's house, pulling into a space in the Currie Park lot. Jimmy got out and walked up to William's porch. William gestured to the bench, and Jimmy sat down beside him.

"Thanks."

Jimmy nodded. "I could hear the security system, but not the door. The kid thought it was a false alarm."

"Good. You sure kept him busy."

"I had a lot of questions," Jimmy said, an astonished look coming over his face. "Do you know what a PlayStation is?"

"Heroin with a remote control."

"Damn right. I'd seen them, but I'd never played one. I mean, I played Atari and Nintendo and some others, but this stuff now is amazing. It's like watching a movie, except you're controlling one of the actors. It's kind of creepy, to tell the truth." He shook his head.

William nodded, and the brothers let the swing carry them back and forth for a little while. They hadn't been this close since Mamie's funeral, carrying her casket from the hearse and setting it down on the machinery that would lower her into the ground. William remembered the rage he felt toward his brother that day, but there on the porch, the image just made him weary. He looked between the houses across the road and watched cars pass on Main Street, trying to clear his mind.

"Do you think you'll get it?" Jimmy asked.

"We'll know in a few hours."

"What do you want to do till then?"

"I have a PlayStation."

"Are you serious?"

"It's two generations old, but it works."

Jimmy stopped the swing and stood. "After you, little brother."

William went inside and pulled the system out of the closet where it typically spent fifty weeks of the year. He hooked it up and proceeded to beat the living daylights out of Jimmy at Madden football until Eagle Pawn had closed for the night. Jimmy smiled and laughed and shook his head, clearly enjoying himself, in spite of the lopsided scores. They played a couple of extra games just to be sure the night's traffic had died down. Eventually, William put the system away, and they walked down to the Charger.

Jimmy's job was to set up in the Shirley's parking lot and be a lookout. The Charger was much too flashy for the job, but William couldn't risk the Corolla being seen. He never drove to Shirley's, and there would be questions if a student or colleague saw it there. Jimmy drove away, and William walked down the greenway. He hadn't gotten to Osgood Oaks before he got Jimmy's text. "Set."

Rounding the bend at the apartment complex, William heard a low buzz he recognized. The trees blocked out most of the city light, but there was still enough for him to make out the shape of Mr. Berry rolling along. William knew the scooter was slowing down before he could really see it. The buzz had changed tone.

When he was close enough to be sure Mr. Berry could hear him, he called, "Out a bit late tonight, aren't you Mr. Berry?"

"I could say the same to you, William."

"I suppose you could."

"I am glad it's you, though. I don't mind telling you I was a little afraid when I saw someone coming toward me in all black clothes. You look like a thief, William."

"It's laundry day."

Mr. Berry slowed the chair to a stop, and William walked right up to him.

"You don't have to say it."

"Say what?"

"I know I shouldn't be out here in the dark. Old man in a wheelchair. I just needed some air. It gets a bit stuffy sitting in that room all by myself."

"I know the feeling."

"I mean, there are other people at the Arms, but they're all old. Older than I am, most of them."

William nodded. *That's my future*, he thought. *Sitting in an old folks' home, wishing I could go out for a walk.* He pushed the thought aside. "Just be careful getting back, okay?"

"I will. Take care, William."

"Goodnight, Mr. Berry."

"Goodnight, William."

The buzz started up, and Mr. Berry rolled the way William had come. William walked on, wondering if Mr. Berry suspected anything. If things went according to plan, it wouldn't matter. He got a second text from Jimmy. "?"

William replied, "Mr. Berry." He wasn't sure Jimmy had ever met the old man, but he couldn't think of anything else to send.

"OK," was Jimmy's reply.

When William reached the back of Eagle Pawn, he texted "?" and slipped on his gloves.

"G."

William took a quick look around before walking up to the door. It was clear, so he knelt down and took out his tools. Billy had watched his father pick locks dozens of times, and he had convinced Ian to teach him at the age of ten. There had been a long speech about ethics and morals and laws, but Billy was a boy who never got into that kind of trouble. His temper was an issue, but his parents trusted him, and he made sure they never had reason to doubt the wisdom in doing so. He opened the two locks in under sixty seconds, and he felt slow and out of practice because of that time. When he heard the thunk of the deadbolt settling inside the door, he turned the knob, swung open the door, took two strides into the room, grabbed the camera, took strides and closed the door.

He was in and out before the system could say, "Rear door entry. Rear door entry."

He had the door locked again shortly after it said, "Rear door exit. Rear door exit."

He put Ian's tools in his pockets and ran.

Around the pine tree and down the trail, William ran as fast as he ever had. At Osgood Oaks, he forced himself to slow down, to jog then walk, to act as if he were just out for a stroll. He wondered if he might catch up to Mr. Berry and listened for the buzz of the scooter. He couldn't hear anything over the sound of his own breathing, the pounding of his own blood through his veins. He walked and forced himself to act naturally, to breathe deeply, to be on an ordinary moonlight stroll. He still got home faster than he should have.

CHAPTER 9

William didn't expect to hear from Jimmy anytime soon. He expected to have a long, uncomfortable wait. The cops would come, and they'd call the owner or whoever the security company had listed. They would look around and make sure nothing had been stolen. They would make sure nothing had been moved. If everything went the way William believed it would, since nothing had been stolen or moved – nothing that belonged there, anyway – in the end, they would declare the whole thing a false alarm and go on about their business.

In the meantime, William popped out the camera's memory card and settled in to see what was on it. The first video showed William stepping toward the back door and out of the shot. The angle caught his back first and then his side, but anyone who knew him would be sure who it was. He deleted the file. He deleted his viewing history. He deleted his Temp folder. He deleted everything he knew how to delete that might possibly give someone a copy of that video.

Then he watched the second file. It showed Doug coming back to check the door. According to the time stamp, Jimmy had managed to delay him almost a full minute. Doug could write, but he wasn't much of a gatekeeper. There were four more files. The next two showed Doug's left arm for less than a second. William couldn't be sure, but he thought Doug must have been getting things from the locked cage above the spot where the camera had been. He had gotten just enough of his body into the camera's motion sensor to turn it on.

The next to last file showed exactly what William had planned to record: Doug punching in the code to set the alarm system before going home. William slowed down the view and watched it frame by frame. The angle caused a slight perspective problem. William thought the code was 2638, but it could just as easily have been 1638 or 1637 or even 2637. The buttons on the panel glowed a dull green-gray, and the outside column was more distinct than those on the inside. He wrote down all four sequences, just in case. The last file showed William approaching, his hand grabbing the camera and covering the lens. He deleted everything on the memory card and repeated the deletion process for the computer.

He took the card out to the garage and put it in the well of his charcoal grill. He doused it with starter fluid and lit a fire. He watched until the card had shriveled and writhed into a small black nugget of plastic. He thought about destroying the camera, too, but it seemed like overkill, and he might need it again. He was being paranoid, he thought, but he was pretty sure paranoia was his friend. He wasn't of the House of Usher, and his paranoia had always served him well.

He went back into the house and studied the numbers. He could remember them easily enough, but he kept the list in case panic made his mind go blank when it mattered. He hoped they wouldn't change the code. He didn't think they would. They had no reason to suspect the code had been compromised. Either someone had broken in and the alarm had scared the burglar off, or the sensors were faulty. There was no problem with the code. He considered getting online and doing a little research on alarm systems. What were the protocols for code changes?

How many chances did you get to enter the correct code?

Ian Baker had done locks, not alarm systems. He had a friend he recommended for that kind of thing. He said it was a waste of money for most people. Good locks, storm doors, and double-paned windows were usually enough. There were too many easy targets for thieves, too many people who didn't even do the basics. William was too paranoid to do the research. If things went wrong, he didn't want that stuff in his search history, and he knew the one he could delete wasn't the only copy. With a warrant, the internet service provider would have to give up every site he had ever surfed.

There was nothing to do but wait, so he settled in his recliner, leaned back, and put his phone on his chest. He slept for almost an hour before Jimmy's call woke him up.

"They're gone," Jimmy said.

"All of them? No chance one of them is hiding in there waiting for someone to come back? No chance they've got a cop pacing the greenway, watching for a second attempt?"

"All the people who went inside came back outside and left. I counted."

"Can you see the trail?"

"Not very well, but if there's someone back there, he walked from your end. No one's come through here."

"Keep watching. I'll be there shortly."

He was about to hang up when his brother spoke. "Miss Marple, the next time you send me on a stake out, remind me to wear a coat."

"I'll bear that in mind."

He hung up and double-checked his tools, his gloves, and his numbers before going back out to the trail. He had walked the west greenway countless times over the years, but he had never made so many trips in so short a time. Most days, he felt young. All the walking kept him fit and energetic, and he was still as slim as he had been in college. Physically, he was more like his students than his colleagues, but he wasn't twenty anymore. He could feel his years on that third walk to Eagle Pawn. On the curve around Osgood Oaks, he heard young people babbling, their words slurred as they called to each other in the parking lot below. The bars had just closed, and Samuels University's students and faculty – some of them, at least – were up to no good. William was glad for the leaves still clinging to their branches and blocking the view of him from the cars and apartments below. He walked on, confident that he wouldn't be seen by anyone sober enough to remember, that he probably wouldn't be seen by anyone at all.

He texted Jimmy when he got close enough to see the pawn shop. "?"

While he waited for a reply, William walked slowly past the shop, scanning the trees for any sign of a hiding policeman or anyone else who might see him. He slipped into the pine tree and scanned its branches to see if by chance anyone had put up another camera, hoping to catch a shot of a thief. It was too dark to see much.

Jimmy texted "Clear."

William used the light of the phone screen to give the pine's branches a better look, but the screen light died less than a foot from his hand. He saw nothing, so he slipped out on the other side, closer to the door, and knelt down. He scanned the edges of the door, looking for any sign of new security measures – anything that might set off the alarm or somehow record his presence. He saw nothing, so he pulled on the gloves, picked the lock, and went inside.

"Rear door entry. Rear door entry."

He stepped up to the security panel. The numbers glowed red, showing the system was on. He typed in 2638. The red lights flashed off and on and off and on again.

"Code error. Code error."

He could hear the voice coming from above the door and echoing around the main store. He ran through his mental list of possibilities and tried to review the footage of Doug in his mind. William thought he would get two more chances before the alarm went off and called the cops back to Eagle, but he wasn't sure. He might only have one more shot. He made the decision and entered 2637. The lights on the panel went from red to green, and William's blood pressure dropped. He was in.

He turned around and got his first full view of the shop's back room. His in-and-out dashes had given him a vague sense of the place, but nothing more. It looked more like a hallway than a proper room. The shelves along the inside wall faced another set that he hadn't noticed earlier. The sight shocked him a little. What else had he missed? A little workstation sat at the far end – a desk with a dinosaur of a computer and a dot matrix printer. William couldn't believe it. He walked over and took a closer look. The printer was loaded with perforated carbon paper, pre-printed with the form for pawned items. The dot matrix made sense then. Up close, he could see a small inkjet on a narrow shelf under the desk.

Getting into the shop was nothing. Getting past the alarm was complicated. Getting into the database would either be a piece of cake or completely impossible. William had gambled it would be the former. He had worked a number of odd jobs over the years. He delivered papers as a kid, when children still did that kind of work. He delivered pizza when he was in high school. During college and grad school, he took a different job every summer, a habit he continued until he got tenure and the salary bump that came with it. Every business he had ever worked in – every office, every factory, every camp, every restaurant – had at least one thing in common: at least one employee who couldn't handle technology. William was betting at least one person employed by Eagle Pawn couldn't remember how to handle the database. For that Luddite's sake, there would be a set of idiot-proof instructions, complete with username and password, stored somewhere in arm's reach of that computer. He might be wrong, and it might be too buried by other stuff for him to find it in the minutes he was willing to stay in the shop, but his gut had told him all along that it would be there. In reality, it was much easier than he had imagined. They had printed it out in eighteen-point font and taped it to the wall above the computer.

"I will sing the achievements of General Ludd," William mumbled to himself.

He sat down at the desk and turned on the computer. It was slow to boot up, and when it finally did, he had to look it over twice to be sure what to do with it. The operating system looked to be three or four generations old. He had forgotten Windows once looked like that. The database was conveniently labeled "Database." When he opened it, he saw several fields with abbreviations that meant nothing to him. He checked the instructions and found an explanation. He could search by name or by item number or a few other options. He needed the item number for his father's gun, so he got up and went into the main shop.

The gun case was locked and dark. William bent down and squinted at the little tag tied to the trigger guard. It was too dark to read the numbers. He pulled out his cell phone, pressed a button to bring the screen to life, and held it to the glass. It didn't help. He went to the end of the shelf and looked for a switch. He was pretty sure there were lights in there to better show off the hardware. He had to check both ends and the middle before he found it. The light was brighter than he imagined, and it threw a glaring reflection of William on the front door. He saw his own furious face staring at him in the glass and switched off the light.

"Bad idea," he whispered to himself.

He went back to the desk and scanned it, then opened the only drawer. No flashlight. He looked down the shelves, but there was nothing that would help. He went back to the main store and scanned it.

"TV," he whispered.

He went over and took the smallest TV from the display wall and walked back to the gun shelf. The cord was just long enough to reach the plug in the wall behind the counter. He turned the TV on and put it screen-down on the display case. It worked. He could see the number. It was too long to remember, so he had to go back for a pen and write it on the back of the paper with the alarm code options. His gloves were too thick and the pen felt awkward in his hand. He turned off the TV, unplugged it, and put it back on the shelf. He walked back to the counter and looked at the TV wall. He couldn't be sure he had put it back exactly as he found it. Hoping no one would notice, he went back to the computer.

Typing was even harder with the gloves. He tried three times to enter the number, each time catching too many keys with the wide canvas fingers. He gave up and used the pen to hunt and peck. The old computer hummed a couple of seconds before showing him what he had gone to all this trouble to learn. The gun had been sold by a Patrick Riley. The named seemed familiar, but William couldn't place it. There was also an address. He was scribbling this above the gun's number when he heard the back door open.

"Rear door entry. Rear door entry."

He froze. The shop didn't offer much in the way of hiding places. He would have to run or do something violent. He was still making up his mind when he heard, "Billy? Billy, what's taking so long?" Jimmy came down the length of the room toward him.

William relaxed for a split second before his anxiety transformed into fury at his brother. "Jimmy, what the hell are you doing? You're supposed to be the lookout. Get out of here. I'm almost done."

He didn't watch to see what Jimmy would do, just bent back down and finished copying the address. He put the paper in his pocket and felt Jimmy pass behind him. He closed the database and shut down the computer. He had wanted to try to erase the search, but he had taken too much time already.

"Jimmy, I've got the name and address. Let's go."

"I want that gun," Jimmy said. He was standing over the case.

"If you take the gun, they'll know we were here. The whole thing is supposed to look like a bunch of false alarms, like their system is faulty. Anything comes up missing, everything will get complicated. We don't want complicated."

"I want that gun," Jimmy repeated. He was shaking the sliding door of the case, trying to get it open.

At least he has gloves on, William thought. They were thin, tight gloves. The kind he should have been wearing.

Jimmy stepped back from the counter and sighed. He walked around to the front of the case and stared at the gun for a moment.

"Jimmy, I'll come back on Monday and buy the gun."

It was too late, though. He hadn't quite finished the sentence when Jimmy raised his right leg and put his boot into the glass. For a fraction of a second, William was impressed by his brother's technique. He had broken through the thick pane with a quick motion and brought back his foot before it went far enough for the leg above the boot to be in danger of the shards. Then the alarm went off – a screeching, whooping sound that came with flashing red lights above the alarm system speakers.

"Gun case breach. Gun case breach."

It had never occurred to William that there might be secondary alarms. He had only seen one security panel.

Jimmy grabbed the gun and tucked it into his belt. "Now we can go," he said.

William's old friend paranoia spoke instructions in his mind, pushing aside the fury, the deep desire to snap Jimmy's neck. "Bags," he shouted over the den of the alarm. "Get bags." He pointed to the jewelry counter.

Jimmy responded, much cooler in the face of the noise and lights than William would have believed. His brother was better at this stuff than he had given credit. William snatched up as many handguns as he could and dumped them into the first bag Jimmy brought to him.

"Why are we stealing these guns, little brother?"

"If we only steal one, they're going to know it was the one you asked about. The one I was looking at when I talked to Doug. They'll be looking for you and maybe even me. If we take a bunch, it looks like a random smash and grab." Jimmy nodded and handed William another bag. William filled that with pistols, and Jimmy kicked the other case.

"Jewelry case breach. Jewelry case breach."

Jimmy dumped the first row of rings and bracelets into a bag and turned to go. "Let's move, Billy." He snapped his fingers.

William gave up the effort and followed, but Jimmy stopped him with a hand on his chest. "Grab the Desert Eagle. No robber would leave that behind." William grabbed it and followed Jimmy out the back door.

"Rear door exit. Rear door exit."

William stopped two paces out, turned and blocked the closing door with the barrel of the Desert Eagle. In all the noise and excitement, he had forgotten to deal with the cameras inside the store. He had planned to avoid them, to stay inside the office and never be caught on video.

"Rear door entry. Rear door entry."

William dumped the big gun into the bag with the others and set his bags by the door. He scanned the wall for the wires. A hole had been drilled above the interior door, and the wires came through it like strands of rope. They weren't connected to the computer he had used. It had been off. He followed the wires to a box on the floor. It looked like one of the servers in the bowels of the Samuels IT department – small lights and ports on the front and the back.

William yanked the wires and tucked the box under his arm, snatching up the bags on his way out.

"Rear door exit. Rear door exit."

He ran about a hundred yards before he could distinguish between the sirens of the police cars and the pawnshop's alarm. At two hundred yards, Jimmy came from some hiding place in the trees and joined him.

"What did you forget?" Jimmy asked. William didn't speak, just hitched the hard drive a little higher. "The files?"

"The video."

"Good thinking, Billy. Damn good thinking."

CHAPTER 10

Together, the brothers picked up speed, not a sprint, but a steady jog. The jewelry jangled, and a sprint just wasn't possible with all the extra weight. The guns clacked together in the bags, hammers stretching the plastic and threatening to poke through. At the bend around Osgood Oaks, William slowed and tried to catch a glimpse of the parking lot through the trees. He couldn't see much, but there were no flashing blue lights, which was reassuring. He thought the cops would assume a getaway car and not even think about the greenway. If one of them did consider it, he expected they would be looking for tracks from a motorcycle or four-wheeler or someone slipping through to a car parked nearby. The Oaks parking lot seemed the outside limit for that. No rational criminal would try to take stolen goods the length of the greenway on foot. What they were doing was just too stupid for anyone to suspect it.

About two thirds of the way down the track, one of the guns finally poked through the bag, so William stopped to deal with it. He dumped the jewelry in with the guns, the rings and necklaces filling the empty space like sand around rocks. Then he tucked that bag into the other, like double-bagged soup cans from Shirley's. The maneuver wasn't easy with the hard drive under his left arm, but he managed. Jimmy stopped and did the same thing, moving a little quicker without the extra burden.

At the edge of the park, William picked a bush and hid the bag and the hard drive. "Wait here." He jogged up to the house. The neighbors' houses were dark. He went in and swapped the black clothes for his uniform, grabbed his shopping backpack, and went back down to meet Jimmy. They packed the server and the Eagle bags into the backpack and went back to the house.

"I need to get my car," Jimmy said.

"Not tonight, you don't."

"That car stands out, Billy. I can't just leave it there."

"That's why you have to. They'll notice when it leaves. We don't want questions."

"Somebody's gonna question why it sat there all night."

"You had a fight with Wendy, had too much to drink, realized you shouldn't be driving, parked it there, and called me. I came down and walked you back here to sleep it off. That's our story. It covers everything – why you were there, why our tracks are on the trail, why Mr. Berry saw me, and why the car sat overnight. Clear?"

"Yeah."

"They'll suspect you, anyway."

"No shit, Miss Marple."

"This wouldn't be happening if you had just done what I asked you to. Just stay in the car and be the lookout. How hard is that?"

"I'm sorry, Billy. You were taking too long. Three minutes is max on a job. The sirens were going off in my head."

"I had it under control."

"You were gonna leave Dad's gun."

"I had to. You know that."

"Well, you've got it now."

"I've got it, but now I can't keep it. It's stolen property. If I keep it, that break-in hangs over me for the rest of my life."

"Seven years. Statute of limitations."

"They could still fire me."

Jimmy nodded and sat down. "I'm sorry, Billy."

"William."

"I'm sorry, William. I'll take it with me. All of it. Hide the stuff till we figure something out."

"No. I'll handle that." William wasn't sure what it was, but he could feel another idea bubbling up from the back of his mind. He hoped it would be more sensible than the last one.

"You got the name, right?" Jimmy asked. He pulled Ian Baker's .45 out of the bag and tucked it into his waistband.

William breathed slowly, pushing away images of violence. No one else could make him so angry so quickly. "I got it." He pulled the paper from his pocket and sat down across from Jimmy. He passed the slip to his brother.

"Patrick Riley," Jimmy said. "That name mean anything to you?"

"It sounds familiar, but I don't know why. Could be a freshman comp student from sometime back. I've had several Rileys and dozens of Patricks. Could be nothing."

"Chapman Road. Where is that?"

"South side, I think."

"White or black?"

William shook his head. Most of the neighborhoods in that part of town were poor, and many were still as segregated as they had been in the 1950s. He had never spent much time in that part of town, just passing through occasionally on his way to somewhere else. He had known people who lived there over the years, students and classmates, but he had never been invited to anyone's house in those neighborhoods. Most of the shootings in Osgood took place there.

"Wherever he lives," Jimmy said, "I wanna have a talk with him."

"We will. But I'm going to do some research first."

Jimmy looked like he was about to argue, but William glared at him. Jimmy raised his hands in surrender. "You sure you don't want me to hide this stuff?" he asked.

"I know a place." William stood to leave, and Jimmy got up with him. William shook his head. "You're sleeping it off, remember."

Jimmy nodded and sat back down.

"Take the front bedroom, if you want."

"Really?"

William nodded and went out to the Corolla. He put the backpack in the trunk and drove down to the old mill. In the dark, he had to stumble around a bit to find a good pile of broken bricks. He cursed the ground, cursed the bricks, and cursed his brother. Only Jimmy could have gotten him into something like this. Only Jimmy could have screwed things up so completely. If he'd just waited in the car, everything would have gone according to plan. Even William himself hadn't really believed in the plan, but it had worked exactly as he had imagined right up to the point of entering the item number into the database. He should have brought a flashlight. That was on him. But he had that under control until Jimmy lost his cool. William realized he was venting out loud. His voice was still low, but he knew he needed to rein it in before he got to a full rant and called attention to himself. The nearest houses were more than a block away, but his voice would carry in the stillness before dawn.

Eventually, he picked a spot and shifted the bricks until he could shove both bags of guns and jewelry into the mound. He covered them up and kicked bricks in different directions until he felt sure the bags wouldn't be seen. He walked back a few paces and took a long look. The bricks now looked like a burial mound, something obviously intentional. He went back and shifted them again, adding and taking away to make it look like they had just fallen there. He walked away and looked again. Knowing what was there, he still saw it as a burial mound, but he hoped it would fool a passerby.

In any case, it would have to do. The first pinks of sunrise were already on the horizon. He had been out there much too long. The adrenaline was wearing off, and he had trouble focusing on the road during the drive home. He hadn't been up so late since grad school. He had never been one to pull all-nighters, even as a young man. When he got back, he tore the innards out of the server and melted them down in the grill, just like the memory card. Inside, he heard Jimmy's snores faintly through the door to the front bedroom. William didn't bother to undress, just kicked off his shoes and fell into bed. It had been almost twenty years since he and his brother had slept under the same roof.

~ ~ ~

William woke up to the smell of coffee six hours later. For a moment, he lay in bed wondering if the machine were broken. It had separate settings for weekdays and weekends. He knew it was Saturday, but it took a few moments to remember all that had gone on the night before. He could hardly believe it had really happened. He hadn't really been himself since Jimmy showed up in his office that Tuesday afternoon. He got up and shuffled his way to the kitchen feeling like he'd been beaten from head to toe. His muscles ached the way they had after tackling drills in high school. Too much running. Too much stress.

Jimmy sat at the kitchen table, sipping coffee and eating a NutriGrain bar, the wrapper still around the bottom. Two other empty wrappers lay on the table. The radio was on, the volume turned very low.

"Did I wake you?" Jimmy asked.

"The coffee."

Jimmy got up, poured a second mug, and put it on the table across from where he had been sitting. He pulled the box of NutriGrain bars from the shelf and set it in the center of the table. "I hope you don't mind," Jimmy said. "You know I don't cook."

William nodded and sat down. The coffee tasted good, better than usual.

Jimmy smiled. "Salt," he said. "Put a little salt in with the grounds."

"I had forgotten that." William took a bar from the box, opened the wrapper and ate.

"I've been thinking," Jimmy said.

William looked at his brother, not sure he wanted to know what Jimmy had been thinking.

"You're right. I screwed up bad last night."

William nodded.

"So I'm going back to Augusta today. You find out what you can. Make a plan, and I'll follow it."

William waited for the catch.

"Just promise me I can be there when you talk to this Riley guy. I need to look in his eyes. Just promise me that, all right? That I can be there?"

"I promise."

William needed two cups of coffee before he felt more or less himself and able to drive Jimmy back to Shirley's for the Charger. In the parking lot, something in Jimmy's body language made William think he wanted to hug – something about the way his shoulders arched back. William put out his hand to shake instead.

Jimmy took it and said, "Call me when it's time. You promised."

"I did."

Jimmy nodded and got out.

William drove away.

At home, he took a long nap. His sleep cycle was well and truly shot, and he knew once he started looking into Patrick Riley, he would obsess and be up all night. He needed information, details, and a plan.

CHAPTER 11

Late that afternoon, William shaved, dressed in weekend clothes, and pulled out his laptop. Samuels' paper records went back to the founding, but the student records William could access went back only five years – since a system change. Patrick Riley was in the system, but he hadn't been in one of William's classes. Because he advised students, William had access to academic transcripts. Three years earlier, Riley had attended two semesters at Samuels, earning four Fs, two Ds, and two As. One of those Fs was in Danny's freshman composition class, and another was in Janet's, when Riley retook the course. William might have heard them talking about him. Maybe not. He still felt the name was familiar, more than just that it was common. He couldn't place it. The database included an ID photo for each student, but the quality of the file was so low William never trusted the pictures to be a reasonable likeness. Riley looked to be right out of high school in his pic, which he would have been, according to the transcript. Black hair, long and straight, like a goth musician without makeup or dye, and covering most of the face. The picture was too grainy and pixelated to be sure of the eye color. Maybe hazel or brown. He had been a chemistry major, and his As were in that subject.

William logged out of the Samuels system and pulled up Facebook. There were a lot of people named Patrick Riley with Facebook accounts. He scrolled through a few dozen profile pictures before he took the time to narrow the search to people in Osgood. The first result was definitely the same kid. He had cut his hair – shaved the sides down to stubble, but left a long swath on the top left that hung down like overgrown bangs across the boy's face. William wasn't sure what kids would call it or what subculture Riley intended to represent. In Billy's teens it would have been a skater's haircut. Or, more likely, a kid who wanted to be like the skaters, but who had never been on a board in his life. The half of his face that wasn't covered by the hair showed a peach fuzz mustache and looked to be pocked with acne and acne scars or maybe sores. It wasn't a close up, and William couldn't be sure. The kid was shirtless and really shouldn't have been. He was rail thin with no muscle tone and the sort of concave chest William associated with the nerdiest boys he knew in his youth. Riley was trying to look tough, something he would never be able to pull off with his skin and his build. The kid surely knew that, which explained the pose he had struck in the pic – shoulders back, elbows locked, and both hands wrapped around Ian Baker's .45. The barrel pointed just to the right of the camera lens, the perspective drawing the eye from the reedy kid to the long metal casing, the filed initials in full view.

William wanted to shove the gun so far down that punk's throat his colon would double as a silencer.

There were other pictures, several with the gun, each in a different pose, all meant to be threatening, none succeeding. The boy might have stolen the gun, but there was no way he had taken it from Ian Baker by force. Even in aged, senile weakness, he would have torn that child apart. William was as sure of this as his own breath. The kid's security settings made his profile pictures public, but the posts weren't visible. There was no real information to be gained from the rest of the page, William thought. He closed the browser, then opened it again for a second look at the pics. They were all stills from a webcam, it seemed, something mounted on or over the computer monitor. What William's students called "selfies." Patrick Riley had no one to take his picture for him. The kid was close enough to the camera that almost no background showed, just a small rectangle on either side of the boy's ugly shape. William clicked to the full screen view, trying to see as much as possible. Over the left shoulder was a patch of gray wall and a small streak of light. Over the right were black lines and letters, too out of focus to process. William clicked through the pics, looking at those spaces. Slowly, he pieced together an image from the small squares that were clear enough to make out. After four or five passes, he was pretty sure the boy was in a furnished basement – cinderblock walls, a small, ground level window on one side, and a classroom-sized periodic table on the other.

"Meth," William said.

He googled the address and planned his route before closing the browser and the computer. He took the Corolla to the south side, trolling the streets in the dusk of the evening. It was a rough neighborhood. Like so much of Osgood, it had once been a mill village. This one had been so poorly maintained, it seemed more like a housing project. William didn't know much of the history, but it must have once been for upper management. The houses were bigger and farther apart than in his neighborhood or the others on the north side. He knew the mill there had been the first to close, sometime in the early 80s. These four-bedroom houses on full-acre lots had once been the homes of Osgood's bosses, but the neighborhood had become a hotbed of drugs and gang activity, the place to go for all things illegal, immoral, and dangerous.

At a stop sign two blocks from Riley's address, a boy of maybe ten, his hair in twists, ran up to William's car asking, "What you need? What you need?" William waved him off, and the boy responded by showing him two short, narrow middle fingers.

The yards were patchy, more dirt and weeds than grass. Roofs sagged, porch rails lay beside crumbling concrete steps, and zigzagging cracks ran through the brick facades. Clumps of young men stood drinking beer and smoking – beside a house here, in front of one there. The groups were more integrated than William would have imagined. A few stared at him as he passed, but most ignored him, engaged in their own conversations. Some cars had been tricked out with rims and tinting and messages in large letters across the windshield. "PIMPIN" and "2CRUNK" caught William's eye, mostly because he knew that slang was long out of style. Other cars were plain, rusted, or just faded. Nearly all of them had rear-window epitaphs, some small in the corner, others filling the entire glass.

Patrick Riley's house was in about the same poor condition as the rest, but the porch rails were shiny and new. A third of the steps' width had been covered by a metal ramp. The house sat two lots down from the corner of a long, seven-house block. In William's neighborhood, two owners would have sold slices of a lot to a third party for a new house, if their lots had been so big. No one with the money or credit to do it wanted to build in this neighborhood. An early 90s Dodge Caravan sat in the driveway, blue paint faded to gray on either side of the pealing woodgrain panels. A handicapped permit hung from the rearview mirror. On the other side of the house, well back from the street, an elderly Trans Am sat on blocks. The golden wings were still visible as William slow-rolled past, but the bird's body had long since faded into the rusted hood. He wasn't even sure what color the car had been. Black, maybe. Evidently, Patrick Riley fancied himself the Bandit. Neither the front nor the sides of the house had the kind of low, basement window William expected to find, based on the profile pictures. He wondered if Riley had moved and given Eagle Pawn an old address.

He watched the house in the Corolla's rearview mirror all the way down the long block, wondering who drove that mini-van, who needed the ramp up to the front porch. It wasn't Patrick Riley, unless he had suffered a serious injury since the pictures were taken. William turned right, driving slowly down the next road, hoping for a view of the house across the lawns of the other homes. The angles weren't very good, and the block was too large to give him much of a look. He made the next right and tried again from the back. The houses on that street didn't line up with the ones on Chapman Road, so he got a clear view from there. He stopped directly behind the Trans Am, maybe one hundred yards distant, and took a long look. He could see it from there, the low window in the left corner of the house. On the other end were three short steps leading from the back door. Next to that, a little closer to the window, sat a low, slanted door that he was sure would lead to a storm cellar. Evidently, it had been finished and made into a bedroom. He wondered if there was an interior entrance. His own storm cellar could only be accessed from an outside door just like the one he was studying.

William heard a close booming sound from behind him and turned to see a kid standing at the rear passenger's side of his car. "What you lookin' at, cracker?" The kid couldn't have been more than fourteen, but he was already posturing as gang-hardened, standing shirtless in the fall weather, the waistband of his boxers showing above his sagging jeans. He must have slapped the rear quarter panel.

William buzzed down the window closest to the kid and said, "I think I'm lost. Could you tell me where Horne Street is?" He had never been to Horne Street Methodist Church, but he knew it was nearby. He had heard it discussed over the years and noticed it on the map when he looked up Chapman Road. It was the closest place he could think of that he might have a legitimate cause to be.

The kid leaned down and propped himself on the door, his head framed by the open window. "You is lost. Go to the end of the block, turn right. Take that to Main, turn right again. Go a little ways. Church ain't on the corner, but it's close enough you'll see it. If church really what you lookin' for." The kid winked at William and waited, still leaning on the car.

William smiled and said thanks. The kid still didn't move, so William turned his head back to the road in front of him and put the car back in drive. He eyed the kid through the rearview mirror, not sure what he would do if the boy didn't back away from the car. The kid moved, though, and William caught sight of a brand burned into the boy's right shoulder. *Not posturing after all*, William thought. The kid really was already in a gang. William buzzed the window back up and followed the kid's directions out of the neighborhood. He went all the way down to the Methodist church and turned around in its parking lot before heading home to plan his next move.

The sun had set by the time he parked the Corolla in his drive way. He went in and made a fresh pot of coffee. There was no way he was going to sleep that night. He was going to have to have a private discussion with Patrick Riley – very private.

Somewhere the screams wouldn't be heard. The punk's own basement room would work fairly well, if not for the fact that a person who needed a ramp to get into the house probably didn't get out much. The kind of discussion William wanted to have was sure to get that person's attention. The only other option would be a kidnapping – a federal offense. The sort of thing that brings out the FBI and news crews.

"Jimmy, you're contagious," William said. Out loud. "And now I'm talking to myself."

If he were going to snatch Riley, he would want to do it in an out of the way place, somewhere few, if any, people would see. The kid looked to be a meth cook or at least a wannabe, which would mean there was a lab somewhere. It wasn't in that basement, William was pretty sure. Whoever lived upstairs would smell it, along with half the neighborhood, probably. With all the crime over there, cops would be patrolling the area too frequently and interviewing potential witnesses too often for that kind of operation to go on very long. Wherever it was, it would probably offer some privacy. To find its location, William would have to stake out Patrick Riley and follow him there. It could take days, and after his encounter with the branded kid, William was pretty sure he wouldn't be able to sit outside and watch for more than a few minutes. He thought about using the deer camera again, but there were no trees in the yard, and even if he found a good spot for it, it would only show him a few entrances and exits. It wouldn't be much help with the actual following. It would also mean several trips in and out of the neighborhood to check the footage. He wrote that off.

Any decent plan was going to require more information, which meant he would have to go back into that neighborhood. His talk with the shirtless boy would likely be forgotten, but if the Corolla were seen two or three more times, someone would notice. Jimmy's Charger wouldn't get through one trip without being seared into someone's mind. He was going to need a different car, something that would blend in. Something that could be parked somewhere nearby without being remembered or stolen. Maybe Jimmy could steal something for that purpose, William thought, then decided against it. The list of felonies was going to be much too long already.

He would need a few other things, too, but he didn't want to buy them in Osgood. Anywhere he might shop, there was a high probability that one of his current or former students would be working the register, and that person might ask questions or remember the exchange at some later date. At William's trial, perhaps. Instead of taking that risk, he made the drive up to Greenville, letting the struggles of the boy wizard distract him on the way. At Target, he picked out an oversized knit cap – what he grew up calling a toboggan – a gray zippered hoodie, a pair of tight-fitting gloves, and four bags of beef jerky. He paid in cash.

The girl at the checkout asked, "Going camping?"

"Yes," William said, smiling.

"We always take jerky when we go camping," the girl said. "My family, I mean."

"Mine, too. It really hits the spot after a long hike."

The girl nodded and told him to have a good night before turning to the next person in line.

At the Walmart down the road, he made almost the same purchases, getting a roll of black duct tape instead of gloves, along with a box of ammo. The woman at the checkout said hello, but she asked no questions. She took his money and told him to "Have a blessed day" before turning to her next customer.

William picked up a Coke from the vending machine out front and ate three of the bags of jerky on the way home. It wasn't the least healthy supper he had ever eaten, but he thought it was probably in the top ten. When he got home, he cut eyeholes in the knit caps. It was still too early for the next thing on his to-do list, so he took a short nap. He was surprised he was able to sit still, much less sleep, after all the coffee and soda he had drunk that day. He was still exhausted from the crazy night before – the emotional roller coaster of the pawnshop and the physical exertion of all the trips up and down the greenway before and after. He wondered briefly, as he drifted off, if sleep deprivation accounted for the madness of what he was planning to do.

He got up at two forty-five, grabbed his father's tools, and drove back to Horne Street Methodist Church. From there, it would be only about a half-mile walk to Patrick Riley's house. William put on the knit cap, and pulled it down till it covered his ears and his forehead all the way to his eyebrows, the eyeholes turned to the back. He put on the hoodie and pulled the hood up over the cap. The hoodie was two sizes too big and blocked his peripheral vision, but it also meant that only a person directly in front of him would be able to see his face.

CHAPTER 12

It was after three in the morning when William started walking toward Chapman, winding his way through the streets and crossing a few yards. The space between the houses made it seem natural to cut through, and a few even had worn places – the obvious paths of the neighborhood kids. Most of the homes were dark, but he saw a bonfire party going on behind one of the broken down mill houses. He went a block out of his way to avoid it. He had to circle around behind Riley's house to get back on track, which gave him a chance to see from a distance whether its lights were on. A faint glow came from the basement window, like the light from a TV or computer. He was too far away to be sure. He worried that the branded boy would still be roaming, but even the gang members seemed to have cleared the streets by that time. Maybe they had business elsewhere.

William looped around as he had earlier and approached the house from the north side. A Corolla at least ten years older than his own sat in the driveway behind the minivan. It had once been white, but the front passenger's side fender had been replaced with one from a candy apple red model, and the rest of the car was pocked with rust and Bondo. William threw back his hood and scanned the area as best as he could while he walked the last fifty yards to the house. He saw no one moving and no lights on in the houses on the street. A Samuels University parking sticker was still affixed to the rear window of Riley's Corolla, now three years out of date. William had forgotten they once looked like that. He squatted between the car and the mini-van and pulled the knit cap down, covering his face and twisting it till the eyeholes were in place. From that spot, he watched the house a few moments and listened. The main floor was completely dark, and the only sound he could make out came from the HVAC unit at the side of the house.

William had only broken into homes he knew were empty. He wondered if he could be quiet enough not to wake anyone who might be sleeping inside. That was the plan, but he wasn't entirely confident. He tried to picture the layout of the house, based on others he had been inside. The mill houses didn't have a lot of variety in floor plans, so he had a good chance of getting that part right. The furniture or pets or anything else unique to this owner would be impossible to guess. From his place between the vehicles, he scanned the area again. Seeing no one, he moved quickly across the drive and up the front steps, avoiding the ramp in case it might rattle against the rail. He picked the locks much faster than he had at Eagle, wondering the whole time if someone might be coming up the street behind him. He knew he would see car lights reflecting off the house if someone drove by, but anyone could be walking to or from the party two blocks over. He listened carefully, focusing his eyes on the task at hand, but the only sound was the click of the lock.

He turned the handle and pushed the door gently, worried about the squeak of old hinges or the pop of a warped threshold. The door swung silently, though. Whoever replaced the porch rails must have had a look at the door too. He stepped in and squatted down to listen, pushing the door closed with his elbow.

What he heard confused him. A rhythmic, mechanical sighing came from the other side of the room, like Darth Vader pondering his next atrocity,

William thought. *Fish tank? Radiator?* His eyes were adjusted for the moonlight and street lamps outside. It took a moment for him to begin to see clearly in the dark room. Heavy curtains blocked the front windows, and a long threadbare couch stretched across the back wall. In the far corner sat a recliner in much better condition, almost brand new, and it was occupied by a matronly woman of no less than eighty years. She was dead asleep, it seemed, but kept alive by the workings of a machine next to her on the end table. She was connected to it by a long, opaque hose and a mask strapped to her face with adjustable bands.

"Sleep apnea," William said in a low voice, then silently chastised himself for speaking at all.

Next to the chair stood a cane, metal with four little feet at the bottom. In the corner facing the chair, a motorized scooter sat recharging. A little row of dim green lights shown against the far wall. This model had three wheels and handlebars, like an overgrown tricycle. William wondered how the ride compared to Mr. Berry's motorized chair and suppressed a grin at the image of the two elderly people racing each other down the greenway.

To his right, along the end wall by the front door, sat a small table, a semi-circle arcing out from the wall. The elderly woman kept a collection of nativity scenes, about a half dozen of them in various sizes. *It isn't even Halloween yet*, William thought. He crept around the table and turned right, down the hallway. Three doors led from each side, all open except the middle one on the left. On the right were a bathroom and two bedrooms. The last door on that side looked to be the woman's bedroom, full of frilly things and more nativity scenes. On the left side were two more bedrooms. Besides the woman's room, the others looked to be guest spaces. Two might once have been boys' rooms, and the third a girl's, but they all had been stripped of personality for some time, it seemed. William wondered why Patrick Riley opted for the basement with so much room upstairs. The separate entrance seemed the most logical explanation.

William thought the closed door might lead down to the basement. He knelt and put his ear against it, but he heard no sound. He put the palm of his hand on it, checking for warmth or vibration. He wasn't quite sure. He suddenly realized he hadn't worn the gloves he'd bought, and he jerked his hand back. He tried to wipe away any fingerprints with his sleeve. *The front door*, he thought. *I've got to clean the front door handle.* He pulled his hand into his sleeve and used that to grasp the handle of the closed door. He turned it slowly, very slowly. The image of an elderly man with cataracts looking at him with one evil eye flashed across William's mind. He had read "The Tell-Tale Heart" too many times. He pulled the door open slowly as well, but it was only a linen closet. He closed the door quietly and crept back down the hall.

A wide, arched entry led off the back of the living room into a large kitchen and dining area. The round, four-person table looked too small for the space. The tablecloth was much too big, hanging to the floor on all sides. William had to squat and inspect them for a moment to be sure, but the salt and peppershakers turned out to be Joseph and a very pregnant Mary on a donkey. William shook his head and looked into the kitchen.

The counters were the stainless steel so common in the mill houses. The cabinets might have been an update – William couldn't tell in the dark room – but all the doors hung slightly open, as if their hinges needed adjustment. The wall that separated the kitchen from the living room had built-in shelves, a sort of open pantry. Just beyond this was a closed door with the tiniest sliver of gray light showing under it.

William knelt and listened. He thought he could hear a faint murmur, like voices from a TV turned way down. It could just as easily be the HVAC, he thought. He hoped the kid would be asleep, giving him a chance to see the layout and make a better plan. A kid that age could be up till all hours, though, especially a tweaker on a Saturday night. Based on the pictures, William was pretty sure the kid didn't just make meth for other people. He pulled his hand back into his sleeve and reached for the knob of the door. He had barely touched it when it swung open with a long, crescendoing squeak.

"Memaw, is that you?"

He cooks meth, poses with a .45 on Facebook, and lives with a grandmother he calls "Memaw," William thought. *This kid is a piece of work.*

William backed away from the door and looked around. The only hiding place was in the far corner of the room, behind the round table, with its chairs and oversized tablecloth blocking the view. He went and squatted there, listening to the kid's steps on the stairs. William considered jumping him there and then. The skinny boy wouldn't be much in a fight, even if he was hopped up on God knows what. But Jimmy had been promised he could be there. This was about information, not action, so William waited.

The boy passed the table and went into the living room, his steps quick and loud in spite of his slight build. The kid must have seen that his grandmother was still asleep, because he turned quickly and went down the hall.

"I hate that fucking door," Riley muttered.

William heard a door close. The bathroom, he thought. He took the chance and came from behind the table, stepping as lightly as he could across the kitchen and down the stairs. Halfway down, they turned back at a narrow landing. The bottom of the stairs faced the slanted door leading to the back yard, a set of six or seven steps going up to it. The periodic table hung on the wall by that door. The far wall had posters of Brian Cranston and Aaron Paul.

"Too much television," William muttered.

In the corner beneath the small window was a full-size mattress and springs on a metal frame, no head or footboard. Dingy sheets had been kicked off the corners, exposing the flower pattern stitched into the old mattress. On the opposite wall, facing the bed, sat a cheap, pressed wood desk, its surface covered with moleskin notebooks stacked haphazardly, like a round of Jenga about to end. An entertainment unit made of the same cheap material sat next to the desk. The TV was sixty inches, and there were three game systems on a shelf underneath. The shelf under that had wireless controllers on chargers. The rest of the shelves held game and DVD cases, stacked in various directions and filling every available inch of space. A single office chair, the kind of thing Samuels issued its professors, sat in front of the TV. Evidently, Patrick Riley played his games alone.

William had seen enough, so he stepped across to the slanted door. In the mill houses he had seen before he bought his own, these doors were secured with a latch or a bar, but this one had a standard knob. He slipped his hand back into his sleeve as he climbed the short set of stairs and went out, closing the door gently behind him. The light was still on in the bathroom window at the center of the house. William scanned the area. Seeing no one, he looped around to the front and wiped the door handle with the tail of his shirt. He took another look around before trotting through the yard to the street.

Halfway down the block, he realized he was still masked. He slowed and adjusted the knit cap on his head, then pulled up the hood. He crossed the street and dashed between the next set of houses. He needed to cross two blocks to get back to Horne Street and his Corolla. Making his way through the next set of yards, he saw a police cruiser slow-rolling the cross street, a spotlight searching the other side. William picked up his pace and crossed the next street, slipping between two houses and hoping he hadn't been seen.

"The hell you doin'?"

William could tell the voice came from his left, but the hood blocked his vision. The voice was male. A grown man, William thought. Only a few feet away. He thought about running. The car was only a block away now, but he couldn't risk having his car reported. He stopped and turned slowly toward the man, trying to get a look without having to show his own face.

"This my yard," the man said. "Ain't no path." He had come closer.

William kept his head tilted down, trying not to be seen, so the first thing in his view was the man's left leg, only three or four feet away. William finished his turn with his head still down, finally facing the man. The man must have thought he was afraid, a kid about to be chastised.

"Look at me when I talk to you, boy."

William could see the man's hands now, both empty. He drew back his right fist, slow and obvious, then snapped out his left foot, kicking the man sharply in the testicles. The fist wasn't just a distraction, though. The man's hands dropped instinctively,

127

covering himself before he could be kicked again, exposing his face. The man had bent down into William's line of sight. He turned his hips with the punch and landed a right cross on the man's chin. He toppled over and curled up, trying to protect himself from the next blow. William drew back his left foot and snapped it out again, this time putting his heel into the back of the man's skull. Lights out.

William was ashamed of himself as he ran through the yards to the church parking lot and his car. The man was only trying to protect his property, possibly his family, from people like Patrick Riley and worse. William couldn't risk the man getting a good look at him or the car, though.

"A wrong is unredressed when retribution overtakes its redresser," he whispered to himself as he drove away.

The Poe quotation didn't cleanse William's conscience, but it did lower the volume. A beat down was probably a minor event in that neighborhood, he told himself. He wondered what the man had been doing in the back yard at three-thirty in the morning. Had he been alone? William couldn't remember any lights in the house's windows. He was certain he hadn't heard anyone else. Surely if someone had been there, that person would have shouted at him or screamed for help when the man went down.

"Damn you, Jimmy," William muttered to himself.

It had been a long, long time since he had hurt anyone, and he was sure it wouldn't be happening now if Jimmy hadn't come back. Without Jimmy, William would never have known about the gun, never have known about Patrick Riley, and none of this would have been necessary. Now that he knew, he couldn't let it go. The wrong had to be redressed. Jimmy was right; he did know William.

"Damn you, Jimmy," he said again. He shook his head, pushing off his frustration with his older brother and trying to focus on the next part of the process, the next stage in his plan.

By the time he got home, he had a rough outline. It wasn't a very good plan. Dozens of things could go wrong, and they could both end up in prison for the rest of their lives. In truth, it only had three things in its favor: It was simple, it would be familiar to Jimmy, and it only required one more purchase – an old car with a big trunk. Of course, the car could just as easily be stolen.

That much resolved, William went to bed.

CHAPTER 13

William forced himself out of bed at his usual Sunday time and did prep reading until lunch. He ate another can of soup, washing it down with coffee. After that, he called Jimmy.

"I've done some research, and I've got a plan."

"You can tell me all about it when I see you," Jimmy said.

William wasn't sure if his brother was with someone or was just too paranoid to talk about it on the phone. Either way, William took the hint. "The problem is my trunk isn't big enough, and I don't think yours is either."

"You want a pickup?"

"No, it might rain that day."

"I can borrow something," Jimmy said.

"Thanks."

"Not a problem. I'll see you Tuesday. I've got work till then."

"Tuesday is good."

"See you then," Jimmy said and hung up.

William wanted to do all his prep reading for the week that afternoon in case things got too complicated Tuesday night. He was still at it two hours later when someone knocked on his front door. He left his American literature anthology on the recliner where he had been sitting and went to the door. Through the peephole, he saw a police officer. A wave of fear rolled through him before it was overwhelmed by logic. If they were coming to arrest him, there would be more than one cop. There would be two or three of them, and there might even be flashing lights.

He took a deep breath and thought things through. The officer had come to ask questions, probably about the pawnshop and where Jimmy was. The key was not to let on that he knew anything. He wasn't supposed to know there had been a break-in. He wasn't supposed to know when or where or what was taken. He took another deep breath and opened the door.

"Dr. Baker?" the officer asked.

William nodded. "Can I help you, officer?"

"Maybe. I'm trying to get some information, and I'm told you're the man to see about the greenway." The officer was young, probably twenty-five or so, and certainly not yet thirty. A little silver bar on his uniform identified him as Phillips. William could tell he was nervous, worried he was wasting an important person's time. He stood at the door like a sheepish freshman, afraid to look William in the eye.

"I walk it almost every day," William said.

"That's what the captain said. You helped with the search a few years back, right?"

"I did." William didn't want to think about that search, and judging by the way Phillips looked down at the porch when he asked the question, he didn't want to think about it, either. "What do you need to know?" William asked.

"Were you out there on Friday night?"

"A couple of times. I had to make two trips to Shirley's."

"Two trips? Did you forget something?"

"No, my brother had a bit too much to drink and parked down there when he realized he shouldn't be driving. I went down there and walked him home."

Phillips tilted his head sideways, like a confused puppy. "You walked? Why not drive down?"

"I always walk, and I couldn't have Jimmy throwing up in my car."

Phillips' head snapped up – a eureka moment. "Jimmy Baker is your brother?"

"He is." William hoped the young policeman could see just how ashamed he was about that fact.

"The captain didn't mention that." Phillips looked down again.

William wondered if the captain had been playing a joke on Phillips, deliberately putting him in an awkward situation. There was nothing he could do, though, so he said nothing.

"You may be even more helpful than I thought," Phillips finally said.

William shrugged his shoulders. "If you want to talk about Jimmy, you'd better come in." He stepped back to allow Phillips through the door. William shut it behind him and led the way into the living room. "Would you like something to drink? Coffee? Tea? Water? Maybe a Coke?"

"I could use a Coke," Phillips said.

William gestured for Phillips to sit on the couch and walked through to the kitchen. He pulled two cans from the fridge and went back to the living room, handing one to Phillips before taking a seat in the recliner. He sat on his book and had to stand again to move it.

"I interrupted your reading," Phillips said. "I'm sorry."

"I'm always reading," William said, sitting. "I've gotten used to interruptions."

Phillips nodded. "I'm having trouble getting my mind around it. Dr. Baker is Jimmy Baker's brother." He shook his head.

"It's never been a secret. Frankly, I'm surprised you've ever heard of either of us. Maybe you're older than you look, but I wouldn't think you were a policeman the last time Jimmy was arrested, and that wasn't even in Osgood."

"He's a bit of a legend for the cops around here. We tell stories about him."

"Osgood's dumbest criminals?"

Phillips went a little pink. "Some of it, yeah, but not all of it. Mostly, it's about how ballsy he was. The kinds of places he'd break into in broad daylight."

William knew what Phillips meant. Jimmy had once walked into the home of the president of the Osgood Chamber of Commerce during a party and walked out with a pocket full of jewelry and a laser disc player over his shoulder. Dozens of people saw him, but no one said a word. He acted like he had every right to be there, just brazened his way through it. That was Jimmy's second arrest.

"He was like that," he said, keeping the story to himself.

"Was?" Phillips asked.

"He says he's done with it. He's been out six months, which is a good long time for him. How'd you hear about me?" William wished he hadn't asked as soon as the words were out of his mouth. He didn't want to talk about the search, and he didn't want to talk about his reputation as a teacher. He hated arrogance in professors, especially himself. It was just too much the stereotype, too much the image of the worst of his own professors.

"Your students," Phillips said. "I went to SC, but I grew up here. They say you're really strict. Very by the book." William could tell Phillips was sugarcoating this out of politeness. He was trying not to say "hard ass" or something more insulting.

"They say a lot worse than that," William said, "and it's all true." He smiled and sipped his Coke.

Phillips shook his head again and took a long drink from his can. "So Jimmy was with you Friday night?"

William nodded.

"Do you remember what time?"

"No. It was some time after midnight. I was asleep when he called."

"Any chance he was lying about why he was there?"

William tried to look confused. "There's always a chance Jimmy's lying. Why do you ask?"

The look on Phillips' face made William think he had pulled off the expression. "Well, to be honest, we've had a lot of unsolved robberies the last several months, and Jimmy is one of the usual suspects. Then Friday, there was a break-in at the pawnshop, and Jimmy was in there twice this week. We think he might have been casing the place."

"That sounds like Jimmy, but he told me he went to Eagle Pawn looking for an engagement ring. He's got a girlfriend in Augusta. He says it's pretty serious."

"He was looking for an engagement ring in a pawn shop?" Phillips asked. He looked a little disgusted by the idea.

"That's what I said." William shook his head. He didn't have to fake his disgust at the idea of buying an engagement ring in a pawnshop. If Ian had done that, Mamie would have slapped him. In fact, if Ian had done such a thing, William and Jimmy wouldn't exist. "For the record, I was in there this week, too. One of my former students works there. He dropped out a couple of years ago, and I'm hoping he'll come back next semester."

"That's good of you." Phillips nodded and took another swig of his Coke. "I guess what I really needed to ask you is if you saw anything Friday night or

Saturday morning that might help us find the burglar. We talked to the folks working at Shirley's that night, and they didn't see a car come or go around the time of the robbery. I thought maybe they came down the greenway."

"A car on the greenway?"

Phillips shook his head. "There weren't any tire tracks. They had to be on foot, if they came that way."

"It couldn't have been much of a haul if they carried it down the greenway."

"Not a big haul, but a dangerous one. Whoever it was got away with several guns, and we really want to get them back before someone gets shot. Stolen handguns are always bad news on both ends."

"I can imagine." William sipped his Coke for a moment, trying to look like he was thinking. "The only other person I remember seeing was Mr. Berry, and I'm sure he wasn't hiding stolen goods under his wheelchair."

Phillips smiled and nodded.

"I take it you've met Mr. Berry."

"Oh, yeah," Phillips said. "I talk to him at least once a week. He calls to complain about the kids who hang out under the bridge on the north greenway. Someone has to go out and take a look or he just keeps calling."

"That sounds about right."

"Well, I think I've taken up enough of your time." Phillips stood and finished his Coke in a long drink, his head tilted back. He tapped the bottom of the can to get the last drops, a sort of three-fingered drumroll.

"I'm sorry I couldn't be more help," William said. He stood and took the empty can from Phillips, setting it on the end table next to his own. He followed the officer to the front door, and the two men shook hands.

"Let me know if you think of anything," Phillips said, stepping outside.

"I will. And good luck." William closed the door and watched through the peephole while Phillips walked down to his patrol car and got in. When Phillips drove away, William rested his head against the door for several minutes, breathing deeply, in through the nose and out through the mouth. He hadn't felt the nervousness, the fear, while the cop was in the house. He had kept it all at bay, walled up in the back of his mind. Now that the urgency of the moment had passed, the wall came down and the emotions flooded his mind. The conversation had gone as well as he could have hoped, and he had no reason to think Phillips suspected him of anything. Having a reputation as a straight-laced bookworm had its advantages. He hoped they would be enough.

He spent the rest of the evening doing his prep reading. The process took five times longer than usual. He found himself reading the same small sections again and again, not processing a word. He wondered how many other cops were working the case, who they had spoken to, what other witnesses there might be – people coming in and out of Shirley's, passing drivers, people who lived along the greenway.

He went to bed early, knowing he wouldn't sleep. He faded in and out of consciousness until the morning alarm, thinking about Patrick Riley, Officer Phillips, Doug, and Jimmy. There were so many variables. Too many. He could plan and plan and plan, but he could no more guarantee the outcome than he could predict the weather. He could only give percentages, an estimation. Forecast: cloudy with a twenty percent chance of incarceration.

~ ~ ~

William managed to sleepwalk through his usual Monday morning routine and got to work on time. He worked with his composition students to create a rough outline of a process analysis paper describing the use of their online submission system. Then he put them into groups to write a draft of the paper, each group taking a major section. By the end of the period, they had managed to produce a very disjointed first draft of the necessary paragraphs, setting them up for a revision project on Wednesday.

In the Major Authors class, they discussed a poststructuralist reading of "The Fall of the House of Usher," leading to another disagreement between Nick and Regina. She argued that from a postmodernist perspective, the actual house was not a metaphor for the Usher family, but instead a symbol of the insubstantial nature of the social structures of the era.

"The center cannot hold. Literally. The house cracks down the middle and slides into the lake. The whole estate is deconstructed."

Nick argued that this was too literal to qualify as a poststructuralist reading. "You're just substituting one structuralist reading for another. The symbolism you describe is still a one-to-one correlation. It's still a traditional metaphor, with one tenor and one vehicle. To be truly poststructuralist, the reading should be pluralistic. It should be messy."

"I think you're understanding of poststructuralism is flawed," Regina said. "As flawed as your parking." Nick had been known to scrape other cars in the parking lot, typically two or three times a semester, and the other students ribbed him about it when the opportunity presented itself.

"No, it isn't," Nick said, ignoring the jab and drawing a breath to continue.

William cut him off before he could exhale his next diatribe. "We're about to descend into ad hominem attacks and semantic arguments that will take us a long way from Poe's story," he said. "Ultimately, your conflict demonstrates the primary problem with poststructuralism and, more generally, with postmodernist thinking. These are philosophies which reject most if not all primary assumptions, even things as fundamental as the meanings of words. Whatever the accuracy of the criticisms they provide, they inevitably lead to breakdowns in communication."

"Like right now," John Kennedy said. "I have no idea what you're talking about."

"Precisely. While we may not actually use language with the kind of universal meaning the modernist presupposes, the assumption of that universal meaning allows for communication, however crude and inaccurate it may be. When we eliminate those assumptions, we no longer have any faith in our ability to communicate, diminishing and sometimes eliminating what little real communication we originally had."

"All right," Nick said, "now even I'm confused."

Regina rolled her eyes.

Charlotte took in a breath, as if she were going to speak, but she bit her lip instead. William and her classmates recognized the action, knew that she was processing, probably formulating a question.

Nick and Regina turned from Charlotte and traded dirty looks until their conflict became absurd, even to themselves, and they started making silly faces, going so far as to use their fingers to push and pull their lips and eyebrows.

William ignored all of this, waiting patiently for Charlotte to speak. If he moved on, she would, too, and her contribution would be lost.

"I don't really get poststructuralism," she finally said, "but I thought I knew what postmodernism was, and I don't see the connection. Isn't it supposed to be about morals and stuff? Like big picture things. Truth with a capital T."

Nick didn't wait for William to respond. "Postmodernists reject the notion of objective truth, or sometimes that humans are capable of knowing objective truth."

"It's a little more complex than that," William said, "but I think that's the part you're thinking of, Charlotte."

"Moral relativism," John said.

"Remind me what that means," Charlotte said.

"It's about whether something is always right or wrong or whether it depends on the situation," John said.

"We need to refocus on the story," William said.

"Then let's talk about the morality of putting your sister in a coffin when she's not really dead yet," Regina said.

"I'm going out on a limb and saying that's immoral," Charlotte said.

"Not absolutely," Nick said.

The back and forth continued, leaving the story behind, and William let it continue. He considered the morality of his own actions. The theft of his father's gun was a violation, a desecration of something he held sacred, a larceny greater than the value of the object itself. If the theft was in any way connected to Ian Baker's death, then the crime was exponentially more severe. William knew he wouldn't have a prayer of justifying his actions to a jury, but he had justified them to himself. His primary goal was an answer. Justice – or vengeance – would be secondary by the slimmest of margins. Not getting caught was tertiary, but only in the strict denotation of the term. Others could call him relativistic if they wanted; he had his morals prioritized to his own satisfaction. Unfortunately, that didn't give him any guarantees that he would still be a free man at the end of his journey. He was lost in these thoughts when he realized the students were looking at him in anticipation.

"I'm sorry," he said. "What was the question?"

"You really spaced out there, didn't you?" Regina asked.

"Yes, I did."

"We were talking about the difference between morality and compulsion," Anna said. "I'm not convinced the story is presenting a morality in Usher's actions. It's just the compulsion to keep his sister as close as possible."

"Didn't we talk about this last week?" William asked.

"That was about the distinction between simple paranoia and actual schizophrenia," Nick said. "This is about the distinction between a decision based on moral concerns and one based on pathological compulsions. In other words, does something have to be conscious, rather than subconscious, to qualify as moral? Are these instincts or pathologies functioning so separately from morality that they can't be discussed as if they were comparable?"

William shook his head. "We've managed to leave a semantic argument, leap over the story, and land in a Freudian debate. Or perhaps a Darwinian debate. Certainly an existential debate. What is the nature of humanity? What is the nature of psychosis? What is the origin of morality? Biologists will give you one kind of answer. Anthropologists another. Psychologists. Philosophers. Theologians. I would argue a fiction writer who offers definitive answers to these questions in a story or novel has ceased to be a fiction writer and become, at best, a parabolist, at worst a preacher. I don't believe it's the place of a literature professor to offer definitive answers to those questions, either."

"That's a copout, Dr. Baker," John said.

"Indeed, it is," William said, "but it's one I can live with. And our time is up." He closed his book and began to pack his things.

"Was your brother really here last week?" Regina asked "On campus?" She had gathered her things and made her way to the front of the room while the other students walked toward the door.

William looked up at her, trying to decide how to respond, and he saw the other students stop and turn to hear his answer. "Yes," he said.

"The villain?" Nick asked.

"Yes."

"I thought he was in prison," Anna said. She looked a bit pale, William thought.

"He was, but now he's out. He's getting married, and he wanted to tell me face to face." *Dad was right*, William thought. *Lying is just as easy as breathing*. The thought chilled him to his very core, and he shivered.

"Scary thought, huh?" Nick asked.

"Very."

Nick seemed poised to ask further questions, but William flicked his hand, dismissing the literature students just as he had Matthew Gibbard on the day Jimmy returned. They understood the gesture more readily than Matthew had.

William went back to his office, grabbed a can of soup, and microwaved it in the break room. He managed to eat it in his office without being disturbed. The afternoon was filled with sophomores who needed papers graded. William forced himself to focus on their work, one line at a time. When the last appointment was finished, he began to pack his things.

"Dr. Baker?"

William looked up to find Doug outside the doorway, leaning back as if he were afraid to cross the threshold. William felt a flash of annoyance. He was eager to get on with the preparations for the next stage of his plan. He pushed that aside as quickly as he could. Doug on campus was a good thing. At any other time, William would have been happy to see him.

"Doug," he said, "it's good to see you. Good news?"

"Yeah," Doug said. "I'm registered for classes in the spring, and I've filed a new FAFSA. They said I should get plenty of financial aid now, since my parents can't claim me as a dependent anymore."

"I'm glad to hear that. You deserve a break."

Doug finally stepped into the office. "I signed up for your nineteenth century fiction course. Do you know what we'll be reading in there?"

"Poe, Hawthorne, Melville, Twain, Stowe. Several short stories. They have the list on the bookstore's website."

"That's already up?"

"I checked it over a week ago."

"Thanks."

William nodded. "I don't want to rush you," he said, "but I've got some things to tend to at home."

"Actually," Doug said, "I was wondering if you heard about the break-in."

William nodded again. "An officer came by the house yesterday."

Doug stepped back again, putting himself just outside the office. "I, uh... I told them your brother had been in the store." He raised his hands, a gesture of surrender. "I didn't say he was your brother. I didn't want you dragged into it. I just... I know his reputation, so I felt like I had to tell them. I hope it's okay." He had kept his hands up for too long and finally lowered them, clearly not sure what to do with them. He rubbed them together and eventually put them in his pockets.

William waited this out, trying to choose just the right response. "You were right to tell them," he said. "When a known felon shows up right before a robbery, there's usually a connection. And I'm not offended. My brother and I aren't close, precisely because of the things he's done to earn his reputation. That said, he does seem to be on a better track now. He's been out six months, which is a good long time for him, and he has a serious girlfriend. I'm not convinced he won't end up in prison again. He's always been prone to make big, stupid mistakes, no matter what anyone says to him."

William could feel his face going red, hear the rise in his own voice. He was still pretty angry about Jimmy mucking up the plan at the pawnshop. He hoped Doug read the emotion as frustration with Jimmy's life choices, not anything to do with the break-in. "In this case, though, he was with me at the time of the robbery. He wanted to talk to me about his girlfriend. He's planning to propose."

"So it wasn't him?" Doug asked.

"Not this time."

"I'm really glad to hear that, Dr. Baker. I felt really bad about..." His voice trailed off, and he shrugged his shoulders.

"I appreciate that, Doug. Really." William finished packing his bag and slung it on. "I really do need to go, though." He met Doug at the office door and shook the kid's hand. "I'll see you in the spring. Before then, if you need something."

Doug nodded. "Thanks, Dr. Baker. I'll see you then." He walked back toward the lobby, and William went the other way, down the back stairs and out of the building.

CHAPTER 14

William wanted to take another look at Patrick Riley's house, but he knew it would be a bad idea to have his car seen the second time – or third, if someone had noticed him in the Horne parking lot. Instead, he decided to drive out to Sumter National Forest. When he was a teen, he and his father sometimes went deer hunting there. They had picked out several good spots to set up their stands over the years, places that were a little harder to find and offered a little privacy. The forest was so big and so rich with deer that a crowd big enough to fill a high school football stadium could sometimes be found trumping through the forest in orange vests or settled into tree stands. William needed a quiet spot where no one would see or hear. He wasn't sure what would become of Patrick Riley. That would depend on what the kid had to say and how quickly he was willing to say it. Witnesses would be a problem in any case. Deer season was well under way, but a Tuesday night/Wednesday morning was not going to be all that busy, William thought.

It took an hour and a half to wind his way back to the area he remembered. The last road in wasn't really a road, just a dirt track hunters and rangers used, mostly in pickups and jeeps or on four-wheelers. The Corolla wasn't really fit for the trip, but William slowed to a crawl and managed to bounce and rock his way there. He got out and searched for evidence of people. His father had come back from Vietnam with many skills, tracking among them. Like so many things, William wished he had learned more about this while his father was still alive. He could distinguish animal types and the size and weight of humans from their prints, but he had never grasped the subtleties that tell a great tracker how long a print has been there. Deer had been through, but he found no human footprints, and the only tire tracks were from a four-wheeler. It could have been a hunter, but since he hadn't seen any vehicle tracks, he thought these were likely the ranger's. A ranger could show up any time for all sorts of reasons, but with all the hunting going on, William doubted a ranger would be back any time soon, since the spot was one the hunters weren't using.

He couldn't turn the Corolla around without risking getting stuck in the soft earth beside the track or wrecking the suspension on the ruts, so he had to drive in reverse all the way to the road, almost a mile. This was even slower than the drive in, so he used the time to memorize the landscape, making sure he would recognize it in the dark. The road to the track was barely a road itself, a narrow strip of asphalt not quite wide enough for two vehicles to pass. William didn't think it had ever had lines, but if so, they had faded before his first trip out there, nearly thirty years earlier. The road was so rough, he had to stay under thirty miles an hour from there to the county road that would take him back to the state highway and on to Osgood. By the time he got to his house, Dumbledore had died and the last disc of book six had come to an end. William was surprised by the intensity of his emotional reaction to it.

On the back steps, he found a small, Styrofoam cooler with a note on top. "Sorry I missed you. I hope this makes for good stew." The signature was completely illegible, but he recognized the shape of it. Fred Dillion or his grandson had killed a deer, and William would soon eat a portion of it. He put the meat in the refrigerator and dumped the ice and water from the cooler into the kitchen sink. The meat would keep until after things had been settled with Patrick Riley. If everything went according to plan, he might even share the stew with Jimmy.

~ ~ ~

Tuesday morning, he discussed Amy Hempel's "In the Cemetery Where Al Jolson is Buried" with his American literature sections. The students almost never understood what was happening in the story – the surface narrative or the layers of fear, loss, and pain. When it was explained to them, they always complained that it was depressing. William went through this every semester, but he refused to take the story off the syllabus. It was just too beautiful. At nineteen or twenty, readers were rarely equipped to appreciate it, but he was convinced some of them would return to the piece in their thirties and forties when friends or relatives died too young. Then they would understand, empathize, and be comforted. He planned to have more soup for lunch, but Janet turned up at his office door in time to stop him.

"Down in the very marrow," she said, "your body has already begun to produce new cells." She held her hands in front of her eyes, the thumb and index of each pinched to show the tiny nature of the event. "An aluminum-like substance that will soon replace the hair on your head and plasticine to replace your skin. At the current rate, over the next decade, your Caucasian shell will become red and white, your salt and pepper coif will become silver, and one afternoon – probably a Thursday – I will slip in while you nap behind that ostentatious desk and pull the tab at the top of your head to discover there is no brain left, no man at all, just a human-shaped bowl of chicken and dumplings, microwavable, sure, but also well past its sell-by date. And I will serve your preservative-saturated innards to the starving, failing students huddled outside your door."

"You've been reading Mary and Percy Shelley again, haven't you?"

"I have. Two great tastes that go great together. We're going to lunch."

"We are?"

"We are."

"All right." He stood and followed, leaving the can of soup on his desk. Janet went toward the back stairs. "Not the caf today?"

"We need to avoid another run in with the dean." Janet tilted her head toward Danny's office and made a sad face. "At least for a few more days."

William nodded and followed her down the stairs. Danny, Kelvin, and Heather were waiting in the parking lot beside Kelvin's Lincoln crossover. The vehicle was at the high end of what might be afforded on an assistant professor's salary, and William had shaken his head in disgust the first time he had seen it. It was Kelvin's second year on the faculty.

"What?" Kelvin had asked.

"Your salary is public record, and that thing is outside your budget."

"I had full rides from freshman year through my Ph.D.," Kelvin said. "This is my reward for not borrowing a dime until my thirties. Besides, the ladies like the luxury." It was none of William's business, so he let it go. Since then, he'd come to appreciate the big, comfortable Lincoln. It was the standard vehicle for any trip the group took off campus. A few times a year, they all went to a Samuels away game or a play in Greenville or Columbia that had struck Janet's interest. All five of them could sit comfortably in the Lincoln. William had even caught himself wishing

Kelvin were driving when he, Danny, and Janet had
gone to English conferences.

That Tuesday, Danny took shotgun, which put
William in the back with Janet and Heather, who
smelled especially nice that day. The only time he had
asked about the perfumes, she had given a coy smile.
"Smell is the most memorable thing about a person,"
she said, "and I'm not sure I want to be remembered
the same way by everyone I meet." She had placed a
finger on her lips, like she was telling a secret. "If the
scent is different, then I could be a different person."
He had never been sure what to make of that. Some of
the scents were more becoming than others, though,
and that Tuesday's choice was perfect for her. He
found himself thinking about her with an intensity
that hadn't been there in quite a long time. He
wondered if the perfume were really that powerful or
if he just needed a distraction from the chaos his life
had become since Jimmy's return. He was a few hours
away from kidnapping someone and whatever would
come after that. A brief fantasy about Heather
Rodgers was a welcome distraction. And she really did
smell good.

Four years earlier, they had come perilously close
to having an affair. Heather drank too much at a
faculty party, so Janet took her keys. Heather insisted
she had to get home immediately to relieve the
babysitter. Since William lived closest to Heather –
about a mile and a half – he consented to drive her
home in her car and walk back to his own house. He
walked her inside, wanting to make sure Eliza –
Heather's two-year-old daughter – was safely down
for the night before the babysitter left. He was pretty
sure Heather would sober up before the baby woke in
the morning. Carl, Heather's husband, was the
women's soccer coach and away overnight for a game.

As soon as the babysitter left, Heather made her move, kissing William like he was shipping out in the morning. He kissed her back. He'd liked her from the first time he saw her – lips and hips and legs for days. She had been a soccer player herself, a division two striker when Carl was a graduate assistant coach. William thought of Carl during the second pause for breath, when buttons and buckles were being undone.

"I can't do this," William said. "You're married." He pulled away from her and dropped onto her couch.

"It's okay," Heather said, sitting next to him. "Carl's cheating on me. He's always cheated on me."

William was pretty sure that was true. There were rumors about what Carl got up to in hotel rooms after away games. No one even bothered to whisper about that anymore. The whispers were reserved for rumors about Carl and his players. William liked Heather's logic, mostly because it meant having sex with Heather, but from his position on the couch, he could see Eliza's toys scattered about the room. A married woman with a small child. It was going too far. And he knew what his father would say when he heard. Somehow Ian Baker always heard. "A married woman who'll screw you will end up screwing you over." He claimed to have had experience in that area before Mamie came into the picture. William buckled his belt and left. He never told anyone, and he avoided Heather as best as he could in the weeks that followed.

Then the unthinkable happened: Eliza disappeared.

Heather woke up one morning and found an empty bed. William participated in the search effort, combing the wooded areas around the greenways. He knew them as well as anyone, and he scoured every inch, doing his best to ignore the whispers of the other searchers. Everyone had a theory: the dad, the mom, a local, a drifter. William had to suppress the urge to choke some of them, the ones who didn't care about Eliza or her family, the ones who just wanted a chance to gawk and brag to their friends afterward. William hoped they would find a clue and not a body, but no one found either.

Almost a year later, drunk teens stumbled onto a shallow grave in some woods near the lake, east of town. The closest house belonged to Thomas White, a local who already had child molestation convictions. The decomposition was too far along to find cause of death, but they believed Eliza was killed around the time she went missing. They found a few of White's hairs in the grave, and, given his record, it was obvious to everyone what had happened. TV newscasts showed images of White over and over, most often the moment of his arrest – cuffed hands covering his face as he denied everything. William stopped watching the news. Ian Baker's wreck was only a few months earlier, and he couldn't bear all the death around him. Heather had taken a sabbatical, and she and Carl divorced. Carl took a position at a college in Nebraska, and no one at Samuels had heard from him since.

When Heather came back to work, it was as if her personality had been on steroids. She had always been crass and cynical, prone to gallows humor, and these things had intensified to an almost intolerable level. That faded back to normal eventually, in part because Janet and Danny made her their pet project, drawing their circle of friends much tighter and forcing everyone to treat her as if nothing had happened. William was comfortable with that. Compartmentalization had become his standard operating procedure, as easy as putting on his uniform each morning.

"So you talked to the police?" Danny asked.

William was brought back to the present by that last word. "What?" He wondered how Danny would have known about the conversation with Officer Phillips. His mind raced through the possible connections.

"Yeah," Kelvin said, ignoring William. "They said they'd file a report, but without any witnesses, nothing will get done."

"Your insurance should cover it," Danny said.

William decided to wait it out and see if the conversation would make sense eventually.

"What insurance?" Janet asked. "What are you talking about?" Evidently, she was less patient than William.

"You didn't see it?" Kelvin asked.

"See what?"

"The three gouges down the side of my baby. She looks like she lost a fight with a wolverine, laid open from bumper to bumper."

"Keyed," Danny said.

"That's awful," Janet said. "Who would do that? Why?"

"Students, probably," Kelvin said.

"Maybe an ex?" Danny asked. "You've got a line of them."

Kelvin shook his head. "I leave them wanting more," he said, "not wanting revenge."

"But you leave your students wanting revenge?"

"Sometimes," Kelvin said. "Chemistry is hard. People fail. Some of them take it personally."

"Do you have an idea who it was?" William asked.

"It happened yesterday, right after I gave back a set of tests. Just one set, in my organic section. I left class, packed my stuff, and found her like this. She was fine at lunch. I'm thinking it was one of the Fs."

"How many?"

"Nine."

"That's a lot of suspects."

"Three of them had failed tests before. My money's on one of them."

"What would you do if you found out who it was?" Danny asked. He looked a little worried at the prospect, William thought.

"Turn him in," Kelvin said.

"Without proof?" William asked. "They couldn't prosecute."

Kelvin shook his head.

"I think I'd have to do something about that," Heather said.

"Like what?" Danny asked. He was losing color.

"Depends on the person," she said. "On what would even the score."

"Revenge doesn't solve anything," Danny said.

"Maybe not," Heather said, "but sometimes it's necessary."

William wondered what she would have done if she had gotten her hands on her daughter's killer. White was serving life without parole and still denying the whole thing. William could picture Heather tearing the man apart with her bare hands, not leaving many big pieces.

Kelvin pulled into the lot at Big Bad Wolf, a local barbeque place on the north side, a couple of miles from campus. William had been so lost in his own thoughts he hadn't even considered where they were going, hadn't even noticed they had left the faculty parking lot. The lunch menu was low on his list of priorities. The restaurant had meat and Coca-Cola, so he was satisfied.

As a kid, he had loved eating there, more for the art than the food. He liked barbeque, but he had never loved it, no matter how good everyone else said it was. Blue Ribbon this and Gold Metal that had little influence on Billy Baker and none on William. He hadn't been to Big Bad Wolf in years, but the murals on the walls were as intriguing as ever, maybe more so that afternoon. The space between the entrance and the counter had been filled with low walls, about hip high to a grown man, arranged in switchbacks to corral the line of customers. Along those low walls, the story of the three little pigs was depicted in storyboard form, the houses of straw and wood being blown down. Unlike the traditional tale, though, when the Big Bad Wolf is unable to blow down the brick house, he sneaks in the back door and catches the pigs by their tails. The final image, stretched over the menu above the counter, showed the little pigs roasting on three spits, the Big Bad Wolf salivating in anticipation. Little Billy Baker, aged ten, thought this version of the story was more realistic and a lot more fun.

"No one wants to eat a boiled wolf," he had told his father, "but everybody loves bacon."

"They sell barbeque, Billy, not bacon," Ian said.

"Close enough," Billy said.

Ian Baker patted his son on the back and led him to a booth to wait for their order.

That Tuesday afternoon, one week after Jimmy's return, William ordered two barbeque sandwiches with no trimmings and no sides, just pork and spicy sauce, before joining his friends at a table. He had lingered over the murals and ended up last in line.

"All right, Will," Kelvin said, "what is your major malfunction? You've been even more ascetic than usual lately. With you, the differences aren't always visible to the untrained eye, but we know you. What's going on?"

William took a moment to gather himself before answering. He had done his best to maintain his normal routine, his normal demeanor. The fact that he had missed whatever signs Kelvin and the others had seen unnerved him. What else had he missed? He prided himself on seeing what others overlooked, on being able to anticipate how others would perceive a given set of facts or events. "What do you mean?" he asked.

"Typically, we only have to drag you out of your office for lunch once a week," Janet said. "You come out voluntarily once, and we let you be as hermit as you want to be the other three days."

"Except during exams," Danny said. "Basically, you've gone exam-monk Will six weeks early."

This was true, William realized, but he hadn't thought they would notice so quickly. He would've expected another week or two of tacit excuses before it became an issue. They were paying him more attention than he had imagined. *Who else is paying me too much attention?* he thought. He remembered the police officer who had been to see him and said people knew he walked the greenway more than anyone else. This was no secret, but he wondered how much someone might have seen, who might have been paying him special attention. A person who had already singled him out, before Jimmy's return, might have followed him, might have seen everything, and William would have no idea. He would have to be more careful, even more than he had been. His friends were looking at him, waiting for an answer he had already taken too long to give.

"Maybe we should mind our own business," Heather said. "If Will had something he wanted to share, he would have. Or he'll get to it in his own time."

"Heather's right," Danny said. "Sorry, Will."

"Sorry, Will," Janet echoed. When Kelvin didn't chime in, she gave him a glare.

"I'm not sorry," Kelvin said. "I'm just asking a question. It's not like I'm pulling out his fingernails or something."

"You always have to go to violent places, don't you?" Danny asked.

"Guys," William said, "it's fine. To tell the truth, I've just been thinking a lot about my dad lately. Since Jimmy came by."

"You should've called the cops that second time," Danny said.

William felt a flare of rage, felt his face flush, and he took a deep breath to calm himself before responding. "I don't like Jimmy very much," he said. "I don't think I ever did. But he is my brother. He's the only family I have anymore. I'm not going to pretend I want to have Thanksgiving dinner with him, but I'm not going to sic the police on him because he drops by the office a couple of times."

"You're out of line, Danny," Kelvin said.

"Yes, you are," Janet said.

Now Danny turned red, too. "I... I...," he sputtered. "The way you talk about him... I just never... I guess I don't think of him as really your family. I'm sorry, Will. Truly, I am."

William took another deep breath and willed his temperature to drop back to normal. "You're right, Danny. I don't talk about him like he's really family. That's my mistake. Something I ought to change, especially now that he seems to be getting himself together. But that's not what's been bothering me. I just keep thinking about Dad dying. There's so much we don't know."

"I thought he had a wreck?" Heather said.

"He did," William said, "but we don't know how or why. We don't know what he was doing in that part of the county. There's no record of him having a job out there. I just..." He hesitated, timing the pause for maximum effect. "I worry that I should have been paying more attention. That I should have gotten him help. Something."

"It wasn't your fault, Will," Janet said.

"We don't know that."

"You need to let that go," Kelvin said. "You'll eat yourself alive with that kind of thinking."

"Kelvin's right," Danny said. "You can't think like that."

"I just wish I knew exactly what happened."

"It wouldn't change anything," Janet said.

"Of course it would," Heather said. "It would change everything. It might not make it any easier. It might even make it worse. But it would change things. I know that much."

"They'd still be gone," Kelvin said. "It wouldn't bring them back, and that's all that matters."

"I just want him to tell me why," Heather said. "Why her? I don't want to know how it happened, what she went through. I just want to know why her. Why my daughter?"

She had lost all color. She wasn't crying, didn't look sad. Both her fists were clenched, the veins on the backs of her hands bulging beneath the skin, her forearms shaking. William thought she was imagining strangling her daughter's killer with a cord. The body language matched, and he could sympathize with the desire – to watch the life drain from someone who took something too precious for words. He still wasn't

159

convinced his father had been murdered, but he was damn well going to find out, come what may.

"I'm sorry," Janet said. "I guess none of us can keep from getting out of line today. Can we talk about something else?"

"We can talk about that gnarly scar down the side of my baby," Kelvin said.

"Something pleasant?" Janet asked.

"Ed Collins, Nick Fuller, and Charlotte Clements had a paper accepted for the Rhetoric Society Conference," Danny said. "They're presenting in Madison next summer."

"That's more like it," Janet said. "What was the paper on?"

William didn't listen to the summary. He was thinking about Patrick Riley.

CHAPTER 15

That night, one week after Jimmy's return, William ate his dinner like any other evening and went over the plan in his mind until he felt confident in it. After that, he sat reading from his mother's battered copy of *4:50 from Paddington* until he fell asleep. Jimmy called a little after midnight to say he was getting close. William got up, put on dark clothes, and packed his shopping backpack with another set of clothes and the things he had purchased in Greenville. He took a twenty from his wallet and stuffed it in his pocket, laying the wallet next to his phone on the end table. He went out to the garage and added Ian's little tool kit before walking down the greenway toward Shirley's, where he had told Jimmy to meet him.

As he walked, the night air was cold and burned his lungs, made his eyes water. He had been too preoccupied to check the weather report. It wouldn't have mattered, he told himself. He didn't own a jacket he would be willing to sacrifice to the project, and he wouldn't have bought one for the purpose, not even something from Goodwill, already worn in and full of other people's DNA. *Maybe that would have been wise*, he thought.

"So many possibilities," he whispered, not sure who he might be addressing out there in the dark between the trees.

He tried to picture what could be seen from the other side of those limbs, how many angles he had failed to consider. There were just too many. Even if Jimmy didn't get out of line again, it was still likely he would have to improvise somewhere along the way. Looping around Osgood Oaks at pace and a half, he tried to imagine all the things that could go wrong, but by the time he reached the other side he had given it up as impossible. There were just too many variables. He might as well try to predict the Ravens' scores for a whole season before the first round of the draft. Even getting close would be a statistical miracle.

At Shirley's, he scanned the parking lot for Jimmy, but he saw no cars like the one he expected – something old with a large trunk. William didn't want to take the full bag into the store, so he hung it from a branch of a dogwood tree, facing the greenway. He was confident no one else would be coming through there at such a late hour.

In the store, he found a six-pack of twenty-ounce bottled waters and a small tub of oxygen bleach. He wished he had thought of this while he was in Greenville, wished he could think of another purchase to go with it so the clerk wouldn't remember Dr. Baker buying bleach in the middle of the night. It was too late, and the bleach would probably be a necessity. The clerk turned out to be a middle-aged woman who had rung him up before, but she had never called him by name or been friendlier than the average stranger in a store. He didn't think she knew who he was or what he did for a living, but he couldn't be sure. That it wasn't one of his current or former students was the best he could have hoped for, so he felt good about that when he walked through the automatic doors and put the receipt in the trash.

Headlights flashed at him, but he couldn't see the driver. Instead of approaching the car, he waved and went over to the mouth of the greenway to retrieve his backpack. He turned back to the lot to find the car pulling up, the passenger's side next to him. The car was an early 80s Chevy Impala, a long, wide car with a big trunk and an even bigger hood. In the dim light of the edge of Shirley's lot, he couldn't tell what color it really was. Something light, baby blue or maybe mint green. He could see Jimmy clearly now, so he opened the door and got in, tossing the backpack into the backseat as he sat, setting the Shirley's bag between his feet.

"Thirsty?" Jimmy asked.

"It's to mix with the bleach." William lifted the tub from the bag.

"You planning to wash the answers out of this kid?"

"It's to clean up his blood. Oxygen bleach destroys hemoglobin, makes it nearly impossible to get DNA – his or ours."

"Seriously?"

"Yes."

"How in the world would you know that?"

"I'm an English professor; I read."

Jimmy nodded and turned right, heading south. William opened the bleach tub and rolled down the window. He opened the first bottle and poured a little of the water onto the street before scooping powder with the little blue cap. He closed the bottle and shook it, and then repeated the process five times.

"Turn here."

Jimmy made the turn, but he looked a question at his brother.

"We need to make one stop first." William directed Jimmy to the old mill. He took his pack from the backseat, pulled on his new gloves and set the ammo on the seat beside him. Jimmy parked on the broken pavement of the mill's lot and turned off the Impala's headlights.

"Five minutes. Maybe less." William took the empty Shirley's bag and made his way around to the back of the mill, to the mound he had made for the things stolen from Eagle Pawn. He removed as few bricks as he could, trying to keep the mound as natural as possible. He pulled the first bag out and separated the outer Eagle bag. A necklace dangled through a hole one of the pistol's hammers had torn into the interior bag. William tucked it back in and slipped the Shirley's bag over it. He sifted through the mess of jewelry and guns until he could pull out what he wanted: two long barreled .38 revolvers. It hadn't rained since he hid the stash, so the weapons were probably all okay, but he wanted the simple, old-fashioned mechanisms of the revolvers just in case. The long barrels were better for accuracy, and the .38 caliber would have some stopping power but not much of a recoil. He had read about people taking several .22 rounds without falling down. The .357 or .44 would take anyone down, but the recoil could cause a second shot to miss, especially for someone like him who hadn't fired a handgun in more than a decade. He tucked the guns into his waistband. He scooped out three handfuls of the jewelry and put them into the Eagle bag before tucking the rest of the stash – now with a Shirley's outer bag – into the mound and replacing the bricks. He counted ten paces, turned, and checked his work. He was pretty sure the mound would still pass as natural.

Watching for signs of other people as he walked, he made his way back to the Impala. Seeing no one, he pulled the guns from his waistband and passed them to Jimmy through the open window. William took a last look around and got into the car. Jimmy was loading the first revolver from the box of bullets, now between his legs. He pushed in the sixth round, snapped the cylinder closed, and passed the gun back to William before loading the other gun. He wedged the second revolver into the narrow gap between the seat and the armrest, the barrel pointed at the backseat. He closed the box of bullets and handed it to William, who stored it in the glove compartment.

"It's pretty much a smash-and-grab job. Only there's no smashing. I'm going to pick the lock. We tape up the kid." William pulled the roll of tape from his pack and set it on the seat between him and his brother. "We throw him in the trunk and go."

"Simple," Jimmy said. "Simple is good." He started the car and drove three blocks before turning the headlights back on. He wound his way back to Main and turned south toward Chapman Street. The brothers passed the drive in silence, William hoping Jimmy wouldn't go off the script again and derail his plan. It wasn't much of a plan, and a lot could go wrong, but it was as close to Jimmy's usual pattern as William could make it, so the temptation to veer from it should have been minimal. Jimmy looped Riley's block twice, once with the headlights on and once with them off. William knew it was still too early to expect the whole neighborhood to be asleep, but the drive to Sumter was long, and he hoped to be back in time to clean up and go to class as if it were a normal day. A few of the houses had dim lights on in a room or two, but most were already dark on all four sides.

After that second loop, Jimmy pulled into the driveway of Riley's next-door neighbor, crossing the yard from there. He veered around Riley's house on the end farthest away from where William expected the kid's grandmother would be sleeping, her breathing apparatus strapped to her worn face. The Impala ran quietly for an old car, but William wondered if the kid would hear the low rumble as it passed his basement window. It shouldn't wake him, William thought, and he might have his headphones on, oblivious to the world outside his video game.

Jimmy turned the car till it was perpendicular to the house and backed it up to within a few feet of the slanted basement door. William pulled Ian's tool kit and the two masks from his pack, offering a mask to Jimmy.

"Got my own," Jimmy said, smiling. He drew it from under the seat.

William tucked the extra in his back pocket and got out of the car. He stood at the Impala's door and scanned the area, checking that no one had come out since their second pass. He pulled on his mask and made sure it didn't block his vision. Satisfied, he gave Jimmy a sign to wait, took the bag of jewelry, and stepped as quietly as he could to the rear of the old Trans Am on the side of the house. He picked the trunk lock and pulled up the carpet, tucking the Eagle Pawn bag beneath it. He had to smooth out the bag twice before the carpet would lay flat. It didn't need to be perfect, William thought, just good enough that a cop would believe Patrick Riley had thought it was okay. That accomplished, he shut the trunk lid gently, the quiet click of the locking mechanism sharp in the cold, dead air of the night.

When he got back to the Impala, Jimmy was masked and standing at the rear of the old car. He had opened the trunk and taken out a few zip ties, along with the duct tape William had brought. William took the tape, slipping the roll over his left hand till it hung like a bracelet on his arm. He knelt and picked the lock on the slanted door, forcing himself to breath slowly and quietly, listening for any sound of movement in the basement, any sign his actions were heard or seen. He heard nothing but the sound of the lock mechanism turning. He put away the tools, stepped back, and dropped the kit onto the Impala's front seat. He and Jimmy had both left the front doors open, ready for them to jump in and drive off, hopefully at a slow, quiet roll, but full of roar if necessary.

He went back to the slanted door where Jimmy waited, Ian Baker's .45 in his gloved hand. William put his right hand on the door handle and lifted his left, the roll of duct tape sliding halfway down to his elbow. He put up three fingers and counted down, dropping his ring finger, his middle, his index. He opened the door, and Jimmy went in first, crouching, the gun in front of him. William followed, leaving the door lying open, its weight on the hinges. He expected the kid to be sitting in that chair, headphones on, controller in hand, thumbs pounding away at pixelated enemies. Instead, Riley was in bed, snoring away. Jimmy had stopped by the bed, waiting for William and the tape.

William slipped the roll over his hand, but he couldn't pull up the tape with his gloved fingers. He bit off the glove, leaving it dangling from his mouth as he started the tape. Jimmy reached down and took the corners of the sheets at the foot of the bed. He pulled them up slowly, exposing the kid's feet. William tried to tear off the tape, but he wasn't able to pinch it tightly enough with his gloved left hand. He stuffed the right glove into his front pocket and bit off the left one.

The rip of the tape echoed in the basement, and Riley's eyes sprung open.

William shoved the tape over the kid's mouth and grabbed his head with both hands, forcing it to stay on the bed. He looked down and saw Jimmy flopped over Riley's legs, wrestling them down and struggling to get the point of a zip tie into the catch. William sprung onto the bed, the left glove still dangling from his mouth, and straddled Riley, trying to keep him still long enough for Jimmy to finish the job. He let go of the kid's head and grabbed his bony arms, forcing them under William's own knees.

He hadn't held anyone down like this since high school, since his last school yard fight. He had pressed the memory as far into his subconscious as possible, so deep that the occasional flashes of it felt more like scenes from a film than a part of his own life. He looked down at Patrick Riley and adjusted his weight, careful not to put pressure on the boy's throat. William wanted answers, and the strangled don't speak well. He couldn't see Jimmy, but he could feel the struggle continue for a few more seconds.

Finally, Jimmy whispered, "Got it. Turn him over."

William shifted his weight again, putting the majority of it on Riley's right arm. He took the kid's left wrist in his own right hand and twisted it back. The kid tried to squirm away from the force on both sides, but he only succeeded in rolling himself over, his left arm twisted behind his back and his right pinned beneath his body – exactly as William had intended. William switched hands, taking Riley's wrist in his own left hand, and then put his right under the kid, searching for the right forearm. When he had a grip, he twisted that out and pinned the two wrists together. He spit out the glove.

"Zip him."

Jimmy got off the bed, the mattress and springs creaking in relief. He zip-tied the kid's wrists, and William took the spare mask from his back pocket. He pulled it over the kid's head, the holes on the backside, the whole thing functioning as a quick and dirty blindfold. William hopped off the bed and put his gloves back on. The kid's phone lay on the floor next to the bed, so he pocketed it just in case. Each of the brothers took an elbow, lifting the kid off the bed. Jimmy swung around the foot of the bed till they were three astride, like contestants in an outlaw version of the fireman's carry.

A crack rang out, the sound of ripping wood followed by an awful clang – metal crashing into something equally solid. The slanted door, too heavy for its hinges, had torn from its frame and slammed into the bricks beneath it.

William froze, but Jimmy kept walking, causing the trio to spin for a moment, till William got his wits about him again. The brothers dragged Riley toward the hole where the door belonged. The kid was light enough, but he was resisting, tugging and twisting as they went. William lost his grip, the gloves not as tacky as human skin, and ended up with his arm hooked around the kid's elbow, now facing the wrong way. Jimmy let go and did the same, so they were dragging Riley along, the kid facing the bed and the brothers facing the door. With all the kicks and moaning, William couldn't be sure, but he thought he heard noise above. He stopped to listen at the foot of the small set of stairs leading to the hole and the waiting Impala. Jimmy stopped, too, and Riley kicked out, trying and failing to free himself from their grip. Light spilled down the stairs from the main house.

"Damn thieves, stealing from an old woman. You ain't worth the air you're breathing."

William looked up toward the voice and saw a pair of ancient, gnarled feet, one blue and the other purple. He stepped up, Jimmy stepping with him and the kid dragging behind. Riley's heels thudded on the first step, and he sank down, sitting on the third step and pulling Jimmy down with him. William tried to drag them both forward, stepping up the few stairs quickly, leaning his body forward like a skier before a jump. He looked back and saw Jimmy clambering to his feet and dragging the kid up the third step.

The old woman had come halfway down the stairs. She moved much faster than the cane and scooter had led William to believe was possible. At first glance, he thought she carried a rifle. She fired, the barrel pointed toward the basement floor. It was meant to be a warning shot, it seemed, but the ricochet tore through the kid's legs, blood bursting out in an instant.

Shotgun, William thought. There were too many holes, each small and red.

Jimmy and the old woman were screaming, words William couldn't process, if they were words at all. He let go of the kid and stepped back down, meeting the old woman at the bottom of the stairs and snatching the gun from her, the warmth of the barrel seeping through his right glove. It was an old single-shot .410, now useless to her. He drew it back, catching the stock with his left hand, already aiming the butt for a blow. The barrel was caught, though, and he turned to see what caused the resistance.

"You don't want to do that," Jimmy said. He let go of the barrel.

He was right. William didn't want to hit the old woman. He was just moving on instinct, his muscles on animalistic autopilot.

"Sit down right there on the stairs."

She had seen the blow coming and stepped back, cowering. She obeyed.

William tossed the gun through the hole into the yard, turned and yanked the mask from Riley's head, showing his face to the old woman, presumably Riley's grandmother. She screeched at the sight, a fearful wail without words.

William pointed to the boy's bleeding legs. "You did that, not us. If you want him to live, you'll sit right there and be quiet."

She nodded, the screech fading into low moans and sobs.

"Is there any rope around here?"

The kid was bleeding quickly, more than William would have expected from the small pellets of a .410 shell.

"Bungee cords in the trunk," Jimmy said.

"Bring them. He's bleeding out. She got his femoral artery, I think."

"Lord, have mercy."

The woman shrieked.

Riley, now free of Jimmy and William's grip, curled himself in a ball, rolling to the bottom of the small staircase. He writhed on the floor, trying to get his hands over his wounds, but unable because of the zip ties. Jimmy stepped back through the hole and tossed two bungee cords down to William.

"Bottle of bleach, too."

"Why?" Jimmy asked.

"Look at your leg."

"Shit. I didn't even feel it," Jimmy said.

"Kid, I'm going to tourniquet that leg, so you don't bleed to death. If you want to live, be still."

Riley rolled over onto his back, and William got a clear look into the kid's eyes. He was terrified. His eyes seemed to have lost their irises – just pupil and bloodshot whites. He straightened his leg, clearly more afraid of his wounds than of the masked man offering to help. William wrapped the cord three times around the kid's thigh, connecting the plastic hooked ends to hold it in place.

Jimmy had come back down, and he handed William the bottle. William opened it and doused the kid's wounds first, then splashed it on the floor around them. The kid squirmed in pain from the peroxide in the mixture.

"Get two more bottles. Toss one down and splash the other around the yard."

"Are you serious?" Jimmy asked.

"I don't want your DNA left here."

"This is Osgood," Jimmy said, "not Vegas. They ain't gonna have the whole cast of *CSI* out here pulling blood samples off four-leaf clovers and shit."

"Just do it."

Jimmy went back to the car, and William took hold of the kid's elbow, dragging him back up the little set of stairs toward the hole. The old woman stood, even in her fear, tempted to fight for her grandson.

"Woman, I told you to sit down." William let the kid go and pulled the .38 from his waistband, pointing it at her first, then at the kid's head. "I mean for both of you to live through this, but it'll work just as well for me if you're both dead in the morning."

She stepped back and sat on the stairs again, her hands trembling and tears streaming down her weathered face. William put the gun away and dragged the kid through the hole, where Jimmy met him with the bleach.

"Put him in the backseat and then do the yard."

Jimmy nodded, so William took the bottle, opened it, and stepped back down to the basement floor. He splashed the bleach over the blood on the floor, not sure if any of it was Jimmy's. *Better safe than sorry*, he thought. He scanned the wall and found a few splatters, so he doused them as well before collecting the first bottle and cap from the floor. He used the remains of the two bottles on the steps as he went up. He tossed the bottles in the open trunk and checked Jimmy's work in the yard. The mixture bubbled in several places, and he saw no evidence of blood anywhere. In the dim light from the inside of the house, he doubted he would see it even if it were there. He went back to the passenger's side of the car, collected another bottle, and closed the door. He splashed that bottle on the grass around the driver's side of the car.

Jimmy had deposited the kid in the backseat and sat waiting behind the wheel. The Impala rumbled quietly in the still, cold night. The door crash and the single .410 shot hadn't caused much of a stir in that neighborhood; William saw no lights on in the surrounding houses. He knelt at the hole and spoke to the old woman.

"If Patrick here tells us what we want to know, they'll be calling you from the hospital in less than an hour. If he doesn't, they'll never find his body. If you call the cops, they won't find yours either. Do you understand?"

She nodded, William thought, but it was difficult to distinguish that from her fearful quaking. He turned and shut the trunk, then climbed into the back with Patrick Riley. He sat the kid up, wedging him into the corner where the seat met the door and propping his head against the window so they could talk face to face.

"Go."

"Where?" Jimmy asked.

"Head toward the hospital. And hand me the gun."

Jimmy handed Ian Baker's .45 over the Impala's bench seat, and William held it out for Riley to see in the light of the passing street lamps.

"Do you recognize this?"

The kid just stared, seemingly oblivious to the gun in front of him. William slapped him with his left hand, keeping the gun right in front of the kid's eyes.

"I asked you a question. Do you recognize this? You've plastered the internet with pictures of yourself posing with it, like you're some kind of badass gangster. You know this gun, don't you?"

The kid finally registered the words William spoke and nodded his head.

"You sold this to Eagle Pawn, right?"

Riley nodded again.

"All right. I've got one more question for you, and you're going to have to speak this time. I'm going to pull off this tape so you can answer. And you're going to answer. You're going to tell me exactly what I want to know, no hesitation, no bullshit, because if you don't – if you do anything I don't like, scream or anything at all – two things are going to happen. First, I'm going to pull off that cord and let you bleed to death right here in the backseat. While that's happening, we'll be turning this car around and going right back to your house, where the last thing your grandmother will see before I put a bullet in her brain will be your dead body being dumped on her floor. Is that clear to you?"

Riley nodded.

"Good." William ripped the tape off. "Where did you get this gun?"

"Kilo. I got it from Kilo. Traded him a batch of meth for it."

"Kilo is a measure of mass, kid. It's not a person's name. I need a name. An actual name, first and last."

"I don't know his real name, I swear. Everybody calls him Kilo."

"That's not good enough." William reached for the hooks of the bungee cord.

The kid jerked away, curling his legs against the door.

"Describe him," Jimmy said. "White, black, Hispanic? How old?"

William pulled back his hand.

"He's white," the kid said. "I don't know how old he is. A few years older than me, I think."

"What does he look like?"

"Black hair. I don't know about the eyes. You don't stare at Kilo."

"How tall?"

"Same as me, I guess."

"Five-ten or so?"

"Yeah."

"Fat, skinny? What?"

"He's ripped. Works out all the time. Played football, I think."

"Where?"

"Osgood High."

"When?"

"He was a senior when I was a freshman. I remember that."

"You went to high school together, and you don't remember his last name?"

"Jones, maybe. I can't remember. I'm sorry, I just don't remember."

"Tattoos?" Jimmy asked.

"A bunch of them. One's a scale, like an old-timey scale, with stuff on both sides."

"What's on it?"

"Money on one side. I'm not sure about the other. Handcuffs, maybe. Or a snake. It's kind of messy, and you don't stare at Kilo."

"Scary mofo, huh?" Jimmy asked.

"Yeah."

"Where?"

"What?"

"Where's the tat? What part of his body?"

"His neck."

"Where can we find him?"

"I don't know. I'm not sure he lives here anymore. He stays in Columbia, maybe. Just comes up here sometimes to sell stuff or buy stuff."

"He buys your meth?"

"Sometimes, if he needs to. He gets better stuff from people somewhere else, but sometimes they run out or can't find a place to cook."

"All right," Jimmy said. "I think that's enough. I think you get to live."

"Did he tell you where he got the gun?"

"No, but he had to have stolen it. No way Kilo could buy a gun in a store. He's been in jail more than he's been out."

"That can happen," Jimmy said. He had driven them across town, the streets empty so late on a Tuesday night, so early on a Wednesday morning. "Hospital."

"Last instruction, kid. We're going to pull up to the Emergency entrance." William pulled the kid's phone from his pocket and tucked it under the kid's arm. He drew out his pocketknife. "I'm going to cut you loose and out you'll go. If you can walk, go straight in. If not, you wait till we're out of the lot and scream for help. Your story is you and some friends were pulling a prank on your grandmother and she accidently shot you. Call her and get her onboard. You say anything else, we'll find out and we'll be back to kill you both. Clear?"

The kid nodded.

Jimmy stopped outside the Emergency entrance. William opened the knife and cut the zip ties. The kid opened the door and hopped out on his good leg. The entrance was deserted, but the brothers passed a smoking nurse on the sidewalk at the other end of the ER's semicircle drive. If she noticed they were wearing masks, she didn't react to it. Two blocks later, Jimmy pulled off his mask, and William did the same.

"Billy Baker, you are the meanest man I have ever met."

"I did what I had to do."

"I know you did," Jimmy said. "Are we really going to kill that kid if he talks?"

"No. If he talks, the police will get an anonymous tip that he robbed Eagle Pawn and find that bag of jewelry in the trunk of his Trans Am. After that, no one'll believe a word he says."

"Cops won't believe he pulled Eagle by himself. That kid's too squirrelly for serious B&E."

"Exactly. His crew are the same ones who snatched him out of his basement tonight. Told him to keep his mouth shut, threatened to kill him and his grandmother if he talked. Masked men asking about a gun he used to have are just the best his meth-addled mind could come up with under pressure. Doesn't mean anything."

"The grandmother?"

"She can tell them what she wants. The story still fits. Falling out with his partners. She didn't see faces, and he's too scared to tell."

"It has holes, Billy."

"It'll be good enough."

"And this Kilo?"

"We'll find him. There can't be that many guys around here who go by Kilo."

"You might be surprised. I've known three in prison."

"All from Osgood?"

"Fair point."

"How's your leg?"

Jimmy looked down. "I'd forgotten it." He poked a finger at the bloody spot on his right thigh. "I think it just lodged in the skin." He rolled his flesh between his thumb and forefinger. "Yeah, it's there. I can feel it. Doesn't really hurt, but it's creepy as all hell. Like when you shot me with that pellet gun."

"I'd forgotten about that."

"I'll never forget it."

"That was the idea."

Jimmy nodded. "What now?"

"Drop me at Shirley's and get rid of this car."

"Not a problem."

"Whose car is this, anyway?"

"Officially, this car does not exit."

"What does that mean?"

"State records show this car was totaled a few months back, stripped for parts, crushed and melted down."

"And unofficially?"

"It belonged to my employer, but tomorrow, it'll be exactly what the paperwork says."

"Who is your employer?"

"Better you don't know," Jimmy said.

"Fair enough." William climbed over the seat and settled into the passenger's side. By the light of the passing street lamps, he could see Riley's blood smeared all over his clothes. He pulled off the gloves and dumped them in the backseat. His backpack was still back there, so he pulled it up to the front. It was covered in blood, too. He emptied his pockets into the floorboard and shed his shirt and pants, dumping them in the backseat. He opened the pack and checked the spare clothes inside. The waterproof pack was blood proof too, evidently. He dumped it into the backseat and tugged on the fresh clothes, putting his keys and things into the clean pockets.

"I really liked that bag."

"Price of doing business," Jimmy said.

William nodded. "Burn all that."

Jimmy nodded. "You'll find out who this Kilo is?" he asked.

"Soon. I'll call you."

Jimmy pulled into the Shirley's lot, swinging around to put William's door next to the head of the greenway. "Thanks, Billy."

William patted his brother's shoulder, got out, and made his way up the path.

CHAPTER 16

W illiam knew he was taking a big risk, trusting
Jimmy to destroy all the evidence. "He's never
been caught in the act," William whispered to himself,
to the trees. He had left his phone at home and had no
way of knowing what time it was. The business with
Riley felt like hours, but he thought it couldn't have
been more than a few minutes, plus the driving – just
a few miles around town. Looping around Osgood
Oaks, he saw lots of headlight beams crisscrossing
through the trees – students coming back from
closing bars, he was sure. *Just after two*, he thought.
He sped up a bit, hoping to get past the area without
anyone seeing him. He wouldn't be recognized
through the dark and the trees, but it would be better
if no one recalled a person passing at that hour.

Striding down the greenway in the cold October
night, the image of the old woman flashed across his
mind. He saw her terrified expression as he raised the
butt of her shotgun in anger. If Jimmy hadn't grabbed
the barrel, he would have killed her. Two quick strikes
with that old wooden stock would have ended her, not
a doubt in his mind, and that was the motion he had
begun. The thought made him physically ill, and he
vomited into the bushes without breaking stride. He
felt certain Jimmy had prevented a blackout and
saved at least one life in the process. Probably two. If
he had killed the grandmother, he was pretty sure
Riley would have followed shortly after.

The last quarter mile of the walk seemed brighter
than usual, a lighter gray than he recalled from other
late-night trips along the greenway. Slowing his pace,
William approached the park with caution, trying to

see what caused the light. When the trees finally opened, he got a clear view across the trimmed lawn and up Harvie Road.

Two police cars sat in front of his house, one on either side of the road, pointed in opposite directions. Their blue lights rotated in a balanced rhythm, one turning toward the park when the other turned away, less like flashing than ebbing. William froze at the edge of the park. He couldn't understand it. He backed up a few paces, trying to make sense of what lay before him. There hadn't been enough time. Even if Patrick Riley had talked, the kid hadn't seen their faces. He shouldn't have been able to give the police a name and send them straight to the house like this. Even if William had missed some piece of evidence, even if there were some way of tracing it all back to him, there was just no way he could imagine them connecting the dots in the time it had taken for Jimmy to drive from the hospital to Shirley's and for William to walk down the greenway.

He scanned the area till he found a tree with low branches, somewhere he could hide and watch. He spotted a pine and crouched in its cover, trying to squint past the blue lights and see people, to see movement of any kind. It took a few minutes for his eyes to adjust. The lights were on in the house next door to his, the first one after the park, every window a pale yellow against the purple mix of brick and police flashers. On the other side, the first house was just as bright, the porch and living room glowing. The police had woken the whole block, it seemed.

"Jimmy," William whispered, reaching into his pocket for a phone that wasn't there. If Jimmy had been stopped, pulled over for any reason – run into a roadblock, an insurance check, or a drunk driving crackdown – they were done for. The kid's blood was all over the car. William's own prints were on the empty water bottles, the tub of bleach, the duct tape, the blood-soaked clothes and backpack. "Too many variables," he whispered. Jimmy would lie for him, he was sure of it, but it wouldn't do much good. He needed to get away.

He needed a car.

He could pick the lock on something in the Shirley's lot, hot wire it, and be gone. He had never had occasion to hot wire a car, but he had read about it many times and even watched a YouTube video on the process. If he could find a car from the 80s or earlier, he was pretty sure he could do it. He would need money, though, which he could steal, but it would be much easier if he had his wallet, if he could make one big withdrawal before they froze his accounts. The wallet was in his house with his phone, things left behind so there was no danger of dropping something, no danger of leaving some trace. His own house seemed to be dark, as far as he could tell from his position in the park. They weren't inside yet.

He forced himself to sit, to take a few deep breaths, to calm down and think clearly. If they stopped Jimmy, they would make assumptions. He was involved in the Eagle robbery. He was involved in Patrick Riley being shot. They wouldn't assume William was involved. Probably the opposite. They would want to talk to him, to find out if Jimmy had been in his house again, if he had seen the Impala, seen the jewelry or the guns. If he had seen Jimmy with Patrick Riley. In the minutes they could have had him and the car full of evidence, they couldn't have analyzed anything, couldn't have run any fingerprints. They would only have the obvious – a car full of blood and three stolen guns – plus whatever Jimmy had told them. Whatever Patrick Riley or his grandmother might have said. William wouldn't be under suspicion yet, not really. If he could talk his way through the interview, they would leave and he could get away. He could figure out what to do next somewhere far away, figure out how to stay out of jail, figure out if there was anything he could do to help Jimmy. He would owe Jimmy for telling whatever story he had told to keep William's name out of it for as long as possible.

Those were long-term issues, problems to be solved another day. In the short-term, the right now, he needed only two things: a way to get back into his house and a believable excuse for not answering his door when the police knocked, for not answering his phone when they called. He assumed they would have called when he didn't answer the door. He got up and looked around. He needed to get over to the next block and slip through to his back door. He would need a place to stop and be sure no one was watching that side of the house.

He went back down the greenway, stopping every few paces to look through the trees and gauge the yards on the other side. The neighborhood on that side was part of the same mill village as his own house. Currie Street had been mostly two-bedroom, one bath places for the lower-level people. Some of them had been remodeled, had additional bedrooms and garages attached. The yards were small, often filled with children's outdoor toys – swing sets, plastic pools, pup tents, and the like. The occasional doghouse. He wanted one of those yards, something with a lot of cover, big things he could crouch behind.

The fifth yard was perfect. It was on a small lot, less than a quarter of an acre, and the back yard was now a quarter smaller than the mill planners had intended because of a large, wrap-around wooden deck. The rest of the yard was taken up by an elaborate playset, a sort of metastasized fort with a wide slide, monkey bars, and ladders all over it. William ducked through the trees and crab-walked his way under the slide, past the deck, and around the side of the house. A few quick strides brought him to the sidewalk, where he stood upright and tried to stroll, like a man out for a crisp walk to ward off insomnia.

At the house behind his next-door neighbor, he slowed his pace and tried to get a view of his own back yard through the gaps between the houses. It was too dark to see much. He passed the next house, the one behind his own, and tried again with no better results. He continued to the end of the block before turning around and trying again from the other direction. The flashing lights gave him quick glimpses, but he saw nothing definitive. He slipped around his rear neighbors' house and crouched behind their boat. No light showed from the windows along the rear of his own house, but the blue glow from the police cars illuminated his back door.

No one was there.

He crept to the stern and checked one side of the house, then crept down to the bow and checked the other. No sign of police or anyone else. No sign of movement inside the house. He slipped out from the shelter of the boat and dashed to the back stoop, quietly took out his keys, and opened the door. He let it swing slowly through the arc of its hinges, listening for any sound, watching for any movement, ready to run or fight, if necessary. He heard nothing, saw nothing, and waited for his eyes to adjust, crouched like a prowler at his own back door.

When he could see the kitchen clearly in the dim blue glow, he went inside, stepping quietly, shutting the door gently. He crab-walked like a burglar, through the living room and into the study at the front of the house. He knelt by the front window and used one finger to push the curtain aside, creating a gap of less than an inch – just enough to see out. Hopefully, not enough for anyone to see in. The porch was empty. He let the curtain close slowly, one millimeter at a time, and stood, making his way through to the front bedroom. He hadn't thought to check it after Jimmy slept there, but he now saw the bed had been made, the foot of the bed done in the hospital corners Ian had demanded when they were children. William moved the curtain in that room just as carefully as he had in the study and saw no one on his lawn, no one on the sidewalk at the street.

On the other side of Harvie, the windows were still lit up, glowing yellow through the curtains. He thought he saw movement behind them, but he couldn't be sure. He began to doubt the police were there for him. If they were, they were doing a very poor job. The Osgood police might not be ready for a primetime reality show, but he had no reason to believe they were completely incompetent, incapable of staking out the right house. He relaxed a bit and began to revise his theory.

Something must have happened across the street, a break-in or domestic violence, maybe. He went to his bedroom, shed his clothes, and thought. He still might need a cover story, a reason he hadn't answered his door. He couldn't be sure they had knocked at all. He found his phone – no missed calls, no new texts. Jimmy hadn't made it to Augusta yet, hadn't dumped the car. He would have called. It was too soon to worry about that, though. The trip should take at least another half an hour, plus whatever time it took to do the work. William considered calling and checking in, but he rejected the idea. He didn't know anything yet.

There was no reason to bother Jimmy, no reason to risk making him nervous and causing a mistake. Calling would be more likely to make things worse than better. He needed more information. He would have to risk going outside and talking to the police himself.

Normally, he slept in his underwear, but he owned a set of pajamas, flannel top and bottom – a gift from his mother that he couldn't bring himself to give away. He pulled the bottoms from a drawer, from beneath a stack of old T-shirts he hadn't worn since grad school. He put the pants on and climbed into bed, rolling around a bit, trying to simulate tossing and turning, trying to wrinkle the pants and his undershirt, to make himself look like a man who had just gotten out of bed. It wouldn't be enough. A good strong knock should have woken him. Why hadn't it? The solution jumped into his mind, and he jumped out of bed, dashing to the bathroom.

The earplugs weren't in the medicine cabinet.

"Suitcase," he whispered. He had stored them in a small pocket when he packed at the end of the conference in Charleston.

He closed the cabinet and turned on the bathroom light to check his hair in the mirror. The sight of himself gave William a shock. He had given himself a respectable bedhead in his two minutes of rolling around, but that didn't bother him. On his neck and the collar of his undershirt, in a dark red rim, was what could only be Patrick Riley's blood. William wondered how so much of it had gotten so high. He stripped off the shirt and stuffed it behind the hamper, stripped off the pajama pants, and checked the rest of his body. He found blood on his ankles and wrists, along his waistband. Dragging the wounded kid around, he had managed to stain himself at every opening, every place his clothes could ride up and expose a strip of flesh. He washed himself in the sink, cleaning his wrists first, then his neck, then his waist. He pulled back the shower curtain and washed his ankles, rinsing the tub to make sure no pink residue remained, no telltale flecks of red attached to the drain.

He double-checked the sink and scanned his body again. He pronounced himself clean and pulled yesterday's undershirt from the hamper, tugging it on. He put the pajama pants back on and went back to the bed, turning on the bedside lamp to check for blood. Evidently, the walk down the greenway and all his skulking through the neighborhood had given it time to dry. There were no stains on the pillow or the sheets. He lay down and rolled around again. In the mirror after that, he believed he saw a man who had just gotten up. He went to the front door and unlocked it, remembering at the last second that he needed the earplugs. He found them in the suitcase, stored in the second bedroom closet, and twisted them into his ears, popped them out, and twisted them in once more. At the front door, he popped them out again and dropped them into a pocket of the pajama bottoms. He went out onto the porch, shading his eyes against the blue lights that still flashed, trying to look confused, trying to look concerned.

An officer stood by the car across the street, talking into a CB mouthpiece, its black coil stretching through the car window. A second officer stood on the porch of the house across the street talking to William's neighbor, a Samuels senior named Sarah Hudgens. William wondered where her roommate was, whether she might be the reason the police were there. Sarah had never been one of his students, but Ashleigh MacAllister had been in his American literature section the previous spring. He liked her more than he wanted to admit, even to himself. She wasn't an English major, and she was a poor writer, but she worked hard, read the material, and could be insightful during class discussions. She was also strikingly beautiful. William was not the sort of professor who got involved with his students, but he had thought more than once about making an exception for Ashleigh. He had enough trouble keeping his eyes off her face, but she habitually wore a teddy bear charm on a necklace, its golden form lying at the peak of her cleavage. Light glinted off its diamond eyes every time she shifted her position, drawing his attention to her.

William stopped pretending to be concerned and genuinely felt it.

He left his front door open and padded down the sidewalk and across the street, his bare feet stung by the cold, rough pavement. Approaching the house, he recognized Officer Phillips, who seemed to be leaving, telling Sarah he would call when he had more information, telling her to call if she thought of anything else.

"I don't want to be nosey," William said, "but I saw the lights. Is everything all right?"

"We were robbed," Sarah said. Tear tracks stained her face, and she looked to be on the verge of crying again.

"I'm sorry. You're not hurt, are you?"

Sarah shook her head.

"Ashleigh?"

"She's not here." Sarah folded her arms across her chest, Ashleigh's absence clearly a point of contention between them.

"I think everything's settled down now, Dr. Baker," Phillips said. "You didn't happen to see anything, did you?"

"Afraid not. I was asleep till just a few minutes ago. Got up to... Well, I got up and saw the flashers. Thought I'd better take a look."

Phillips nodded his head sympathetically. "I hate that. In the middle of the night. Just started for me."

Sarah made a face, clearly not sure why the two men were talking about nocturnal urination when she had just been robbed.

"One of the costs of being a grown man," William said, smiling at Phillips, then Sarah. "I'm sorry this happened, but I'm glad you're okay. If you need anything, I'm just across the street."

"Thanks, Dr. Baker." Sarah turned and went inside, closing the door with a polite wave.

William thought he saw a small shiver come over her just before the closing door blocked her from view. She probably shouldn't be alone, but it wasn't his place and he had other concerns. He stepped down from the porch and waited for Phillips on the sidewalk. The officer joined him a second later.

"She wasn't assaulted, was she?" William asked.

"No. She heard the burglars and thought it was the roommate. Came out and found two guys snatching their TV. She locked herself in the bathroom and called 911."

"Smart girl."

Phillips nodded. "Better safe than sorry."

"Any evidence? Prints or something?"

Phillips shook his head. "We don't really do that when no one's been hurt. Just don't have the budget for it. Break-in like this, it's just about finding the stuff. We'll check the usual suspects, check the pawnshops, check Craigslist and such. Hopefully, we'll make a connection. Soon, I hope. I'm getting tired of these break-ins. Makes us look bad, to be honest. Worse, it makes people nervous. We'll have accidental shootings next."

William had to strain to keep from smiling. He put his hands over his face and faked a yawn to cover. "Excuse me," he said.

"No problem. Sorry we disturbed you."

"Well, I was already up." William tilted his head to convey the annoyance of getting up at night to pee. This wasn't really a problem for him yet, but he knew it was an ailment of middle age that garnered sympathy with almost anyone.

Phillips nodded.

The other officer shut off his blue lights and joined them on the sidewalk in front of Sarah and Ashleigh's porch. "No luck," he said. His nameplate said he was Dunn. "A couple of people saw them running with the TV, across Main and onto campus, but they must have had a car there. Too much traffic at that hour to spot any one vehicle, with everybody coming in from the bars."

William and Phillips nodded.

"I'll leave you to your work," William said. He started down to the street.

"Thanks, Dr. Baker," Phillips called after him. "And keep an eye out."

"Will do. I hope you catch them." He waved from his side of the street, went up the walk and into his house. He closed the front door and leaned against it, breathing a sigh of relief. All the worry, the planning, the sneaking around in his own home was for nothing.

"Too many variables," he said.

He pulled the earplugs from his pocket and flicked the wax from them with his thumbnail, walked to the bathroom, and put them in the medicine cabinet. He stared at himself in the mirror and shook his head in dismay. It would be days before he could be sure he'd gotten away with the Patrick Riley business – if ever. He wondered how he could find out how the kid was doing without giving himself away.

The grandmother, too. That poor woman, cowering and trembling in her own basement. He had nearly killed her for protecting her family, her home. That shot had been a warning, a threat. If the roles had been reversed, William wouldn't have fired into the floor. He was sure of that. The kid was a drug dealer. He deserved whatever came his way, but the old woman was an innocent. William would have to make it up to her somehow, make things right. The man he beat up on Saturday night deserved restitution, too. That wasn't right, and William knew it. He didn't know what to do about it. He would need to think about these things for a while.

CHAPTER 17

In the meantime, there was the matter of Kilo. Kilo Jones, maybe. For the first time, William considered the possibility Riley was lying. Kilo could have been the first word that came to the terrified meth cook, a figment of his drug and adrenaline-addled imagination. *Why did I believe him?* William asked himself. Standing in the bathroom, he closed his eyes and focused on the memory of the kid's face in the light of the street lamps. Riley was scared. Scared down to his marrow, William thought. And he didn't hesitate, didn't shift in his story or stumble in his description. Of course, the kid had been making and selling drugs to guys a lot tougher and meaner than himself for several months, maybe for years. Surely he had learned to think on his feet, to talk a good game. His product couldn't be all that good, or he wouldn't still be living in his grandmother's basement, still be driving an old Corolla and tinkering with that ancient Trans Am. He had to be able to bullshit. He could have been lying.

William didn't think so. He believed Riley, and Jimmy had, too. At bottom, he was just too sure that even in the early stages of dementia, even in the middle of dementia, if it had progressed that far, Ian Baker would have torn the kid's arms off and fed them to him before letting go of that .45. William took a last look at himself in the bathroom mirror, shook his head, and went to get his laptop.

He knew it was a longshot, but he googled "Kilo Jones Osgood" to see what would come up. Right at the top, the very first search result, was a link to an article from the Columbia newspaper. "Kevin 'Kilo'

Jones was shot and killed by store owner Piyush Patel during an attempted robbery." The article was dated ten days earlier, three days before Jimmy's return.

Billy shook, barely able to contain the urge to smash the computer, slam it to the floor and stomp it into small pieces. He set it aside and stood, pacing the room in an attempt to calm himself, to bring his mind under control. He clenched his fists and roared, an animalistic fury erupting from his throat, like a mama bear on finding a wounded cub. He wanted to tear someone open with his bare hands. He wanted something to break. He snatched up an American literature anthology, an old paperback volume as thick as a phonebook – the first thing he saw – and tore it in half like a sideshow strong man. He roared again and hurled the pieces, the loose pages flapping and fluttering through the room like over-sized confetti, the bound end knocking over a lamp, mangling its shade and shattering the bulb. He roared a third time and sank to his knees, his rage finally spent. Looking at the damage he had done, he knew he would miss the anthology, that he would spend hours recovering his notes from it, transferring his notes to another text. The lamp had come from Walmart and would be easily replaced, a small bright side to look at for a fleeting moment.

He crawled over and collected the laptop, reading the rest of the article on Kilo Jones. Kilo had been an All State linebacker as a senior at Osgood High and committed to play for the University of Georgia. He was arrested for distributing meth the following summer, and the scholarship was rescinded. Various drug charges after that. Two B&Es. There was a mug shot, the scales tattoo wrapping around the left side of his neck. There was money on one side, just as Riley had said, but the other side was too far toward the back of his neck and couldn't be seen. He was twenty-seven when he died. He must have been pretty small-time in the drug trade if he still needed to rob convenience stores, not much higher up the chain than Patrick Riley. Kilo's death made the paper, but not the six o'clock news, William thought. He felt like he'd remember if he had seen that, felt certain he would have recognized the name when Riley said it. To be sure, William checked the Columbia TV stations' websites. He found nothing. He dropped "Kilo" from the search and tried to find other information on Kevin Jones. There were archived articles on football games that mentioned his name and an old write up from the Osgood paper about Jones making All State. William couldn't find anything recent, though, not even a funeral announcement.

He remembered his father's, remembered how painful it had been to fill out the form the mortuary had given him. Ian Baker was a father, a husband, a businessman, a soldier, a war hero, and his whole life was expected to be reduced to a few lines on a single, pre-printed sheet of paper. It felt profane, a desecration of all Ian Baker had been. Sitting on the floor in his study, William wondered what it had been like for his father when he filled out the same form for Mamie. However painful it was, he had never said a word.

"I should have done more," William said, not sure what he could have done. He was doing it now, he supposed, for whatever good it would do.

He closed the laptop and put it away. The broken lamp and the larger pieces of the bulb went into the trashcan. For a moment, he thought of waiting till morning to vacuum up the rest, thinking the neighbors might be woken by the noise. Then he remembered his roars and knew it was too late to be concerned about that. He prepared his explanation while he got the vacuum, plugged it in, and cleaned up the mess he had made with his outburst. He had stubbed his toe, he would say, yelled in pain, jumped around trying to shake it off and accidentally knocked over the lamp. He would apologize for all the racket, look down through most of the story, and will his cheeks to turn a bit pink in embarrassment. With the lie as firm in his mind as the truth, he put away the vacuum and began organizing the torn pages of the anthology. He had gathered them and stacked the pages in order up to 127 before his phone rang.

"Did I wake you?" Jimmy asked when William answered.

"No. Why?"

"You sound like you're half asleep. Hoarse, I guess."

"I'm up. Did you make it home okay?"

"I'm relaxing by the fire," Jimmy said. "Watching *Fast and Loud* on my DVR. I don't think this Chevy is worth the trouble. It ought to be a cube by now."

William could hear machinery in the background. He didn't want to ask, but he could picture his brother in some junk yard, standing by a fire that burned in an old oil drum like a homeless person, watching some behemoth of a car compactor put an end to the pale Impala.

"I've never watched that show, but it sounds interesting. Thanks for the heads up."

"Glad to do it."

William waited silently, hoping his brother would keep talking. He didn't know how to tell him about Kilo Jones, wasn't sure he should tell him at all. Not yet. The grinding in the background became a screeching and then stopped.

"You really ought to see this," Jimmy said. "It is a sight to behold. You wouldn't believe the transformation."

"I can imagine."

"You make any progress since I saw you?"

"Not much."

"Well, you're pretty resourceful, little brother. I'm sure you'll figure it out."

"I'll do my best, but I think we may have hit a dead end."

"A dead end? Really? That sounds bad. I thought it was just a little snag, nothing that couldn't be fixed."

William wasn't sure why he and Jimmy had been speaking in code every time they had to use a phone. It had come naturally, like a game they might have played when they were young. There was no benefit to it, though. He knew that. If anyone was listening, recording their calls with a plan to use the conversations against them, that person knew enough to parse out their simple code. No one was listening, though. William was sure of it. Nothing he had ever done before Jimmy's return would have brought that kind of attention, and the little burner phone Jimmy carried was untraceable. A person would have to put the bug right in the thing or sit somewhere nearby with a parabolic microphone to overhear their conversations. People with that kind of time, people with that kind of budget, just wouldn't be interested in the sorts of things Jimmy got up to. Their little game was a waste of time and energy, and William didn't have any left to waste, not now, not when the whole exercise had come to nothing.

"He's dead, Jimmy. We're too late."

"He ain't dead," Jimmy said. "I saw that wound. Nicked an artery, sure, but it wasn't enough to kill him. You were just yanking his chain about that, putting the fear in him."

William wasn't so sure, but that was beside the point. "Not Riley, Jimmy. Kilo. Kilo Jones is dead. I looked him up. He died ten days ago. Shot dead robbing a gas station."

"Shit," Jimmy said, and William heard the phone hit the ground, followed by a stream of profanity and what William was sure were the sounds of his brother beating a fifty-five gallon drum into a new shape. Jimmy's outburst went on much longer than William's had, so long William worried that Jimmy would hurt himself.

"Jimmy," he called into the phone, not really believing he would be heard. "Jimmy, calm down."

Eventually, Jimmy spent his rage and picked up the phone. "So that's it," he said. "The end of the line."

"Maybe not." While his brother was venting, William had been thinking. "He has to have friends or associates or whatever they call each other. People he works with to sell drugs. Riley said Kilo only bought from him when other sources were dry. It will take some time, but we can find those people. Maybe one of them will know how Kilo ended up with Dad's gun."

"Not likely to find the one that does."

"I'll take my time."

"All right."

"How's the leg?"

"Sore, but it'll be fine. Thanks for asking."

"Good. I've got class in the morning. I'll call you when I know something."

William hung up and went to bed, forgetting to take off the pajama bottoms. They twisted as he tossed and turned, unable to shut off his mind and get to sleep. He needed a plan, some way to narrow the possibilities. He couldn't make his ideas take shape, though. He was too wound up, too spent from the adrenaline rushes of the night – the break-in, the kidnapping, the shooting, the cops outside his house. He needed sleep, but he couldn't get there.

After an hour, he gave up, got out of bed and went back to his study. He finished organizing the torn anthology pages. When they were back in order, he put a rubber band on them to keep them that way, wondering if it would be more efficient to copy his notes to another book or to tape the pages back together. There were hundreds of pages, but there were also hundreds of notes. The thing had been marked up like a high school yearbook, note after note, ink in several colors filling white space from cover to cover. He'd had it for years, and he could even see changes in his own handwriting over time. The letters had gotten closer together, and at some point he had added a slash to his sevens and z's, like the Europeans. He didn't know why.

He had dated a Spanish professor from Barcelona at one point; he might have picked it up from her, but he couldn't remember. She was only at Samuels for a semester, and the relationship was less than half that long. The university no longer produced yearbooks, but in that moment, William wished they did. Was Isa Serra really as beautiful as he remembered? He would have to look her up on Facebook and compare his memory to the reality. He pulled it up, and there she was, gorgeous as ever. He clicked through a few of her pictures, finding a husband after only a few seconds.

He shook his head and searched for Kilo Jones. There were no entries. He tried Kevin Jones and got dozens. He narrowed the search to Osgood and got nothing. He tried Columbia and found several, but none with a tattoo of scales on his neck. He pulled up Patrick Riley and checked the list of friends. No luck.

The yearbook idea stirred in his mind, though, tilting and turning until it snapped into place. He could check the old Osgood High yearbooks and see if anything stood out. Maybe even talk to the football coach. He only had an hour before he had to be up for class, so he shut down the computer and went back to bed. He knew he wouldn't sleep, but he thought an hour of lying still with his eyes closed might do him some good.

CHAPTER 18

When the alarm went off, William wasn't sure lying down had been worth the effort. He wished he had a bigger mug for coffee as he walked to campus that Wednesday morning. He needed all the caffeine he could get. *What I really need is sleep*, he thought. The sleep deprivation made him a little nervous and gave him chills, like the early symptoms of the flu. Caffeine would keep him awake, keep him functional, but it would also make him a little jittery, a little distracted, like students who had been diagnosed with ADD. William wasn't sure he believed in ADD; maybe those kids just needed less soda and energy drinks, less TV and video games, and more sleep, more time in front of a book. He couldn't keep his thoughts going in a straight line. If he didn't take the time to rest, he would start making mistakes – more mistakes, bigger mistakes. There were already too many.

In his composition section, they worked on the process analysis project again. William wanted to rearrange the paragraphs. The order made sense in the outline the students had produced on Monday, but the paragraphs they had written worked better in a slightly different order, he thought. The students didn't seem convinced, but they went along with it. He was the professor, after all. He wondered if the idea was just a product of the sleep deprivation, if he would want it the other way when he looked at it again. The order settled, he took them through a sentence by sentence rewrite of the first paragraph, correcting for specificity, tone, and grammar. On the best of days, the students had little interest in this sort of work.

They had been raised on texting and saw any sentence that conveyed a basic message without causing accidental offense as a "good" sentence.

William wondered if Kilo Jones had left behind a cell phone, where it would be now, ten days after the shooting, and whether it might have anything useful on it. At twenty-seven, a former All State linebacker with the training in self-preservation that came with prison time, Kilo Jones might have been able to best Ian Baker in his weakened state. Maybe. He realized he was already thinking in terms of a murder, agreeing with Jimmy's theory without any evidence to back it up. He wasn't sure if that was the sleep deprivation or an instinct, but finding himself agreeing with Jimmy always made him nervous.

William divided the students into groups again and instructed them to revise the rest of the essay in the same way he had done the first paragraph. The various versions would be reviewed in class on Friday. In his experience, there would be little difference in them because there would be little difference from the original. Freshmen abhor revision, he had found, but the seeds he planted usually grew into something fruitful before graduation. He had seen it over and over again.

When he entered the classroom for the Major Authors section, all the students were already there. They fell silent on his entrance, the unison enough to make choral conductors jealous, William thought. They had been talking about him, he was sure.

"Well," he said, "you may as well just spit it out."

The students looked at each other, clearly trying to come to a tacit consensus. William set up his things at the front of the room, did the roll, and waited for someone to speak. He expected it to be Regina, who was the boldest of the group, but Nick would have been his second choice. Nick rarely seemed bothered by the formalities of student-teacher relationships. He spoke to professors in much the same way he spoke to other students.

In fact, it was John Kennedy who voiced the class's concern. "Well, Dr. Baker, we were just wondering if... well, if..."

"Just speak your mind, Mr. President. I don't have nukes in Cuba."

Kennedy laughed at this, which told William that he was nervous. He almost never laughed at JFK jokes. "I know we're supposed to start looking at 'The Cask of Amontillado' today, but we were wondering if we could continue our discussion of moral relativism and post-modernism."

"Did we ignore something that interested you the other day?"

"Yeah, we did," Regina said, laughing.

William knew something was off, that Kennedy was beating around a difficult bush.

"What the Commander in Chief is trying to say," Nick began.

"Is that we were wondering about your brother," John said.

"My brother is certainly a moral relativist," William said, "but as he isn't a character in a Poe story, I'm not sure how he's related to this course."

"That never stopped you before," Regina said.

"I only tell stories about my brother when they illustrate a point that's relevant to a course," William said. "And I'm starting to think even that was a mistake."

"Why?" Anna asked.

"Honestly, I'm not sure I've been fair to him. I'm also wondering if the fact that the stories were about my brother made you miss the points, remember the wrong thing – that my brother was a criminal – and not the lesson I was trying to teach you."

"You're probably right about that last part," Regina said. "That's all I ever remember from those stories."

"The stories aren't really the point," Kennedy said.

"And the point is?" William asked.

"Well, there was a robbery at that pawn shop by Shirley's."

"The one where Doug works," Nick added.

"Eagle Pawn," William said. "I know about that."

"There's a rumor going around that it was your brother who did it," Kennedy said. "Doug said he was in the shop right before it was broken into, like he was casing it, maybe." He looked around at the other students, like he wanted someone else to say whatever was next. He found no takers and hesitated, picking up his pen and tapping it against his lips.

William wasn't sure what would come next, but he felt it would be better to get it in the open sooner rather than later. He might have another mess to clean up. "I know all about that," he said. "I spoke to the police over the weekend, and Doug came by my office on Monday."

"That's just it," Kennedy said. "You talked to the police."

"And?"

"Well, my cousin's a cop, and, well, he's not supposed to tell me stuff like this, but he said you told the police that your brother was with you when the robbery happened. You're his alibi. I don't know. It just seems like maybe they wouldn't trust that. I'm not saying you lied. I don't think that, really." Kennedy had gone red in a flash, realizing he had just accused his professor of lying to the police. "Oh, God." He put his head in his hands.

"Relax, Mr. President," William said. "It's harder than that to offend me. Finish your thought."

"I just, well, I'm sure you're telling the truth, but I just wondered why the police would just take your word for it. Wouldn't they expect family to lie? Wouldn't they – because they don't know you – wouldn't they assume you're just lying to protect your family?"

William wondered the same thing. "It's been public knowledge there's bad blood between us," he said, thinking out loud. "I guess they assume I wouldn't want him around, that I'd be happy to see him go back to prison."

"Would you?" Charlotte asked.

"No. I really don't want that. I've always hoped he'd get it together and make something of himself."

"It's a little late for that now, isn't it?" Regina asked.

"It's never too late to set things right," William said, "one way or another. Not until you're dead."

"Can we talk about the story now?" Anna asked.

"Yes," William said.

"Just so you know," Kennedy said, "I was just wondering. My cousin doesn't think you lied. He said that break-in was too complicated for Jimmy Baker. No way he could have pulled it off."

"Well," William said, smiling, "that's probably true. And, as Anna pointed out, we need to talk about the story now." He launched into his lecture for the day, thankful for the notes he had prepared before the semester even began. He felt the generation gap as strongly as ever when discussing "The Cask of Amontillado" with students. When he was a boy, teachers discouraged fighting, especially at school, but they always seemed to understand it. In Billy's day, there were things a boy could say that warranted a punch in the face, even in the eyes of adults. There might be punishment for it, depending on where it happened and when, but there was rarely much judgment.

Most Samuels University students had grown up in a very different environment. The ones who came from the bad neighborhoods in Greenville, Spartanburg, and Columbia understood revenge in terms of drive-by shootings – usually resulting in injury or death for innocent bystanders. There was no precision in it, no sense of intimacy, no looking the other person in the eye. It was a box to be checked. For the students who came from middle and upper class areas, vengeance was something you read about in books and comics or saw on TV and in movies. They were taught that violence doesn't solve anything, that people should always listen, look for compromise, and talk things out. They were taught to never, ever resort to physical confrontation. Kids who crossed that line were sent to in-school suspension, expelled, or arrested. They were in need of immediate reform, lest they become perpetrators of the next Columbine, the next Newtown. The idea that insult or even a thousand injuries could justify killing someone was part of a fairy-tale world for them.

William often wondered if they were really reading the same story he was.

He lost his train of thought several times during the session, fading to blankness from exhaustion or getting distracted by thoughts of Kilo Jones. Someone knew something. William just had to find out whom.

He had only one appointment that afternoon, so after class he emailed the student to reschedule and put a note on his office door saying he wasn't feeling well and wouldn't be available for office hours that day. He had done this only a few times in his entire teaching career, while some colleagues did it with astonishing regularity. He was pretty sure he could get away with it. After an email to the department's administrative assistant about the note, he packed his things and went home. The consistent professionalism that gave him license to leave early meant that someone would think him genuinely ill. He knew his friends would call or email to check on him, so he turned off his phone before lying down for a much-needed nap. He was only able to sleep about three hours. Thoughts about Kilo Jones infiltrated his dreams and kept him from really resting.

In Billy's day, Osgood High School had kept decades of yearbooks in the reference section of the library, a wall of gold-embossed volumes next to encyclopedias and unabridged dictionaries. The bedside clock read one twenty-seven, so the high school would still be open. He hadn't set foot in the building since he graduated, but he was pretty sure an alumnus would be allowed to go through those books without having to answer a lot of questions. The high school was outside his usual walking radius, out on the east side of town. Until the mid-eighties, Osgood High took up a full block of the downtown grid, just two streets south of the Samuels campus, but a new, bigger version was built on cheap land beyond the town's core. Billy's class was only the second to spend all four years in that facility. The university bought the old structure, razed it, and put a new dormitory on the site. The Cornell building where Kelvin taught went up between them, unifying the Samuels campus. William got in the Corolla, pausing to eject the last disc of HP6, which had started over. He turned on a local station that advertised "hits from the 80s, 90s, and today," hoping to hear something from his high school days, but he got Taylor Swift instead. He turned off the radio and drove across town.

During school hours, the Osgood High parking lot kept its gates closed and guarded. There had never been a shooting on campus, but the country's rash of school violence over the previous decade had the administration taking no chances. William had to provide ID. He handed over his driver's license and his Samuels faculty badge.

"And the reason for your visit?" the security guard asked.

"I'm doing research for a book, and I think the library has some stuff that will help. At least, they used to, when I was a student here. I'm sure the librarian can help me."

"She'll help," the guard said. He smiled, picked up a phone, and dialed an extension. "I've got a William Baker out here. A Samuels professor. He wants to look at some stuff in the library." He paused, listening to a response William couldn't quite hear. "Dr. Baker? The English professor?"

William nodded.

"Yeah," the guard said. He listened again, and then said, "I'll send him in." He wrote the date and time on a piece of green card stock and handed it to William. "Put that on your dash and park in a visitor space." He pointed to the marked spots left of the main entrance, then he handed William a clip-on visitor ID. "Wear that at all times. The library's – "

"Through the main entrance, take the first right, double doors on the left. I remember."

The guard nodded and waved William through.

He parked and went inside, pausing to take in all that had changed in the more than twenty years since he had been there. The lobby floor had been some sort of fake marble laminate, but now it was a tile checkerboard of green and gold – the school colors. The walls had been green and gold, but now they were an institutional gray. A banner, clearly painted by students, read "Go Eagles, Beat Dorman." William shook his head at the comma splice. The metal detectors were also new. He had to drop his keys, pocketknife, and phone into a basket for a second guard, who checked his visitor badge with a scanner. He set off the detector and had to dump his change and belt in as well. The guard took the knife and offered the basket to him.

"You'll get this back when you leave," she said.

"It was a gift from my dad. Keep it safe."

"I will," she said with no trace of irony. She slipped it into her pants pocket and patted it.

William nodded and went to the library. It had changed, too. The carpet was new, redone in a checkerboard like the lobby but with industrial fiber in three-square foot blocks – easily replaced after a spill or vomiting incident. The walls were equally institutional, and the old card catalog had been replaced with a bank of computers, all narrow towers and seventeen-inch, flat-screen monitors. Some of the stacks had given way to computers as well, but the outer walls were still lined with shelves and study carrels.

He wondered if the one with "CP ♥ BB" carved into its left rear corner had survived. He hadn't thought of Cassie Patterson in many, many years, and the image of her that flashed in his mind – strawberry blond curls spilling around her freckled, cherubic face as they tried to pass a LifeSaver from a toothpick in her mouth to the toothpick in Billy's – made him smile from ear to ear. The sensation was unfamiliar. He had no idea what had happened to her. They had first met in sophomore English, working on a group project during a unit on *Julius Caesar*, but nothing had happened between them then. The eventual relationship was brief – just the few weeks from that Senior Day game until she left for a summer camp counselor job in North Carolina – but it was as lovely as she had been, without demands or disappointments.

"The evil that men do lives after them," he whispered.

"The good is oft interred with their bones," said the librarian. "Quoting Shakespeare under your breath? And you call yourself a Poe scholar?"

"I call myself William these days."

"That suits you. I never thought you were much of a Billy."

William didn't recognize the woman. He felt his head tilt in confusion and forced it upright again.

"It's okay," she said. "We didn't really know each other. I was a senior when you were a freshman."

"But you remember me?"

"I was at that game," she said. "Home from SC for the weekend with nothing better to do."

William nodded. "That game" needed no explanation. Billy Baker had been the second string tight end for Osgood High his junior year. During the third quarter of their eighth game, an opposing linebacker hit the Osgood quarterback in the head – a late hit with a high shoulder meant to knock Matt Cunningham out of a tight game. Matt and Billy weren't close, but the sight of him laid out and twitching in a concussion-induced seizure sent Billy over the edge. Twenty-five years after the fact, he still had no memory of his last blackout, but he had heard dozens of accounts from other players and people in the stands. He had come off the bench, tackled the linebacker, ripped off the guy's helmet, and beaten him unconscious with it before he was pulled off. His own teammates had gotten to him first, saving him from a beating at the hands of the other team and probably saving the linebacker's life. Some said Billy should have been arrested, but the coaches on both teams were afraid of the precedent. Billy was banned from all sports. He vowed he would never lose control like that again, and in all the years since, he had not. He didn't like talking about it.

"Did they get a deal on the mental-ward gray?" he asked, pointing at the walls. "I like the floors, but the walls in this place are like lithium for the eyes."

The librarian smiled. "Exactly," she said. "It's supposed to be calming. Some consultant said it would prevent school violence. They say it's working. Incidents are down since the remodel." Something in her expression and tone made William think she was skeptical.

He pointed at a corner of the ceiling. "Did they put in the cameras and metal detectors at the same time?" he asked.

She smiled and nodded. She was pretty, black hair streaked with gray, slim but not skinny, with eyes the same color as the water in ads for Caribbean cruises, William thought.

"I'm William Baker," he said, extending his hand, "but you knew that."

She shook his hand, firm and professional but lingering a little longer than strictly necessary. "I'm Mary Harmon," she said. "What can we do for you? Max said you were doing research."

"Yes. Just toying with an idea about student athletes."

"I can't imagine what we'd have that you couldn't get through the Samuels library." She seemed confused, but not skeptical.

"When I was a student here, there was a collection of yearbooks going back to the twenties, I think. I wanted to look at a few of them, if I could."

She smiled. "I think we can help you with that." She turned and walked around the main counter, gesturing for William to follow.

A lanky kid in a Men Without Hats T-shirt stopped her. "Mrs. Harmon, have you seen today's paper? It's not in the rack."

She shook her head. "Check the study carrels, Alex."

"Anachronistic," William said as Alex walked away.

"They do that now. Old bands. Old movies. They say they're being ironic." She shook her head again and led William to a side room that he remembered as an AV closet with filmstrip projectors, boxes of old slides, and VCRs. The outdated equipment had been replaced with rows of shelves that housed old periodicals in plastic bins with names and years written on the side. On the back wall, she showed him the current collection of yearbooks. "Your memory is good. They go all the way back to 1922," she said. "Some of the old ones are pretty fragile now, so be gentle. You can be gentle, can't you, Dr. Baker?"

William wasn't sure if she was flirting or teasing him about his violent past. "I think so," he said.

"So what's this book you're working on? Is it a sociological thing or a novel or what?"

"I'm not sure yet. I just wonder if there's a connection between high school sports and who we become as adults. I'm always seeing these news reports on the games and how it builds character and teamwork and prepares you for life. I thought I might look at some guys who played and see how they turned out."

"Interesting," she said, leaning a bit too close.

Definitely flirting, William thought. He looked down to check for a wedding band, squatting to the lower shelves as cover. She was wearing a ring. He wondered who Mr. Harmon was and what he would make of his wife's interest in a man she only remembered for giving a savage beating. William pulled a yearbook from the shelf at random. 1976. Lots of long hair and wide lapels.

"Mrs. Harmon? The paper isn't in the carrels. I really need to see that paper. There's a review of our play."

"Theatre geeks," she whispered. "I'll be right back."

"Take your time," William said.

When she left the room, he went straight to Kilo Jones' senior year. The index listed Kevin Jones as appearing on eight pages. The first was a group shot of the football team. William used his phone to take a picture of the roster beside the photo. On the next page, an individual shot honored Jones as the Defensive Player of the Year. He didn't have the tattoo yet, but he was the same guy pictured in the newspaper article. The third shot was Jones' senior picture, his tux too tight in the shoulders and his bow tie crooked, wedged between a Kenneth Jones and a Lori Jones. The other pictures were candid shots in the back of the book. Jones and another guy arm wrestling in the cafeteria. Jones and a girl in a cheerleader uniform holding a banner at a pep rally. Jones and two other guys with arms around each other's shoulders in front of a classroom white board. Jones and the same two guys with two others, all in uniform, jumping up and down on the sideline during a game. Jones and three other guys leaning on a restored 70s era Camaro in the Osgood High auto shop. William snapped pics of each of the captions and put the volume back. He set an alarm on his phone and programmed it to go off five minutes later.

He pulled down his own senior yearbook and flipped over to Cassie Patterson's picture. *Just lovely*, he thought, smiling. He put it away and pulled down the volume for his junior year. He was in the full team shot, taken before he had been kicked off the squad. The picture was so small he couldn't really see his own eyes. He wanted to look into them and see who he had been. So much had changed since then, and William could hardly imagine the kid in the shoulder pads was actually the same person he saw in the mirror each morning. They had precious little in common. He was still staring at the picture when Mrs. Harmon returned.

"Someone has made off with this morning's *Herald*," she said. "I don't know what a high school student wants with a newspaper in this millennium, but there it is."

William nodded, not sure if any further response was warranted. She came over and stood beside him, leaning close to see the yearbook in his hands. Her chin brushed his shoulder, and he could smell her perfume – something with strawberries, he thought.

"You don't have that one?" she asked.

"Somewhere," he said. "In a box, I guess. I haven't looked at it since the summer before college."

"Where'd you go?"

"Johns Hopkins."

"Grad school?"

"Vanderbilt."

"Nice." She seemed impressed.

"I liked it."

"You could've gotten a position anywhere, but you ended up at Samuels, right back here in Osgood." This was clearly meant to be a question.

"It was the right thing at the right time." William wasn't going to talk about his mother's illness with a stranger and certainly not with Mary Harmon. He could hear his father's voice in his head. *A married woman who'll screw you will end up screwing you over.*

Mrs. Harmon nodded. "You're sort of famous around here, you know."

William didn't know what to make of that. "How so?"

"You're the tough teacher no one wants to take."

"So I've heard. I didn't realize the dread of me had fallen on the high school, too."

"The Samuels freshmen tell the seniors not to take you."

William nodded.

"I mean, the normal students," she said. "Our best students, like anachronistic Alex out there, they want to take your class, but..."

"But they don't go to Samuels."

"Yeah. I've always been curious, though." She looked at the floor, then into his eyes. *She has great eyes*, William thought. He waited for whatever was next. "I guess I just thought, after that game, I mean... I just thought you'd end up like Jimmy. I never met him, but I heard the stories. So what happened? How'd you end up a hard-ass professor instead of a hardened criminal?"

The alarm on William's phone went off. He pulled it out, gave a quick glance, and said, "I need to take this." He walked out of the room, out of the library, and into the hall. He held the phone to his ear and

215

counted to twenty before stepping back into the library, the phone cradled to his chest.

"I'm sorry," he said, "but I have to go. Student issues." He waved the phone. "It was nice to meet you, and thanks for your help."

"Come back," she said. "Anytime."

William got his knife from the guard at the main entrance and left, stopping briefly at the gate to return the green card and his visitor badge. Max the guard smiled at him, repressing a laugh.

"What?" William asked.

"You had to get away, huh?" The guard let out the laugh. "She's pretty frisky."

"Indeed. I guess we'll be reading about it in the papers soon enough."

"Let's hope it doesn't come to that."

William nodded and drove away.

CHAPTER 19

At home, William checked his email and responded to the messages from Danny, Janet, and Kelvin, each asking if he was okay, if he needed anything. He cut and pasted the same reply for each: "I'm just worn out. Nothing some sleep and hot tea won't fix." The student had been happy to reschedule the grading. Her paper could use more work, she wrote. Those duties out of the way, he settled in to research the people pictured with Kilo Jones. After nine years, it was a bit of a long shot that any of them would still be close friends, longer still that William would be able to pick out the one who could tell him how Jones ended up with Ian Baker's .45. It was the best idea William had at the time, though, so he did the work.

Jones arm wrestling opponent was Joe Kinard, who had grown up to be an accountant in Charlotte, according to Facebook and LinkedIn – not a likely candidate for Jones' partner in crime. William dismissed the cheerleader for the time being. The pep rally photo didn't make them look like friends. They were turned away from each other, facing the crowd, a ten-foot banner between them. He knew Janet would call him sexist, but he couldn't see the girl being part of Jones' criminal activities.

Cory Ledford and Troy Hessel, the guys in two of the pictures, seemed more promising at first glance. They were teammates and, based on the classroom photo, they were friends off the field. Ledford had no LinkedIn, but his Facebook profile put him in Augusta, working for a nightclub as a bouncer. He had been a big kid, and he was an even bigger man. The photos on his profile showed him in a gym and at the beach, shirtless, bulging muscles lined with rivers of fat veins. William was pretty sure there were steroids involved. Lots and lots of steroids. The patrons at Club Diamond would be well behaved. None of the photos showed Kilo Jones or any guns, and none of the posts mentioned Osgood or Columbia. If Ledford and Jones were still connected, it would take more effort than online research to find out. William decided to send Jimmy to follow the guy if nothing else came up.

He moved on to Troy Hessel. In his profile picture, the guy couldn't have looked more like a gangbanger without being shown in the commission of a crime. Hessel wore a workman's shirt with "Killer" stitched over the right front pocket. The shirt was unbuttoned, and he had tugged the left side under his arm to expose his chest. Chains hung from both sides of his sagging jeans, tight-rolled to expose his lace-less Adidas sneakers. His neck was tattooed with a chain, every other link cracked, as if he were well on his way to breaking free of it. The tail of a snake poked through one of those links. The rest of it was entwined through the eyes and mouth of a skull that covered the left half of Hessel's chest. William couldn't be sure if the snake's tail were meant to be connected to the chain image or if there simply hadn't been enough room to keep the tattoos from overlapping. He leaned toward the latter. This guy was either a criminal or he was the biggest poser east of the Mississippi, William thought. He went through all the pictures and posts, all of which supported the theory that Hessel was involved in illegal activity, but nothing showed any connection to Kilo Jones. Hessel listed Osgood as his current city, so William made a note of the garage in the background of some of the pics – Nellie's – and moved on. He could dig deeper if nothing else panned out.

The two other guys in the sideline photo had moved away, Jake Olsen to Denver, where he worked as a cell phone salesman, and Charlie Whaley to Nashville, where he was a recording engineer. The three guys in the Camaro pic were busts as well: Ted Graves was a foreman at the Hyundai plant in Alabama; Tyronne Stitt sold BMWs in Charleston; and Derek Smith worked in IT at Coca-Cola headquarters in Atlanta. William wondered if that job came with a soda allowance. He considered working his way through the full team roster, but he decided the garage where Hessel worked was probably more promising. There would be others like him at that place. Maybe one of them had a connection to Jones.

William googled the name, but nothing came up. He checked the Osgood phone book, but there was no listing in the yellow or white pages. He pulled Hessel's Facebook page up again to be sure he hadn't misread the name. This time, he found what he was looking for. On the left side of the screen, beneath Hessel's basic information – city, profession, relationship status, etc. – there was a little block of nine photos of his friends, like the opening credits for the *Brady Bunch*. Evidently, it was populated randomly from people on a longer list. William hadn't noticed anyone of interest there on his first visit to the page, but the group had changed for the second viewing. The center pic in the right hand column, right where Peter Brady belonged, was a shot of Kilo Jones. For a moment, William thought Jones had a Facebook profile he had missed, but the name was Robbie Martin. William clicked to the Martin profile page, where he learned the pic was a sort of memorial. Martin's posts claimed he was Kilo's best friend, homey, dog, and a list of other slang terms William didn't recognize but interpreted as synonyms. There were pics of Martin looking almost as thugged-out as Hessel, alone and with others, including several with Kilo Jones. Many of them were taken in Nellie's garage.

"If there are answers, we'll find them there," William whispered.

Nothing on Hessel's or Martin's page gave an address for Nellie's, so William spent several minutes pouring over the pictures, hoping to get some idea of the location from the things in the background. When that failed, he started going through the profiles of their mutual friends. He had to use his laptop and his tablet to check for names on both lists of friends, but he found several, one of whom was a Frank Nelson. Nelson's page had more pics of the garage, inside and out. From the posts and comments, William gathered that "Nellie" had been Frank's father, who left the garage to Frank. There was no address on the profile, but Frank Nelson's address and phone number were in the white pages.

William shut down the electronics and went to take a look. According to the phone book and Google maps, Frank Nelson lived south of Osgood on Highway 67, a narrow old state route through the tiny towns between Osgood and the Georgia line. Deep in the forest along the Savannah River, it joined a US route that went over the water and through some of the tiny Georgia towns between Athens and Augusta. Billy had been down that way several times in his youth, but the bypasses and four-lane highways that had been built since then rendered Highway 67 useless to anyone who didn't live out there. He drove the Corolla south through town, past the turn to Patrick Riley's house, past the turn for Horne Street Methodist Church, past the last of the mill village houses so ill-kept they looked like decayed inner-city housing projects, and finally veered right down 67.

The Nelson housesat three-quarters of a mile down the road on the left hand side, in the last row of tight houses before Osgood petered out completely. William slowed to a crawl and took a long look. He knew very little about building codes, but he felt sure the Nelson house wouldn't pass an inspection. The wide front porch sagged more than six inches between each support, its screen had fallen from the rotting wood of the front roof support, and holes the size of basketballs dotted that roof. The main structure appeared to have been a two- or three-room shotgun house, but several slapdash additions had metastasized around that, each sinking and sagging in all directions. On the south side of the house, three rows of broken down cars and trucks lined a field for thirty yards or so, some twenty or twenty-five rusting hulks, by William's estimate. A semi-circle drive bounded the small junkyard, and Nelson's garage sat behind that.

William drove on, wondering if someone inside had noticed him already. He took 67 another ten miles southwest, thinking about what he had seen and what he might have missed. The sun had dipped below the horizon, but the last glow of day showed him enough that he didn't yet need headlights. He turned around at an old service station, its elderly red pumps still standing. The dials showed gas had been fifty-nine cents a gallon on its last day in business. He couldn't even hazard a guess at when that might have been.

Ten minutes later, approaching Nellie's, he slowed again, this time noticing the small barn on the south edge of the junkyard. He wasn't sure if it belonged to the Nelson property or to the next-door neighbor. It was in better condition than the Nelson

house, but not by much. He couldn't see a door, so
that must face away from the road, which wasn't any
help establishing whether it was Nelson's or went with
the well-kept double-wide trailer on its other side. The
garage had a high A-frame roof, three wide bays, and
what appeared to be an office door on the south end.
That building had been well-maintained. William
estimated the roof was no more than five years old,
and the paint looked even more recent. Only the
center bay stood open, and a 40s model Ford truck
had been backed in. William couldn't see much from
the road, but the primer gray roof made him think the
truck was being restored. Nelson's Facebook pictures
had shown work of that type, cars and trucks being
transformed from rusty relics into shiny classics by
the Nellie's crew.

William drove on, wondering what sat behind the
garage, beyond the trees he could actually see. At the
main highway, he turned right. US 25 would take him
all the way to Augusta, the way Jimmy had gone just
fifteen hours or so earlier. Watching the houses on his
right and checking the odometer, William drove until
he was sure he had found the other side of the patch
of woods behind the Nelson place. Only a handful of
homes sat on that side of the road, each larger than
the next, each on several acres of land. There would be
an entry point, William was sure, some path he could
forge across one of those plots and through the woods
to the garage.

He continued south for another mile, until he
came to a service station, this one modern and
functional, where he turned around. This time, he
watched the opposite side of the highway, looking for
a place to park for a little while. That side was
populated by a group of businesses: a propane
distributer, an antiques warehouse, and a storage-

building dealer. He pulled in at the antiques place, taking a spot at the end of their parking lot. He took out his phone and pulled up the navigation app. With the satellite view, he was able to see exactly where Nellie's sat – just through the woods, behind a large brick home across from the storage building dealer. If he parked behind one of the larger storage buildings, he would be able to keep the Corolla out of sight of passing drivers, but there would be a long exposed stretch from there, over the highway and across the yard, before he could get to the cover of the woods. The satellite image was taken when the trees were full, so he couldn't see if there would be any fences to scale along the way. He decided to go home and rest up for another round of after-midnight reconnaissance.

At his house, he double-checked his notes on the story he would be discussing in his American literature sections Thursday morning, Raymond Carver's "Are These Actual Miles?" Everything was in order, so he packed his work satchel and left it by the front door before lying down for a nap. He set an alarm for midnight, just in case he actually fell asleep, and kicked off his shoes. He lay on top of the covers, still fully dressed, eyes closed, with his hands folded over his stomach.

The satellite view had given him the layout of the buildings on the Nelson property and its rear neighbor, but William wanted the floorplan of the garage, the schedule of the people who worked there, and some evidence that would prove to his satisfaction whether Hessel and Martin were actual criminals or just inked-up poser mechanics. If they were the former, he would have no problem doing whatever it took to find out how much they knew about Kilo Jones and Ian Baker's .45. If they were the latter, a softer touch would be required. He couldn't be sure about Nelson, whether he was a proper business owner or a criminal using the business he inherited as a front for whatever he and the others got up to.

"Too many variables," William whispered.

He had no idea what traffic would be like on that part of Highway 25 at that hour. Light, surely, but it wouldn't be empty. He might be seen crossing the road from the cover of the storage buildings. The people who live in the house could be awake. He saw no animals, but there could easily be a dog or other pets he hadn't seen. He estimated 150 yards would have to be crossed before he would have the cover of the woods. There was nothing for it. He would just have to make the dash and hope for the best. Without any look at the back of the garage, he had no way of knowing if there were windows or even a door back there. He would have to use the trees to make sure he wouldn't be seen until he knew there were no views from that side. He tried to imagine routes and angles, what the terrain would be like, but he simply didn't have enough information.

"Too many variables," he said again.

He tried to clear his mind, to wipe it blank and allow himself to really rest, body and brain, until it was late enough to go out there. His phone woke him three hours later. William felt like he hadn't slept at all, like no time had passed. For a moment, he thought the noise was the alarm he had set, but when he tried to turn it off, he saw Jimmy's number on the screen. He still had three hours to wait.

Jimmy asked if he had learned anything, and William gave him a quick summary.

"I'll go with you," Jimmy said.

"No, I'm just going to have a look. I want to check it out and make a plan. We'll go tomorrow or the next day, depending on what I find out."

"A plan, huh?" Jimmy asked. "We've been at this for nigh on two weeks, and ain't one thing yet gone according to your plan."

"Half of that's because of you."

"A third. I'll accept the blame for one third. The rest is just life. There ain't much you can predict."

"Too many variables."

"That's as good a way of saying it as any."

William thought for a moment. He had tried to plan everything before he broke into Eagle Pawn, and Jimmy ruined the plan. Not everything had gone right before that, though. He should have had a flashlight, and only the improvisation with the TV had kept him on track. He had made a mistake in his choice of gloves, and turning on the gun case light could have brought someone other than Jimmy to check on it. Things with Riley had worked out, but it hadn't gone anything like his original plan. All the effort he had put into finding a good spot for the interrogation had been wasted. Even after his scouting visit to Riley's house, he hadn't known about the grandmother's shotgun, and he would never have guessed an elderly woman who used a scooter could have made it from the living room to that basement as quickly as she had. He wanted to be careful, to develop a good plan, but Jimmy was right. In real life, even a good plan can go awry.

"All right. Come on up."

They agreed to meet at the storage-building dealer at twelve-thirty, and William hung up. He dug out the clothes he had changed into after the business with Patrick Riley, some of them stained by the streaks of Riley's blood William had found on his neck, waist, wrist, and ankles. He put them in the washing machine and set out for Shirley's, getting back forty-five minutes later and starting the wash with a couple of scoops from a new tub of oxygen bleach. He had left the first tub in the Impala, and he was thankful he hadn't seen the same clerk. His other purchase, a thick porterhouse steak, he cut into four strips and dumped into the plastic Shirley's bag, doubling that with the bag the bleach had been in. The task reminded him he hadn't eaten anything all day, so he warmed a can of soup and drank a Coke with that. The shoes he had been wearing the night before had been splattered with Riley's blood, too, so he set about cleaning them while the washer finished its cycle. He tried to dry them with the clothes, but the noise from the tumbling shoes made him stop the machine. He would just have to manage with damp shoes for a few hours.

When the clothes were dry, he put them on and tucked his mask and gloves into his pockets. He put his father's tools and the porterhouse on the passenger's seat of the Corolla and drove out to the old mill. He rearranged the guns and took another batch of jewelry in an Eagle Pawn bag, making sure the mound was still believable. That accomplished, he went to meet Jimmy.

CHAPTER 20

At the antiques place, William pulled off the road and cut his headlights, waiting until the road cleared of traffic to pull around and hide the Corolla behind one of the larger storage buildings, angling the car to see the northbound lanes of the highway. Ten minutes later, he heard the rumble of the Charger in the distance and watched Jimmy drop his lights a quarter mile out, edging off the road and coasting into the antiques lot. Jimmy paused there, just as William had, then rolled the Charger behind another large storage building.

William got out and walked over. Jimmy met him halfway, holding out an object, something black that William couldn't make out in the dark. He took it, and the weight and shape gave him the idea.

"Where did you get this?"

"Crooked screw dug them out of storage," Jimmy said. "Let some of his boys use them – guys with money who couldn't take care of themselves. I collected a few over that last stretch and hid them in my old TV."

William tested the action of the blackjack in the air. "Nice."

"Be gentle with that thing," Jimmy said, "unless you want to leave a vegetable or a body. A good wrist snap is all it takes."

"Didn't think to bring these last night?"

"Forgot I had them. Don't use that TV anymore. Got a nice flat screen. Bigger than yours."

William nodded. He stepped around the corner of the storage building to point. "The garage is through those woods. I don't know if there'll be a fence or dogs or anything. That's what I was coming to find out."

"We'll find out together." Jimmy took a .38 revolver from his waistband and handed it to William. Evidently, it had been left in the Impala, but Jimmy didn't comment.

William nodded. He jogged back to the Corolla and put the gun under the seat. This was a scouting mission. A gun was overkill. He collected the steak, the tools, and the Eagle bag. "Porterhouse." He shook the bag as he returned. "Just in case."

"Good thinking, Billy."

"William."

"Good thinking, William."

They watched the highway for a moment, waiting for it to clear. At that hour, the traffic was very light, but it seemed there was at least one car in sight at any given time, headlights blazing. William took the moment to look at the houses, none of which had lights on in the front. The house they would need to pass had a security light over its driveway, like a dimmer version of a streetlight, its power wire snaking from the bell of the lamp up to the eaves of the house.

"Go around on the left and hope for the best," Jimmy said, evidently having the same thought process.

William nodded, pulled the mask from his pocket, and put the blackjack in its place. He slipped on his gloves and pulled the mask over his head. The bleach had left parts of it blue and parts of it a pale purple.

"You washed that?" Jimmy asked, pulling on his own mask and gloves.

"Yeah."

Jimmy shook his head. "Just when I was impressed."

A southbound car's taillights were dimming in the distance, and a northbound car flashed its brights.

"Now, while they're focused on each other."

William ran, not waiting for Jimmy, but he heard his brother's footsteps behind him on the pavement. The jewelry jangled in the Eagle Pawn bag, and he wondered if it were as loud as it seemed. He leapt over the ditch and looked up at the side of the house as he crossed the side yard. No lights. He rounded the corner of the house and checked for lights on the back. Nothing. He crouched behind the edge of the house and waited for Jimmy to catch up, opening the bag of meat in case a dog came toward him in the dark.

Jimmy rounded the house two seconds after William and stopped, panting and holding his sides, shaking his head. "Stupid," he said. "Running... gets... attention. Walking... is... boring."

"Seemed like the thing to do at the time."

While Jimmy caught his breath, William looked around the back yard. An old-fashioned clothesline hung between two poles, fifty feet apart. He was glad he hadn't tried to run straight into the woods. He pointed to them.

"Walking's safer, too," Jimmy said.

"Point taken."

The brothers started into the woods, stepping carefully in the dark, not willing to use even their cell phones for light. The woods weren't deep or especially thick, and William soon saw a bit of light coming through the trees from the other side. The crunch of leaves and branches beneath their feet seemed like fireworks to William's ears, each snap and crack exploding in the still night air. Halfway through the woods, they came to a barbed wire fence, marking the property line, William assumed. Just two strands strung on metal posts. The brothers pushed down the top wire and stepped over. From there, William could see the light that came through was cast by a security light just like the one in the rear neighbor's yard. He had misjudged the path and come through perpendicular to the barn on the south edge of the Nelson property, at an angle to the garage, giving him a view of the junkyard. The light sat on a pole in the center of the grid of rusting vehicles, its own power cable snaking toward the garage. On that end, the side where the office door should lead, was a small window. No light shown through. The barn's two great doors were pulled closed, as was a smaller door cut into the left great door. The rear wall of the garage had no door, but there was a large window high up, near the peak of the angled roof. It was also dark.

William stopped and pointed. "There's something up there."

"Like an apartment, you think?"

"Maybe."

The brothers walked on, veering toward the corner of the garage, each looking up at the back window every few steps. At the corner, William signaled Jimmy to wait, and he slipped over to the other end to have a look at the main house. He saw a dim light in one window, maybe a bathroom night light. He couldn't be sure at that distance. The north side of the garage had no windows or doors. He went up to the front corner to check and found all three bays closed. He walked back around the building, keeping an eye on the house until he rounded the corner, being careful to stay against the back wall and out of sight of anyone who might be looking out of the high window. He met Jimmy at the other corner, and the brothers went to the front corner of the garage's south side.

Jimmy kept watch while William took out the tool kit. The office door was triple-locked: the knob, a deadbolt, and a pad lock. None of these was a problem, but the combination took much longer than William would have liked, standing still in the glow of the security light. Thirty long seconds of work opened the door, and he and Jimmy went inside. The office was about eight feet square, with a desk in the corner, facing the garage bays. A picture window and a door took up the wall between the office and the bays. A chair sat behind the desk, and two chairs faced it. William expected to see a filing cabinet, but there was no other furniture in the small office. He dropped his bags on the desk and sat behind it. He tried the drawers, while Jimmy opened the door to the garage and went in.

The desk drawers were stiff and squeaky but unlocked, and it only took William a few seconds to find what he was looking for: a payroll register. He found Hessel and Martin in the records, but both listed the address as the Nelson house. Either they were Frank's roommates or the address was bogus. William suspected the latter. After what happened with Patrick Riley's grandmother the night before, he wasn't excited about breaking into a house without knowing exactly who lived there and what weapons they might have. The pellet in Jimmy's leg seemed like all the cautionary tale a sane person would need. William put the records away and closed the drawer.

He heard footsteps and called to Jimmy in a whisper. "Find anything?"

There was no response, so he went over to the door and peered into the bays. The glow from the security light came through small windows in the bay doors, casting enough light for him to see three vehicles, the old truck and two muscle cars – a

Chevelle and a Challenger – but no Jimmy. William stepped through the door and turned to his right. Along the back wall, he saw stairs leading to an attic trap door.

He didn't see the punch that knocked him down.

He felt the blow above his right eye and felt the strike of his back on the concrete floor. Ian's training kept William's head from snapping against the floor next, kept his head on straight. In the next fraction of a second, he registered Troy Hessel coming at him and scrambled back, gauging the height of Hessel's knee and planning the kick that would give him time to stand and punch. Ian had shown him all sorts of techniques for fighting on the ground, but Billy was always more comfortable using his fists. Hessel crumbled, though, his knees going out and his body folding down on itself like an imploded building. Jimmy had hit him with the blackjack.

"Steak'll be good on that eye, I bet."

"A little warning would have been nice."

"If you'd stayed in the office two more seconds, it wouldn't have mattered."

"Fair enough."

"Is this the one we're looking for?"

"No. Where did he come from? Up there?" William pointed to the stairs.

Jimmy nodded. "I guess he heard you opening those drawers. You'd think a mechanic would know how to use grease."

"I'm not sure they're really mechanics."

"Oh, they know their stuff," Jimmy said. "They're rebuilding the engine on that Challenger, and somebody's doing some serious body work on that pickup. For all I know, I just concussed a righteous man. You sure this is the place?"

"The guy we're looking for works here. I found his payroll records. The book says he lives in the main house. This guy, too."

"So you're saying there could be more of them up there?" He gestured at the attic with the blackjack.

William nodded. "Did you see any rope or anything?"

"Duct tape on that tool rack," Jimmy said. He tucked the blackjack away and drew Ian Baker's .45. "He'll be out for a little while, though."

Jimmy waved at William to follow, and they went up the stairs to the attic room, Jimmy leading with the gun. William pulled the second blackjack from his pocket. A few stairs from the open trap door, Jimmy stopped and raised the .45, putting the barrel through the hole and waving it around, trying to get a reaction, it seemed. When nothing happened, he went on up, keeping the gun raised and his back to the outer wall. He hadn't cleared the last step when he began shaking his head.

"Nobody here."

William followed Jimmy through the hole and took a look for himself. The room was small, clearly an addition, not original to the structure. The south wall ended in the middle of the large windowpane, probably causing the shadows William saw from below. There was just enough space for a cot, a few stacks of clothes, and an empty, military-style duffle bag with Hessel's name printed on it. William checked under the cot and sifted through the clothes, but he saw nothing of interest, nothing that would connect Hessel to Kilo Jones or anyone else. He went back down the stairs, Jimmy right behind him.

William collected the duct tape from the tool rack and went back to Troy Hessel, who was still unconscious. The end of the roll had been folded over to make it easier to start. "I should've thought of that," William whispered as he rolled Hessel onto his stomach and pulled his hands behind his back. He wrapped the wrists and ankles with the tape and cut it off with his pocketknife, setting the roll on the hood of the Challenger.

Jimmy pulled a chair from the office and helped William set Hessel in that. He was much heavier than Riley had been, a grown man with some meat on his bones. William knew that punch would leave a mark. Jimmy picked up the duct tape and added a strip to Hessel's mouth, tearing the end easily even with his gloved fingers.

"Where did you get those gloves?"

"Crooks R Us," Jimmy said, winking.

Shaking and patting Hessel's face brought groans, but he didn't wake.

"Is there water anywhere?"

"Sink over there," Jimmy said, already walking toward the opposite corner of the garage. He came back with a wet rag a moment later. "No cups," he said. He dropped the rag over Hessel's face, which brought more groans but didn't bring the man to consciousness.

William pulled the rag from Hessel's head and wrung it out, letting the water dribble over the man's face. He began to rouse, blinking his eyes and shaking his head sideways, like a swimmer with water in his ears. Jimmy gave him a few backhanded pats to speed up the process. Awareness came on Hessel in a flash, his eyes snapping open, filled with pure terror. He jerked away, and the brothers had to grab the chair to keep the bound man from going over and taking another blow to the head. He kicked out with his bound feet, catching Jimmy on his wounded leg.

Jimmy inhaled to howl in pain, but he covered his mouth with both hands and muffled the sound.

William dropped his elbow into Hessel's groin, and the bound man curled into the chair, his groans muffled by the tape. William took the opportunity to tape Hessel's legs to the chair. Jimmy pulled the other two chairs out of the office and set them in front of Hessel before sitting down.

William took the other chair. This wasn't part of his plan, not by a long shot, and he couldn't even think of a way to blame Jimmy. They were in it now, and he would have to see it all the way through. "We've got some questions for you. If you answer them quickly and truthfully, you won't get any more injuries from us. If you don't, well, it'll be a long night. Do you understand?"

Hessel nodded.

"Very good." William stood and pulled the tape from Hessel's mouth, then sat back down. "Have you ever seen this gun?"

Jimmy held out the .45.

"Maybe," Hessel said. "I've seen a lot of .45s."

"This one has initials that someone tried to file off and some distinctive scratches."

Jimmy dumped the clip and emptied the chamber, putting the ammo in his pocket. He held the gun in one hand and shined light from his phone onto the side of the .45. "Familiar?"

Hessel shook his head.

"Are you sure?"

"If I've seen it, I don't remember. I'd tell you if I did."

"Do you know Kilo Jones?"

"Yeah. He's dead, though. Got shot a couple weeks ago."

"So I've heard. He had this gun and traded it to someone. I want to know where he got it."

"Man, I don't know. I haven't worked with Kilo since before I went to McCormick. Whatever he done since then got nothing to do with me." Hessel was shaking, still scared.

William believed him. "Is that your room upstairs?"

"Yeah."

"Where does Robbie Martin sleep?"

Hessel hesitated.

"You can protect him or protect yourself." William got up and raised the strip of tape.

"Okay," Hessel said. "He stays in the house. Right there." He nodded toward the main house.

"With Frank?"

"Yeah."

"What about Frank and Robbie? Would they know more about what Kilo was up to before he died?"

"I don't know."

Jimmy put the magazine back in the .45, racked it, and dropped the clip. He added the round that had been in the chamber to the clip and put it back in.

"Maybe," Hessel said. "I don't pay any attention to what they do. I don't wanna know anything about it. See no evil, you know?"

"Are they home?"

Hessel said nothing.

William raised the tape.

Hessel still said nothing.

William put the tape over Hessel's mouth and stepped around to the back of the chair. Hessel tried to pull away, throwing his weight forward, but William seized both his shoulders and pulled him back.

Jimmy stood and put the barrel of the .45 against Hessel's head. "Be still."

William reached down and took Hessel's left pinky and bent it back until he heard a nasty crack. He wasn't sure if the noise had been tendon or bone, but it didn't matter. Either would be efficient. He let Hessel whimper and moan for a few moments before pulling the tape off.

"I warned you. I'm showing mercy by only breaking the pinky this time. There will be no more mercy. Are they home?"

"No."

"Where are they?"

"I don't know exactly. They break into houses. Steal stuff. I stay out of it. I ain't going back to prison. Not ever."

"Amen."

"It looks like you guys do good work here. You should be making money. Why would they steal?"

"Robbie does it for the rush. He's crazy. Frank just does it so Robbie won't think he's a pussy. That's their shit, man. I ain't got nothing to do with it."

"When will they be back?"

"I don't know. Soon, I guess. What time is it?"

Jimmy looked at his phone. "A little after one."

"They're usually back by three. The headlights always wake me up."

"Do they have guns?"

"Robbie does. Not Frank. He can't shoot straight without his glasses, and he can't wear them when they break in places. Might get lost and come back to bite him."

"When they come back, what do they do with the stuff?"

"Depends on what they steal. They don't boost cars much, but when they do, they put it in here, strip the VIN, turn it into something different. Other stuff they put in the barn until they decide what to do with it. Some of it Robbie collects. Some of it they sell. Some of it goes to Goodwill. Robin Hood shit, Robbie says."

William looked at Jimmy. "Anything else?"

Jimmy shook his head.

"All right, Troy. You've done okay." William put the tape back over Hessel's mouth. "We've got some questions for your friends, so you'll just have to sit tight for a while."

"If you need to take a leak or something," Jimmy said, "you just go right ahead. There ain't no shame in it."

William picked up the roll of duct tape and wrapped it a few times around Hessel's chest, taping his torso to the chair. He pulled off another short strip and covered Hessel's eyes.

Jimmy set the .45 on the hood of the car and gripped Hessel's mangled finger, giving it a quick jerk.

Hessel's screams echoed in the garage, in spite of the tape.

Jimmy tore off another strip and taped the pinky tightly to the ring finger. "That should hold you till you can get it seen to." He patted Hessel on the back and sat down.

William shook his head. "Keep an eye on him. I'm going to take a look at that barn."

Jimmy nodded.

CHAPTER 21

William went through the office and outside. He knelt a moment and looked for headlights, listened for approaching cars, before jogging over to the barn. The great doors had been secured with a tightly wrapped chain and a heavy-duty padlock. The small door had been outfitted with a dead bolt and a padlock, which William picked. He slipped the pad lock from the latch, and the door fell open, banging into something he couldn't see. The sound seemed incredibly loud in the stillness of the night, and he watched the windows of the doublewide beyond the barn, expecting to see lights. He saw no movement, no swishing of curtains or shifting shadows, so after a count of thirty, he stepped inside and closed the door. It swung open again as soon as he let go, but he caught it with his left hand and held it closed until he found a latch, an old fashioned metal slide bar about three inches long. He could barely operate the small mechanism with his gloved fingers, feeling his way in the darkness of the barn.

That secured, he used the flashlight app on his phone to scan the interior. He wished he had thought to do this in the pawnshop. The dirt floor was smooth and even, as if it had been packed and leveled with a road roller. Tarps hung over all the exterior walls, giant things in blue and brown and black, a rippled blend of plastic and fiber. William pointed the phone at the roof and saw similar tarps. They had made the inside watertight, or at least water-resistant, probably to protect the things stored inside. The outside still projected the image of something broken down and disused. Flood lamps had been mounted on the rafters, a power cable curling down the center support, where a switch had been mounted. The barn once had six stalls, it seemed, and each of these had been transformed into a storage closet for stolen goods.

"They could stock their own pawn shop," William whispered.

Nelson and Martin were organized. The first stall had TVs, the second DVD players, and the third game systems. Dozens of each. On the other side, there was a stall for jewelry, a stall for guns, and what had to be the miscellaneous stall, full of random items: cameras, phones, lamps, stereos, trophies, and one window unit air conditioner someone hadn't bothered to carry all the way into the stall – this last had been the cause of the noise when William entered.

There was too much merchandise for all of it to have been stolen in Osgood, William thought, and the sheer volume of it made him wonder if any of it was actually stolen for the purpose of being sold. He went to the first stall for a closer look and found some of the TVs were old, box style units – things that would be tough to get rid of for a few dollars at a yard sale. He couldn't find any VCRs in the second stall, but he was pretty sure that was just because they hadn't broken into the sort of houses whose residents still used VCRs.

He skipped the game stall and went across to look at the jewelry. They had set up little displays, like a museum or a jewelry store, with felt trays and mannequin heads. William wondered where they got the heads, whether in the homes of people as strange as the thieves or from a store, bought or stolen. He shined the light on each head, inspecting the necklaces. He wasn't sure why he did this, just an instinct, some message from his subconscious mind.

There were gold chains and strings of pearls and even a few elaborate diamond pieces – the kind of things worn by royalty and film stars. He doubted any of them were real, but he had no way of knowing. On the back row, off to the right, he found what he hadn't realized he was looking for – Ashleigh's teddy bear around a pale plastic neck, its diamond eyes glistening.

He moved on to the gun stall, thankful he saw no ammo with the dozens of guns: pistols, rifles, shotguns, and what looked to be a few army-issue M16s. He hoped they were replicas, but decided not to inspect them. The cameras in the miscellaneous stall were all old Polaroids, a personal favorite of one of the thieves, William guessed. He hadn't seen one in years, and he picked one up from the shelf. He couldn't see anything through the viewfinder. He pushed the button anyway, but the old camera didn't respond. He set it back down and took a closer look at the lamps. No discernable pattern, no clear preference on the part of the thief or thieves. He gave up trying to make sense of Martin and Nelson's choices and went back to the jewelry stall. He slipped Ashley's necklace off the mannequin and put it into his pocket. He was sure he could find a way to return it without giving himself away.

The rumble of an engine told him he had taken too long in the barn. It sounded like another muscle car, something well over 300 cubic inches. William went to the door, and the sound was louder there – just outside, he thought. He put his phone away and wished he had brought the .38. Someone slammed a car door, then another. The small barn door rattled against the latch.

"Troy, are you in there?"

William thought a moment, tried to picture the two men entering, how to handle them both. He remembered the blackjack in his back pocket.

"I'm gonna beat his ass." A second voice, deeper and with a heavier Southern accent.

William slid the latch and stepped back into the shadows, letting the small door swing open and bang into the air conditioner again.

"You still haven't put that thing where it belongs?" The second voice.

"It's my barn."

"It doesn't belong out here. You know that."

Someone came through the door, moving quickly to the switch at the center support. The flood lamps blinded William for a moment. He squinted and raised his left hand to shade his eyes. He caught sight of the fist in time to avoid it, leaning to his left and letting it go by his head. The second man through the door, the one who had thrown the punch, stumbled past William, the momentum of the swing taking him to the stall divider, where he caught himself. William drew the blackjack, ducking a swing from the other man, and snapped a blow against the man's knee. He couldn't be certain what was the clacking of the blackjack and what was the breaking of bone, but he guessed he had wrecked the man's patella. The man folded into a pile on the ground. William gave him a short rap on the back of the head with the blackjack to knock him out and stop the screams before they started.

The one who threw the first punch had righted himself and turned back to William, getting ready for a second attempt. He stopped cold at the sight of the blackjack. He knew what it was, had been hit with one before. William could see that in his eyes. Martin stood frozen with fear and indecision. William was able to recognize him then. Nelson was the one he'd lamed, the one out on the ground.

"You a cop?" Martin asked.

William shook his head, waiting for Martin to move, looking for a clear opening.

"That's a cop's weapon," Martin said.

He put his right hand in his pocket, and William swung the blackjack, stepping to meet Martin, not willing to wait to see what Martin was reaching for, a knife or a small gun, maybe. Martin saw it coming and raised his left arm to try to block the blow. The blackjack caught him on the wrist, and he cried out from the pain of half a dozen small bones breaking. William drew back the blackjack, readying a second blow. Martin pulled his right hand out of his pocket, and for a moment it seemed empty, like he hadn't found what he was looking for. Then the blade flashed out, Martin already swinging.

William swung the blackjack at the knife and missed, the blade slicing through his sleeve and opening a gash on his forearm. The follow-through nicked Martin's ear, but the force of the blow came down on his collarbone. It snapped with a sharp crack. Martin slumped to that side, dropping the knife. William saw the opening and landed a left hook on Martin's chin.

Lights out.

William heard footsteps and turned to see Jimmy coming through the door, the .45 raised. "Late again."

"You know, I could just shoot you," Jimmy said.

"Fair enough."

"Which one is the one we want?"

William pointed at Martin, blood splashing onto the dirt when he moved his arm. He pulled back the sleeve and looked at his wound. The cut started a few inches below his wrist and ended just before the elbow, getting deeper as it went. He rolled up the sleeve to get a better look, stepping to the nearest flood lamp. It probably needed stitches, but it hadn't gotten into the muscle, he thought, thankful for the loose skin and body fat that came with middle age.

Jimmy tucked the gun in his pants and came over to have a look. "You've had worse," he said.

William nodded. "Did you see a first aid kit in there?"

"No, but I wasn't looking."

Jimmy left the barn, and William followed, leaving the unconscious men in the barn. He thought better of it and returned to watch them. With the flood lamps on, he was even more struck by the sheer volume of stolen property. He picked up Martin's knife and cut the power cord from the old air conditioner, using that to tie Martin's hands. He went over to the TV section and pulled off a few power cords, using them for Nelson and for Martin's feet.

Jimmy came back with a small, red first aid kit, the size and shape of a paperback book, and the Eagle Pawn bag full of jewelry. "I assume you've got plans for this," he said, shaking the bag.

William nodded and took the kit. He cleaned his wound, stuffing the bloody pads in his pocket. He had to let Jimmy tape gauze over the wound. It couldn't be done properly with only one hand.

"Did you notice if we woke the neighbors yet?"

Jimmy shook his head and stepped out to check.

William added the jewelry to the collection in the stall, the tags still on each item. He wanted to leave the Eagle Pawn bag for good measure, but he still needed it. He checked the ground for blood, scooping up the wet clods and dumping them into the bag.

"No lights," Jimmy said, coming back inside. "If they're spooked, they're still in the dark." He had the roll of duct tape he had used on Hessel, and he used that to cover Martin and Nelson's mouths. Both groaned a bit when he moved them, but they didn't wake up. "You want to bring the other one out here or take these two in?" Jimmy asked. "I don't like leaving any of them alone."

"Garage. I have an idea."

William took Nelson under the armpits, and Jimmy got the man's feet. They lugged him out of the barn and around an old Camaro. It looked to be from the same era as the one in the yearbook photo, but it hadn't been restored. The brothers went back through the office to the garage, setting Nelson on the floor, stretched out beside Hessel, who was still taped to the chair. The tape over his eyes had come loose – from tears, William thought. Hessel stared down at his friend, but he didn't try to speak. The brothers went back and brought Martin in the same way, but they put him in the chair William had been using. Jimmy taped Martin down while William searched the garage for the equipment he would need, eventually finding it in the trunk of the Chevelle.

"Bring him over here."

Jimmy turned the chair and pulled it over to the third bay, Martin's feet dragging across the floor. William met them by the Chevelle's hood, which he opened and propped up.

"Oh, Billy," Jimmy said, "you really scare me sometimes."

"Wake him up."

Jimmy patted Martin's face while William connected the jumper cables. Martin didn't wake up, so Jimmy got the rag and wet it again, wringing it out over Martin's face. That didn't work, either.

"Hold these." William held the cables out to Jimmy, careful to keep them separated. Jimmy took them, and William got into the Chevelle. The keys were still in the ignition, so he started the car and let it idle. He thought about Sarah Hudgens, hiding in the bathroom while these animals looted her home. He found the cigarette lighter and pushed it in. After a count of thirty, he pulled it out, guessing that would be enough. He got out of the car holding the lighter up.

"Billy, Billy, Billy," Jimmy said.

William stepped over and took Martin's hand, turned it palm up, and planted the lighter in the middle. It had the desired effect. Martin's eyes sprung open, and he jerked forward, trying to free himself from the chair. The tape muffled the sound, but his screams still echoed in the garage. He tried to reach for his injured collarbone, but that hurt, too, and he wriggled back into the chair, trying to find the least painful position, it seemed.

"You're going to want to be very still." William set the lighter on the Chevelle's roof. "The more you jerk around, the worse that's going to get. I imagine a part of that bone is crushed or has multiple breaks. Your wrist isn't much better. You won't be working on cars or breaking into houses anytime soon."

The tape muffled the response, so William stepped over and pulled it off.

"Fuck you," Martin said.

William took the cables from Jimmy. "Show him the gun."

Jimmy drew the .45. "Recognize this?"

"Fuck you."

"You have a limited vocabulary. That could be a problem."

"Fu – "

Jimmy cut this off by putting the tape back over Martin's mouth.

"Me. Yes, I understand." William brought the ends of the cables together until small sparks flared from the ends, then pulled them apart again. "I've seen your stash in the barn, so I know you've stolen a lot of guns. I think you may have stolen this one. You're going to tell me when and where and exactly what happened." He nodded at Jimmy, who pulled back the tape.

"I've seen a lot of guns," Martin said. "I'm not gonna remember one from another."

"Nipples or nads?" Jimmy asked.

"Nipples first. I don't want to see his nads if I don't have to."

Jimmy put the tape back over Martin's mouth. He pulled out his knife and cut open Martin's shirt. He was gentle, but Martin still moaned from the pain of the movement.

"We've never done this before. There's a good chance we'll get it wrong."

"You could die."

Jimmy stepped back, and William touched the ends of the jumper cables to Martin's nipples. William wasn't sure how much of the convulsions were from the electricity itself and how much were from the pain of moving Martin's broken bones. He only held the cable to Martin for a count of one-one-thousand, but the writhing and muffled screams went on for quite a while after that.

"I believe you do remember." William gestured toward the barn with the red cable. "That collection out there isn't just a hobby; that's an obsession. Every item is a trophy. You know where you got each and every one. And you're going to tell me, however long this takes."

When Martin finally settled down, Jimmy pulled the tape back.

"Show me the gun," Martin said.

Jimmy held it up, close to Martin's face, giving him a clear view of the scratches and the filed-down initials.

"Where'd you get that?" Martin asked. "That's mine."

"Yours?" Jimmy asked. He put his thumb into Martin's broken collarbone. Jimmy said something after that, but William couldn't make it out over Martin's screams.

William waited for the screams to subside. "Was it part of your collection?"

"Yes."

"When did it go missing?"

"A few months ago. It was down low, so I might not have missed it right off."

"Right after a visit from Kilo Jones?"

Martin thought about that for a moment, and the anger on his face was all the answer William needed.

"So now we know how you lost it. But what I really want to know is where you found it." William tapped the cables together again, and Martin jerked back, screaming with the pain of the movement.

"Norwood Street. Brick house with a pool. It was in a dresser in the bedroom. Big thing with a mirror and lots of perfume. Weirdest house I've ever been in. No TV. No computer. No jewelry, either. Gun was the only thing worth stealing in the place. There weren't even any pictures on the walls. Felt like a hotel in there, like nobody really lived there anymore. I mean, there was food and stuff and a dog in the back yard, but the inside was just creepy."

William handed the cables to Jimmy and disconnected them from the Chevelle's battery. He closed the hood.

"You believe that bullshit?" Jimmy asked.

"I do." William rolled up the cables and put them back in the Chevelle's trunk. He shut off the engine and replaced the cigarette lighter before walking over to Hessel and cutting his bonds with Martin's knife. "You're going to want to clear out. The cops will be here in a little while."

Hessel looked confused, but he didn't argue, didn't fight, just got up and pulled the rest of the tape off, dropping it in the bed of the old truck and going up the stairs.

"Did I miss something?" Jimmy asked.

"Yeah." William went outside, back to the barn, and began digging through the phones in the miscellaneous stall.

Jimmy came in a moment later. "You need to talk to me, Billy."

"William."

"William, what are you doing?"

"I'm looking for one of these that still works."

"Just use one of theirs."

William nodded. "I want pictures. All this."

Jimmy went out, and William smoothed over the holes where he had dug up the blood-soaked dirt, wiped away the tracks he and Jimmy had made carrying Nelson and Martin. Jimmy returned with an old flip-phone, its dime-sized camera glinting in the light of the flood lamps. He showed William what he was doing as he snapped photos of each of the stalls.

"Get the outside walls and the Nellie's sign."

"What do you want me to do with this?"

William pulled out his wallet and found Phillips' card. He gave it to Jimmy. "Text the pictures to him." He closed the door behind him and locked the deadbolt, put the padlock back on.

"They'll tell him about us."

"So what? No prints. They haven't seen our faces."

"What's that house he was talking about? What's that mean to you?"

"Someone I know. We'll talk later."

"All right, Miss Marple."

William took the Eagle bag full of dirt to the garage and collected the sack with the steak in it. Hessel was packing upstairs, and the Chevelle's trunk was open again. Nelson had finally woken up, but he couldn't stand. He writhed on the floor, trying to reach his wounded knee. William thought of Ashleigh's necklace in his pocket, what might have happened if she had been home. He was tempted to break Nelson's other leg. Instead, he took out the blackjack and gave him a quick rap on the head, knocking him out again.

"Him, too?" Jimmy asked.

William nodded, and Jimmy went over and knocked out Martin. William untied Nelson and put the power cords in the back of the pickup. Jimmy started to unwind the tape from Martin, but William shook his head. "Just the cords. Maybe they'll think this one did that to him."

"Not likely."

"Best we've got. Did you send the pics?"

"Yeah."

William went over to the stairs. "You about ready?"

"Coming down now." Hessel emerged with the duffle bag and came down the stairs.

Jimmy pulled Martin's chair out of the way and opened the bay door.

Hessel put the bag in the Chevelle's trunk and closed it. "Who are you guys?" he asked.

"I'm Batman," Jimmy said.

Hessel shook his head. "He sure as fuck ain't Robin."

"No. He's the devil."

Hessel nodded, got in the car, and cranked the engine. "Thanks," he said.

William nodded, turned and went into the office.

Jimmy met him there. "What do you want me to do with this?" he asked, holding out the flip phone.

William took it and put it in the center drawer of the desk. "We clear?"

Jimmy stepped into the garage and took a look around. "Yeah," he said, stepping back into the office.

William raised a finger to his lips and took the office phone off the hook. He laid it on the desk, dialing 911. He took his bags and walked out, Jimmy right behind him.

CHAPTER 22

The brothers ducked into the woods, over the barbed-wire fence, and across the back neighbor's property. They stopped again at the corner of the house to watch the highway. It was empty then, well into the dead of night. They crossed and went behind the storage building where William had left the Corolla. He dropped the bags in the passenger's side floorboard.

"So where are we going?" Jimmy asked. "Where's this house?"

"Not tonight."

"Why the hell not?"

"Jimmy, this is a delicate situation. I need to think it through."

"What's to think about? We drag somebody out of bed and ask questions. You ain't had a problem with it so far."

"This is different."

"How?"

"It's a woman."

Jimmy nodded and pulled off his mask.

William had forgotten he was wearing one. He pulled it off and dropped it next to the bags in the car.

"Another professor?" Jimmy asked.

"Yeah." He hadn't been in Heather's house since before Eliza went missing, but Janet had often spoken of how Spartan it had become.

"How well you know her?"

"Pretty well."

"In the Biblical sense?"

"No."

"Almost?"

"Yeah."

"I see."

"It's too close, Jimmy. Something happens to her, I'm already in the suspect pool. Not high on the list, probably, but there'll be questions. 'Did you know this? How often did you that?' Once they start looking at you, they're likely to find something. We need to be careful."

Jimmy nodded. He understood police attention. "Tomorrow night," he said. "Just a conversation. We'll ask her some questions. Gentle like."

"Jimmy, I don't know. If she killed Dad, I can't promise... Woman or not."

"I'll be there. I'll keep things calm."

"You're sure?"

"I'm sure."

"All right. Six o'clock."

"Where?"

"Just come to the house."

"Really?"

"No law against it."

"I'll be there." Jimmy nodded, turned, and walked to the Charger. He got in and drove off, not pausing to check if anyone was passing. No one was.

William stepped around the corner of the building to watch the road. Through the trees, he could see a bit of the blue lights from the Nelson property, the police arriving to answer the 911 call. He closed the Corolla's passenger side door, went around and got in. He started the car and pulled around the building, keeping the lights off until he was sure the highway was clear.

~ ~ ~

Turning onto Wilson, he saw Ashleigh's car parked on the street in front of her house, right where Officer Dunn had put his cruiser the night before.

William wanted to give her the necklace in person, to see the look on her face when she saw it. He could tell her he found it in his yard, that the thieves must have dropped it as they fled. He pulled around the corner to Harvie and parked in his own driveway. He took the Eagle bag and dumped the clods of dirt into his own yard, crushing them into the rough grass at the edge of the driveway pavement. If Ashleigh knew he found the necklace, she would have to tell the police. There would be questions. William knew he didn't need that. He scanned the street and saw no lights, no passing vehicles. He walked down to Ashleigh's car. It wasn't locked, so he opened the driver's side door and tucked the necklace into the gap between the seat and the back, deep enough to seem hidden, but out enough to be found.

He walked back to his car, took the steak and the mask, and went inside. He hoped no one had seen him in the street, his sleeve bloody, his hair disheveled from the mask, still wearing his gloves, the blackjack still tucked into his back pocket. He sniffed the steak and decided it was still good. He put it in the refrigerator and burned the Eagle bag in the sink, washing the ashes down the disposal. He stripped out of his clothes, dumping them into the washing machine and starting the cycle.

He had managed to wall off any thought of Heather Rodgers up to then, but the dam finally broke. He couldn't imagine her having anything to do with his father's death, couldn't remember if they had ever met. She was exactly the sort of person Ian might have tried to help – a grieving mother with a philandering husband – but William couldn't believe that help would have included the .45 or that Heather wouldn't have told him if it had. The deeper he went into the problem, the less sense it made. How long had Heather had the gun before Martin stole it?

"Too many variables," William said, shaking his head.

He went to the bathroom and relieved himself. Afterward, in the mirror, he saw another problem. Hessel's punch had left a nasty swell, the early stages of a great black eye. The ridges of the mask's material had scratched his face in several places, dragged across the skin by the momentum of the blow. He would need a story to cover that. He pulled off the bandage Jimmy had taped onto his arm. The wound was deeper and wider than he had thought. He really needed stitches, but that wasn't an option. If Martin told the truth, his lawyer would have to check the hospitals for similar wounds. William couldn't leave a record. He cleaned the wound and taped it closed as tightly as he could manage with one hand. Tomorrow, he would have to buy butterfly bandages, pull them tight and tape gauze over that. He would have to remember not to roll up his sleeves in public for the next several months. He was thankful for the oncoming winter, such as it was in South Carolina. He put ice on his eye for twenty minutes and put the clothes in the dryer. His phone had come through the night unscathed, so he checked his alarm, got ready for bed, and called it a night. He hoped he would sleep, and to his surprise, he did.

~ ~ ~

In the morning, he filled his insulated coffee mug and ran a second pot while he showered. He put the extra coffee into an old thermos that had once been Ian's. He drank the first batch on the way to class and sipped the second during his Raymond Carver lectures. Students were always put off by the depictions of stretch marks in the story, too young to have them, too immature to imagine them as natural, something other than a deformity, a repulsive mark of decay, of that revolting thing they could only label "old." William tried and failed, as he had every time he taught the story, to show them how it could be a part of a relationship, part of aging together gracefully – or failing to, as in the story. He wondered if Heather had stretch marks, the evidence of the daughter she lost, of the union now divided.

Thoughts of her – of how to ask the questions, of what he might do if she gave him the wrong answers – distracted him. The throbbing of his wounded arm didn't help. In the first section, he forgot to explain Carver's minimalistic departure from the traditional narrative arc. He forgot to discuss Carver's connection to Gordon Lish in the second section. Both were major oversights, things that would be on the next exam.

There were looks and whispers, but no one asked him about his face.

He ate soup alone in his office, thankful his friends left him undisturbed. He dwelt on Heather Rodgers, failing to come up with a plan. John Kennedy turned up just before scheduled office hours, checking to see if William had gotten around to writing the recommendation letter for SMU.

"I'm sorry, John. I've had a lot on my plate this week."

"No worries. You'll get to it. There's still plenty of time." He clearly noticed the black eye, but he didn't ask.

"I appreciate your understanding, Mr. President."

"I appreciate your help, Dr. Baker." He saluted and walked away.

William graded papers with three students that afternoon. Each of them noticed his eye, but none of them had the confidence to address it. The grades were higher than usual, and he was pretty sure he was missing errors, putting too much effort into protecting his arm to focus and catch the small things. The students didn't seem to mind. He was packing up to leave when Doug knocked on his door.

"I always catch you trying to leave," Doug said.

"Quirk of our schedules, I guess. What can I do for you?"

"I just came by to apologize."

"For what?"

"They got the guys who robbed the store. A couple of mechanics, it turned out. I didn't get the whole story. The cops called Mrs. Griffin to double-check the list of what was missing." Doug looked at the floor, ashamed. He took a deep breath and looked William in the eye. "Anyway, the point is it wasn't your brother. I just wanted to tell you face to face that I'm sorry. I shouldn't have dragged his name into it."

"I appreciate that, Doug, but you didn't do anything wrong. You did your job. I never thought otherwise."

"I just feel bad about it."

"What would make you feel better?"

"I don't know. I wish I could make it up to you. To him, too."

"Well, I don't know what you have in mind, but I think he's still looking for an engagement ring. If you get something good in, give me a call and I'll pass it on. He wants something old fashioned, diamond with rubies or sapphires on the side. Something like that."

"I remember," Doug said, perking up a bit. "I'll keep my eyes open."

"I'm sure he wouldn't say no to a discount, if you find something."

"Don't push it," Doug said, smiling. "It's not like they arrested him or anything."

William returned the smile. "Proportionality is important. You don't want to overreact."

"Thanks, Dr. Baker."

"You're welcome."

"You okay?" Doug asked, pointing to the black eye.

"Caught a limb in the face on the greenway. Teach me to walk in the dark."

"Sorry."

"I've had worse," William said, thinking of his arm.

Doug nodded, waved goodbye, and walked away.

William finished packing his things and went home. He still had no plan, so he took a nap in his recliner, hoping he might dream up a solution. A knock at the door woke him, but he was no closer to a plan than he had been two hours earlier. He expected Jimmy, but he found Phillips instead.

"Afternoon, Dr. Baker."

"Officer Phillips, what can I do for you?"

"I was just across the street delivering some good news for a change, and I thought I should update you on those break-ins we discussed. What happened to you?"

"Force equals mass times acceleration."

"I'm sorry?"

"I was walking home from Shirley's last night – fast because it was chilly. It was dark, and I caught a branch across the face."

"You okay?"

"I'm fine. You were saying?"

"We made an arrest last night. Found a whole stash of stolen goods. A lot of people are getting their stuff back for once."

"That's great," William said, hoping his smile looked grateful and not prideful. "I knew you'd get your man."

"I wish I could take credit. Someone texted me pics of the evidence, and we got a 911 call from the location with no one on the line. They're not talking, but as best as we can tell, the thieves had some kind of falling out with their partner. He beat them senseless and put us onto them."

"He beat them? More than one? I thought you told me Sarah saw two men?"

"There was a third man living there. We're pretty sure he was involved."

"Did you find him?"

"Not yet, but we will. He drives an old muscle car. Easy to track down."

William nodded, trying to keep his thoughts from showing. He didn't want Hessel taking the blame. Hessel was innocent, dragged into this mess just like Riley's grandmother.

"Looks like they're the ones who hit Eagle, too," Phillips said. "We're still going through all the stuff, but we found some of the jewelry. Had to be the same crew."

William nodded again, putting the Hessel issue aside for the moment. He wondered what time it was, if Jimmy would show up while Phillips was still there, what Phillips would make of that. The sun had already set. "Can I get you a Coke?" William asked, trying to keep things light and friendly.

"No, thanks. I've got to get going. I've got more good news to deliver." Phillips smiled and backed down the porch steps.

"Thanks for the update. I appreciate your work."

"Thanks, Dr. Baker." Phillips waved goodbye and walked down to his cruiser.

William waited for Phillips to turn his back before closing the front door. He watched through the peephole until the squad car had pulled around to Wilson Street and out of sight. He went back inside and checked the time: six-fifteen. Jimmy was late. Not surprising under normal circumstances, but a little odd given how eager he had been the night before.

William still didn't have a plan. He decided he didn't need one. Jimmy was right; nothing ever went according to plan. "Too many variables," he whispered.

He went to the kitchen and got a NutriGrain bar and a Coke. He knew he needed food, but he couldn't imagine eating a meal. He was halfway through the snack when he heard the rumble of the Charger, first on the street and then in the driveway. Jimmy knocked on the back door, and William let him in.

"Ready?" Jimmy asked.

William raised the snack in his hands.

Jimmy nodded. "What did the cop want?"

William was chewing. He raised his eyebrows.

"He was parked out front when I first got here," Jimmy said. "Saw him from Main Street, so I went on by. Saw him on your porch on the second pass, so I waited at Shirley's for a bit."

William finished his bite and washed it down with a big swig of Coke. "He wanted to let me know they caught the robbers. The ones who hit Eagle." He smiled.

Jimmy smiled back. "Brought you this," he said, pulling a small tube from his pocket. "Liquid stitches."

"Thanks."

"Wendy."

William nodded and set the Coke on the table. He stuffed the last of the NutriGrain bar in his mouth and went to the bathroom. He came back with tape, gauze, and cleaning pads. He rolled back his sleeve, cleaned his wound, and let Jimmy apply the liquid stitches.

"Do you have a plan?" Jimmy asked as they waited for the liquid to dry.

"I'll ask politely."

Jimmy nodded. He pulled the .45 from his waistband and laid it on the table in front of William. "You can get further with a kind word and a gun than with a kind word alone."

William raised his eyebrows again.

"Al Capone," Jimmy said. "You should put it on your office wall."

William nodded and drank the rest of his Coke.

Jimmy cut the new gauze and taped it down.

"I'll drive." William tucked the gun in the back of his waistband.

CHAPTER 23

The brothers took the Corolla down Harvie and around the corner, three blocks south and two blocks east, before turning into Heather Rodgers' driveway. The trip was less than a mile and a half, something William would have walked if he were alone and not carrying his father's gun.

"Wait here. I'll knock on the window if there's something you need to hear."

"All right," Jimmy said.

William got out, went to the front door, and rang the bell. He scanned the neighborhood while he waited, wondering who might be looking back. There were lights on up and down the street and a few kids playing in yards, in spite of the dark and the light chill in the air.

"Will, hey, how are you?" Heather asked. She wore an aged knit sweater and gaucho pants, the soft fabrics clinging to her curves. A hint of strawberries wafted out from her.

"I'm okay," William said, trying to focus, trying to ignore the attraction. On each hip, a small band of skin shown between the top of her pants and the bottom of the sweater. He wanted to put his hands there and cover her mouth with his. He could see a touch of shock in her eyes, and he wondered if she had the same thought or if he had just failed to turn around quickly enough, if she had seen the gun against the small of his back.

"What happened to your face?"

"Caught a wind-whipped branch on the greenway last night."

"That's why I use a treadmill."

"I'll bear that in mind."

She smiled and leaned back, clearing a path. "Do you want to come in?"

"Please, thanks."

"I was just making dinner. It's just some pasta and sauce, not the home-cooked meal you really need, but you're welcome to it." She led the way through the living room, and William closed the front door behind them.

"I already ate," he said, "and I'm sorry to disturb your dinner."

"It's a nice surprise, actually. If you won't eat, how about a drink? Beer, wine, soda?"

"No, thanks."

"You seem really serious, Will. What's going on?"

"It's a long story, but I need to ask you about something. Can we sit?"

"Sure."

Furious barking came from the back yard.

"That's odd," Heather said. She pulled back the curtain on the dining room window. Jimmy stood on the concrete sidewalk that bordered the pool, sucking the back of his thumb, and scowling at Heather's boxer. The dog had quieted to a low growl. Heather threw open the back door. "What do you think you're doing out here?"

Jimmy looked up. "I was trying to figure out how they got in, when this little one decided he liked the taste of me."

"What? How who got in?" She looked at William, then back to Jimmy. Looked again. "Is that your brother?"

William nodded. "He was supposed to wait in the car." He readied himself to push away the anger he always felt when Jimmy did these things, to calm himself and focus on the task at hand. To his surprise, the anger didn't come. Instead, he found himself smiling at the sight of Jimmy being taught a lesson by an ordinary guard dog.

Jimmy came over and stopped just outside the door. The dog resumed its barking.

"Hush, Butch," Heather said, and Butch did.

"I've never been very good at following instructions," Jimmy said.

William laughed. "Heather Rodgers, this is Jimmy Baker."

"Can't say I'm glad to meet you. I guess you'd better come in. You're disturbing the neighbors."

Jimmy stepped in, passing between Heather and William on his way. William noticed the ends of the zip ties sticking out of Jimmy's back pocket. He hoped they would stay where they were. Heather closed the door and followed Jimmy into the living room. She sat in a chair, but Jimmy remained standing, peeking out the front windows. William met them there and sat on the couch. He closed his eyes and tried to remember how it had looked the last time he was there, Eliza's toys scattered about and her picture in an oval frame on the end table. All of that was gone now, the living room less personalized than a typical office lobby.

"Will, you need to tell me what this is about."

"I need to show you something, but there's no need to be alarmed." He showed her his hands, like a suspect showing the police he is unarmed. She nodded, and he reached back and took the .45, placing it in the center of the coffee table.

Heather gasped at the sight of the gun.

"Do you recognize this?"

"No," she said. "Why would I?"

William sighed.

Jimmy snorted, suppressing a laugh.

"Heather, it's important that you tell me the truth."

"I am."

Jimmy snorted again.

"We know this gun was here, in this house, just a few months ago. In your dresser."

"Did you break in here?" she asked, standing. "I think I need to call the police."

"No, you don't," Jimmy said, turning to face her. He kept his distance, but he put his body between her and the kitchen.

William looked over and saw her phone lying on the counter, next to an open box of dry pasta.

"Is that why he's here?" she asked. "To intimidate me?"

Jimmy laughed out loud this time, bent forward and slapped his knee.

Heather looked to William, confused.

"Just relax." William raised his hands again, a gesture of calm. "Sit down."

"Lady, you don't know my brother very well, do you?" Jimmy said, wiping his eyes.

"What does that mean?" she asked, sitting back down and eyeing the gun on the table.

"I'm not the one you should be scared of," Jimmy said.

Now Heather laughed. "Will wouldn't hurt a fly," she said. "He's too moral."

Jimmy shook his head. "Have you ever seen him in shorts?"

Heather shook her head.

Jimmy bent down and lifted the leg of William's pants. William sighed, but he let his brother expose the scar. Jimmy dropped the pant leg.

"Is that a bite?" Heather asked.

Jimmy nodded. "Neighbor had a chocolate lab. Big dog. People think pit bulls are bad. Dogs ain't bad. People are bad. Dogs do what you train 'em to do. Neighbor was a nasty old man. Made himself a nasty dog. Took a bite of Billy one day. Six years old. You know what Billy did?"

Heather shook her head.

"He tackled that dog, held him down, and took a hunk of *his* leg. Bit right through the fur and muscle and took a piece right off. A bite for a bite. He's like that, our Billy. Always was. Always will be."

"This is not why we're here." William glared at his brother for a moment and turned to Heather, his face softening at the sight of her. "The gun belonged to our dad. It was stolen from this house. Stolen from you, by a couple of thugs. I guess you didn't report it. I really don't care. I want to know where you got it. I need to know. You need to tell me."

"Will, I just don't know what you're talking about."

"Heather, please." William shook. He could feel himself coming loose. He picked up the gun, dropped the clip, racked the shell from the chamber.

Heather drew back into the chair, pulled her legs up against her chest, hugged them tightly.

"Lady," Jimmy said, "you don't know me, but you need to trust me. Whatever you're hiding ain't as bad as what we're after. Least we don't think it is. We're pulling at a thread, and you don't want to be at the end of it. You don't want to get in the way, neither. Billy here is at the end of his patience."

"Did you kill my father?" William's voice was quiet, shaking with suppressed rage. He was on the edge, and he knew it. "Did you run him off the road and take this gun from his truck?"

"Of course not," Heather said. "How could you possibly think that?" She had started to cry, tears splashing into the knees of her pants, turning the fabric a darker shade of black. She whispered something William couldn't hear.

Jimmy stepped toward her. "What did you just say?"

"He couldn't have. There's just no way." She was still whispering, but her voice was strong enough to hear now.

"Who?"

She looked William in the eye and then shook her head. "No," she said, still shaking her head. "He just..."

"Who gave you the gun, Heather?"

"I never used it," she said. "I only touched it once. I put clothes on top of it until... until it wasn't there. I was glad to be rid of it."

"Who?"

"It was years ago. When Carl and I were separated. He just thought I might need something. To protect myself if Carl found out. If he got rough. Not that I would have shot him. Just to scare him off. He could be rough sometimes. He never hit me. Just shook me sometimes. Left bruises on my arms."

"Who, Heather?"

"Nick was just trying to help. Just being sweet."

"Nick who?"

"Fuller."

William couldn't make the connection. He didn't think they knew each other, didn't think Nick had ever taken one of her classes. "Nick Fuller gave you that gun?"

"Yes."

"Why would he... Were you?"

Heather looked away, pulled herself even tighter.

"You slept with a student?" William couldn't believe it. "How long?"

She didn't look at him, didn't answer.

"Was he even eighteen when it started?"

She buried her head between her knees, her crying becoming audible sobs.

"I knew things weren't good with Carl, but... Heather, I thought better of you." William covered his face with his hands, shook his head.

"He's just so sweet," she said, speaking into the space between her knees, her voice muffled by the fabric of her pants, by the lurch of her sobs. "He's so beautiful. He makes me feel special. He never asks for anything. Never tells anyone."

"Present tense? This is still going on?"

"I don't expect you to understand our relationship."

"That isn't a relationship, Heather. It's a psychosis. You're overcompensating for what happened with Carl, picking someone you see as weak, someone who couldn't hurt you if he tried."

Heather sniffed. "You're not a psychologist, Will. What do you know?"

Jimmy snorted again. "He's an English teacher, bitch. He reads shit." He picked up the gun and reloaded it. "Billy, it's time for us to go. We got what we came for."

William stood, still shaking his head. "Goodbye, Heather."

"Goodnight, Dr. Rodgers," Jimmy said. "Can't say I enjoyed meeting with you, but I thank you for the information."

Heather finally looked up, catching William's eyes. "Will," she said, "are you going to tell anyone?"

"I don't know, Heather. Are you?" He left her to ponder this and went out to the car.

CHAPTER 24

J immy closed the front door behind them and joined William in the Corolla. "She's bawling," Jimmy said, "you're looking like somebody died, and I've got Van Halen going in my head." He drummed a section from "Hot for Teacher," his gloved hands pounding the Corolla's dash. "'*Class dismissed.*' This situation gets more fucked up by the hour."

"Indeed."

"You know where this Fuller kid lives?"

"No, but I can find out." William drove them back to his house, got his laptop, and logged into the university system. His class rosters included hyperlinks on each student's name, connecting to a page with links for transcripts, schedules, and contact information – phone numbers, email, and addresses, home and local. William could feel himself boiling over, losing control. He took long, deep breaths, a slow inhale and a slower exhale.

Nick Fuller was a local kid, but his page listed two addresses, one in a lower-middle class development on the north side of town, the other in the same mill village with William's own house. About half a mile to the west, right over the ridge from the Osgood Oaks complex. William had passed behind it too many times to count, probably caught glimpses through bare trees each winter. The houses in that stretch had belonged to line workers, the bottom of the mill power structure. It would be a small place with two tiny bedrooms, maybe half the square footage of William's house. There was a roommate, a history major named Logan. Nick occasionally spoke of him in class. No one used his first name, and William couldn't remember it. The kid delivered pizzas for Four Brothers, and William only knew him from two-minute conversations at the front door. He had never been in one of William's classes. Rumor was he had a habit of consoling the girls Nick rejected, sometimes in bed.

William wondered if either of them were home and who else might be there. He wondered if Heather had called after he and Jimmy left her place. Jimmy paced William's living room impatiently during the research.

"All right. Let's go."

"What's the plan, Miss Marple?"

"Jimmy, this isn't a murder mystery; it's a revenge tale."

"You driving?"

"We're walking."

"Give me two minutes." Jimmy went outside and returned in much less time than he requested. He had put on a jacket and collected duct tape and the blackjacks. He offered one to William, who shook his head. Jimmy tucked the extra blackjack under William's sofa and put the tape into a large outer pocket of his jacket. "You still have that bleach?" he asked.

William pointed to the washing machine in the kitchen, the bucket sitting on top.

"Not good for travel," Jimmy said. He opened drawers until he found a freezer bag and poured some of the powder into it, standing over the sink to catch the spill.

William came behind him and closed the drawers. He rinsed the spilled powder down the drain.

The brothers left through the back door, William leading the way through the yard, around the neighbor's boat, between two houses, all the way to the sidewalk on the street where Nick Fuller lived.

Lights were on in most of the houses on that street. All
the yards were empty, the evening chill having chased
the neighborhood children into their homes. A group
of teens were gathered at the park swings, a couple
kissing and their friends chatting and teasing them.
One of them sang a song about cold sores to the tune
of "On Top of Old Smokey." Jimmy laughed and
waved, but William strode on, determined.

Nick's place sat in a row of once-identical mill
houses on lots so small an average man could spit
from his porch to the middle of the street. Beyond
Nick's, the houses were duplexes with even less living
space per residence. All the front yards in the area
could be cut with three short circuits of a push mower.
There were no driveways. Cars lined both sides of the
street, mostly older, some dented and dinged, others
already showing rust. In front of Nick's house sat an
early 90s Caprice Classic, white, the sort of thing that
might have been a police cruiser when it was born. It
showed no signs of that, no faded outline of an
emblem, no impressions on the backs of the seats
from the dividing cage.

William stopped and looked the car over. Every
panel had been dented, parking lot scratches on all
four doors, foreign paint on all four fenders. A row of
Samuels parking stickers lined the bottom of the rear
window. The trunk was held down with a bungee
cord. He crouched down and inspected. The driver's
side damage was relatively light, red paint on the front
fender, green on the back one. The passenger's side
rear fender showed two layers of damage, a collision
with something black and another with something
green. The front fender had been battered inside and
out, multiple collisions and someone taking a rubber
mallet to the underside to remove the dents. It had
been sanded and touched up, and then picked up

someone else's green paint. The front bumper was twisted and rippled, like it had been hit multiple times and then forced back into shape somehow – with hooks and a tow wench, William guessed. Nick's family didn't have money. The old car probably had minimal insurance. He'd covered up the evidence as best he could.

It was all the proof William needed.

He let go and came undone, giving in to his worst self. He charged the porch almost at a run, not knocking on the front door, just throwing it open. The little house had no foyer, and the door opened on the southwest corner of the living room. Nick and Logan had arranged it like an office lobby in a bank or an insurance agency: desks sat in opposite corners, facing the center of the room. An old couch sat under the front window, to the right of the front door, facing a small TV stand with an old, box 19-inch on top. The kitchen door was to the right of that, at a right angle with the entrance to the alcove – too small to be called a hallway – where doors to the bathroom and two bedrooms were.

Nick sat behind the desk in the southeast corner of the living room. Evidently, Heather hadn't warned him. He was too surprised to speak when Billy burst into the room. There was no thought, just action – blacked out for the first time in more than twenty years. He seized Nick under the arms and swung him over the desk, feet thudding across the top, scattering books and papers, pens and paperclips. He slammed the kid into the floor, knocking the wind out in a wet gush. He kicked Nick in the stomach, toes first like an old fashioned placekicker, and the boy slid across the hardwood floor into the other desk. Nick curled up, protecting his middle.

Billy kept kicking, punctuating his words with his foot. "You. Do. Not. Fuck. With. My. Family."

He grabbed a stapler from what must have been Logan's desk, raised it, and swung for Nick's head. The boy had the presence of mind to roll away from the blow, and Billy missed, the stapler breaking open against the floor and launching staples around the room. He drew it back for another swing and didn't see Jimmy, just felt the arms slip around his neck, the sides of his head. He was too feral to think, just wrestled against the hold, unintentionally wresting himself deeper into it until he passed out.

~ ~ ~

William came to some minutes later, finding himself on Nick's couch, his hands zip-tied behind him, his feet zip-tied in front of him. Jimmy stood off to his left, right arm extended as far as possible and waving smelling salts under William's nose. The last clear memory was of standing at the corner of Nick's car, but William knew what must have happened.

Jimmy jumped back from him, ready to defend himself. "You all right?" he asked.

"How bad was it?" William wasn't sure he wanted to know. He turned to his right and saw Nick on the floor, propped against the wall between the desk and the alcove entrance, hands and feet zip-tied in front of him, unconscious.

"Well," Jimmy said, "you were about to stomp this piece of shit right to the gates of Hell, and I still want to know why he killed Dad."

"Sleeper?"

Jimmy nodded.

"Him?"

"Blackjack."

"Wake him up."

Jimmy pulled a fresh smelling salt pack from his pocket, went over to Nick, and cracked it open under Nick's nose.

"Where'd you get those?"

"Wendy. After the trouble we had waking those two last night, I thought they'd come in handy."

"Good thinking."

"Thanks."

Nick roused slowly. He looked around the room like he wasn't sure where he was. "Dr. Baker?" he finally said. "What's happening?"

"You're gonna tell us a story," Jimmy said. He took Nick under the arms and set him in the chair behind the desk, rolling it out and parking it in front of the TV. Jimmy sat on the corner of the desk.

"What happened?" Nick asked. "Did I dream that?"

"Dream what?"

"You kicking my ass."

"That was one hundred percent real life," Jimmy said.

Nick looked at William, confused. He tilted his head sideways like a dog. "But... I always thought... I mean... I thought you were a pussy."

Jimmy laughed. "Now that's where you're wrong. Billy's ruthless. He's always been ruthless – half bloodhound and half Rottweiler. It's just that there's only a few things in this world he gives a shit about. Steer clear of those, and he'll give you anything you ask for. No worries. Cross the line, and things get ugly."

"So what is this about? What do you want?" He addressed the question to William.

"Once again," Jimmy said, "you have gotten the wrong end of the stick. You're not dealing with him. You're dealing with me."

Nick looked at Jimmy. "What do you want?" he asked again.

Jimmy snapped his fingers and grimaced. "I forgot something. Give me a minute." He went into Nick's kitchen, out of William's view. Nick turned to watch, his face showing confusion and fear. "I've never been the most organized," Jimmy called. "Momma used to say I'd forget my head if it wasn't attached. She's probably right about that."

Other sounds came from the kitchen. The opening and closing of cabinets. Running water. Drawers being opened and closed. The rattling of silverware. The ripping open of a paper package. Stirring in a plastic cup. Something dropped into a sink, already full of dishes – a spoon, William thought.

Jimmy came back with a large plastic cup, a souvenir from a Clemson football game. He set it on Logan's desk. "We wouldn't want that to get spilled," he said. He pulled the chair from behind that desk and rolled it over to the corner of Nick's desk. He straddled the seat, facing backwards, and folded his arms across the seat back. "Billy here's been doing some investigating. I helped. Some. And we have come to the conclusion that you killed our father."

"I didn't – "

"Hush your mouth," Jimmy said, standing. "I'll smack your teeth through the back of your neck."

Billy struggled against the zip ties, his blood boiling, all thought lost.

Nick pushed back the chair, wedging himself in the space between the TV stand and Logan's desk.

"I don't expect you knew the man," Jimmy said, sitting back down. "He was as good as they come. War hero. Good husband. Hard worker. Real good dad. Didn't deserve the shit I put him through. Hell, even Billy here wasn't the son Ian Baker deserved." He looked at his brother. "No offense. It just couldn't be done."

"I'm sorry," Nick said.

Billy tried to stand and couldn't. Jimmy had hooked the zip tie around his ankles to the leg of the couch. He couldn't move without dragging it with him. He took deep breaths, tried to calm himself, and sat back down.

"We know what you done," Jimmy said. "Run him off the road. Took his gun out of the truck. Left that with your cougar girlfriend. What I want to know is why. You're gonna tell me."

"I didn't," Nick said. "Really, I don't know what you're talking about."

Jimmy stood, pulled the .45 from behind him, and whipped Nick with it. The kid turned his head, trying to avoid the blow, and the gun caught him across the side of the neck, the sight tearing the skin just under the ear. A thin trail of blood trickled down. Jimmy sat, laying the gun in his lap. He breathed slowly, the same technique Ian had taught Billy.

"Denying it won't help you, boy. We talked to the lovely Dr. Rodgers just a little while ago. We seen your car outside. You tried pretty hard to cover that up. All them other accidents." He used air quotes on the last word.

Billy shook. "I'm going to kill you."

"Well, maybe," Jimmy said, holding out a hand, the gesture a request for patience.

"Please," Nick said.

"I told you to hush." Jimmy picked up the gun and stood, pushing the chair away from himself, letting it roll into the kitchen. He began to pace the room, twisting his wrist back and forth, letting the barrel of the gun bump his thigh with each stride.

Nick looked back and forth from Jimmy to William to the front door.

"Expecting someone? Roommate due back soon?" Nick didn't answer.

"You don't want that," Jimmy said. "I'd hate to do it, but if anyone interrupts, I'll just shoot him. No one's gonna save you, boy. You will die tonight."

Nick shook his head and began to sob.

"Well, I guess we know who the pussy is," Jimmy said.

"Please," Nick said again.

"You can cry and beg," Jimmy said, "and it ain't gonna change nothing. But I'm gonna give you a choice."

Billy stood again, jerking the couch toward Nick. The kid lurched forward, falling out of the chair. He crawled across the floor and under his desk.

"Relax, Billy," Jimmy said, raising his voice. "I have a plan."

Billy growled and went back to breathing. He sat down.

"Like I said, I'm giving you a choice." Jimmy went over to the desk and picked up Nick's recorder. He pressed Play, and Danny's voice came out, some tangent about Cicero. Jimmy stopped the tape and pressed Rewind. "I want to know exactly what happened that night. Every last detail. You're going to tell me, talk right into this thing for posterity. Did I use that word right? Posterity?"

William nodded.

"No," Nick said. "I can't."

"The last thing you will learn in your short, shitty life is to do as you're told." Jimmy grabbed the corner of the desk and spun it around, exposing Nick, who scrambled back to the wall and banged into his chair. It tipped over, covering him, and he slid around, trying to put it between himself and the brothers. Jimmy picked up the chair and set it upright. Its momentum carried it across the floor until it bumped into the TV stand. "Like I said, you have a choice. You're going to die. The question is how. My brother here is a moral man. He's very Old Testament about things. An eye for an eye. He has a tendency to lose his temper, but even then his code comes through." Jimmy took the chair and rolled it back toward Nick, seized the kid by the shoulders, and set him upright on the seat. "If I were to cut him loose, I imagine he would bend you backwards over this desk and beat you till all your ribs was broke." Jimmy squatted in front of Nick and leaned close, speaking nose to nose. "Then he'd press the jagged end of one of them bones through your lungs and watch you drown in your own blood, hanging upside-down and praying for somebody to help you. It would only be right."

The little recorder made a sharp pop when the tape finished rewinding, the button shooting up to its proper place like blackened bread from a toaster.

Jimmy stood and backed away. "But that's Billy. I'm a practical man. I know you've got to give a little to get a little in this world. And I want to know why." He pushed the desk back into position and set the recorder in the center. "In that cup over there is a little something I cooked up for times like this. My own special recipe. If you drink that down, your eyes will get heavy, you will stretch and yawn, and soon you'll be dreaming." Jimmy mimed this, letting his head loll onto his shoulder and fluttering his eyelids. "A little while later, your heart will slow down and stop. And you will wake up." He opened his eyes and looked at Nick. "In Hell." He turned and went into the kitchen, rolling the second chair back out and sitting down. "So what's it gonna be? Dreams or drowning?"

"Why would you record it?" Nick asked.

"That's your suicide note."

Nick nodded. He was still looking at the front door, still hoping for rescue, it seemed.

"Do we have a deal?" Jimmy asked.

Nick nodded again.

Jimmy stood, looked to his brother, and placed a finger over his lips. William nodded, and Jimmy pressed the record button. He sat back down.

"He saw the body," Nick said.

William opened his mouth to speak, but caught himself and just let out a sigh. He had calmed down enough to think a bit. He looked the question at Nick.

"Eliza," Nick said.

Billy stood, seeing red again, but Jimmy met him, raising calming hands.

"I didn't kill her," Nick said. "It wasn't my fault. I just hid her. That's all."

The brothers sat down, and Jimmy gestured that Nick should continue.

"She was in the pool." He covered his face, rubbed his eyes, like he was trying to wipe the image from his mind. "She was supposed to be asleep. It was late. Carl was on a road trip, and we were taking advantage." He shook his head. "I panicked. I don't remember thinking about it. Heather was in the shower. I tried CPR. I did. But it was just water. Chlorine and acid. I can still taste it. She was dead. She wasn't coming back. She was so small."

Jimmy stopped the tape. "The way you're telling it, you found a little kid drowned in a pool. Why didn't you just call an ambulance?" He pushed the record button.

"I couldn't let anyone find out about us. Heather always said so. If I called 911, there would be cops, questions. She would get fired, leave town. She might have blamed herself. Blamed me. I panicked. I just wrapped her in a beach towel. Hid her between the bushes and the fence." He had started crying again, tears streaming from both eyes.

William realized the earlier sobs had been faked, for his benefit. This was real.

"Heather said my breath stank. Said I might have acid reflux. After, I mean. When she got out of the shower. I told her goodnight and left. Told her I was leaving. I put Eliza in the trunk and just drove around, trying to figure out what to do. Where I could bury her."

William stood, trying to get to the tape recorder. He had the presence of mind not to speak. He shook his head in that direction until Jimmy got up and stopped the tape. "That was months before Dad's wreck. You're lying."

"No," Nick said. "That was later."

Jimmy put a finger to his lips again, and William sat down. Jimmy started the recorder.

"I ended up hiding the body at the old mill. There are all these bricks, and I moved them and dug a hole."

William pictured the guns in the Eagle Pawn bag where he had planted them.

"This was the next night. She sat in my trunk all night. In my parent's driveway. That's why I moved in here. I just couldn't. After." He wiped his nose on his sleeve. "That's where she was. For months. Then I heard they were going to tear the mill down. I thought they would find her. I had to move her."

William understood then. He could see the rest of the story in his mind. There was no need for Nick to continue, but he did.

"They had searched the creek bed when she first went missing. I didn't think they'd look again." He wiped his nose again. "I pulled over, under some dogwood trees with low branches. Turned off the lights and waited. I rolled the windows down and listened for cars. For anybody else out there. It was quiet. Silent. I didn't even hear any crickets. I popped the trunk and started to get out. Then I heard the truck. I closed the trunk and got back in to wait it out, but the latch didn't catch. I just didn't close it all the way, I guess. I was scared. He came right up behind me, headlights right on her. He slowed down, but he didn't stop. I knew he had seen. He had to." Nick began to shake, his voice quivering. "I chased him. He wasn't running, I don't think. I think he was trying to get the gun. I just rammed him. It was raining. Not much, but it was slick out there. All those patches on the road. The truck just spun out. Flipped over two or three times. I don't know." He stopped speaking, wiped his eyes and nose.

Jimmy stood up and stopped the tape. "You stopped?"

Nick nodded. "I went over there. I didn't mean to kill him. I didn't. I don't know what I was thinking. I was scared. But I couldn't help him. He was too bad off."

"Did he say anything to you?"

"No. He just looked at me. Sad. I stepped on the gun on my way back to the car. His windows were down."

"That's enough," William said. "I don't want to hear anymore." He knew the rest of the story. Thomas White's property was just a mile or so from that creek bed. Whether or not Nick had picked White on purpose didn't matter. When the tape got out, another wrong would be set right.

Jimmy nodded. He got up and took the Clemson cup from the other desk, setting it in front of Nick. "Drink up," he said.

Nick leaned forward, using his weight to bring the chair up to the desk. He took the cup, but the ties on his wrists made it impossible for him to tilt it to his mouth. He sat it back down.

Jimmy pulled out his pocketknife and opened the blade. He stepped up to Nick, as if he were going to cut the tie. He stopped, turned and bent down, cutting the tie that held William's feet. "In case you get any ideas," Jimmy said. He went back to Nick and cut the tie on the kid's wrists.

Nick picked up the cup and drank. He grimaced at the taste of the solution, but he finished the cup and set it back on the desk. "I'm sorry," he said.

"It's too late for that," Jimmy said.

"How long will it take?"

"A few minutes." Jimmy went into the kitchen and returned with a rag, which he used to wipe off the cup. "Pick that up again," he said, and Nick did. Jimmy wiped down the desks from top to bottom, then the chairs and the TV stand. "Will you be all right?" he asked his brother.

"Yes."

William stood, and Jimmy cut the tie that held his wrists. Nick already looked drowsy, his eyelids drooping, his chin lolling. William stretched his arms and legs, trying to get the blood flow back to normal. Jimmy wiped down the hard surfaces on the couch.

"No chance they've got a vacuum," Jimmy said.

William went through the alcove and checked the first bedroom. It was decorated with Clemson gear, a pennant and pictures of cheerleaders and football players. "Logan," he said. No vacuum. He wiped the light switch and the closet door handle with his sleeve before crossing to Nick's room. The walls were bare, the bed a lumpy mess with threadbare sheets and a blanket. There was no vacuum in the closet, so he wiped down what he had touched and met Jimmy in the living room. The elder brother had mixed up some of the bleach and was wiping up the blood on the floor.

Nick had put his head down on the desk.

"Is he faking?"

"No," Jimmy said. "After what he drank, there's no need to fake anything."

"Are we good in here?"

"As good as we're going to get."

"Front door?"

"Got it."

CHAPTER 25

William went through the kitchen and out the back door. Jimmy followed, wiping the handle inside and out. They crossed the back yard and ducked between the trees until they came out on the greenway. William wasn't sure what time it was, so he pulled out his phone and checked.

8:43.

He couldn't believe he had talked to Phillips less than three hours earlier. He wondered where Logan was, when he would come home and find Nick. Wondered if he would play the tape. Would anyone? Would Phillips or some other officer come and stand on his porch and tell him they finally found out who killed Ian Baker? Would they be able to tell he wasn't surprised? Would they suspect him of anything? He didn't think so. A student suicide is a tragedy, but it's not unusual. It happens somewhere every semester. There were too many variables to be sure, but he thought he would be okay. He would just have to keep his mouth shut, keep his thoughts to himself. He could do that. It was something he was good at.

"Thanks, Jimmy."

"Don't thank me. You did most of the work."

"But I wouldn't have, if you hadn't pushed me."

"You're welcome."

The brothers walked the rest of the greenway in silence, through the park, and up to William's house.

"Do you want to come in? Maybe have a drink?"

"I'd love to," Jimmy said, "but I've got a couple of errands to run."

"What would you need to do *now*?"

"Better you don't know."

"Fair enough."

"I'll see you soon, though. Promise."

"All right."

William put his hand out, but Jimmy seized him in a hug. His right hand was trapped between their chests, but William put his left arm around his brother and returned the hug as best as he could. After a moment, Jimmy released him and went to the Charger, got in and started it, let the engine rumble for a moment, then backed out and drove away. William went inside, showered, and turned in early.

He was very weary.

~ ~ ~

William slept poorly, with fitful dreams of his father, of Nick, and of Heather. He got up very early and made himself a proper breakfast, eggs and sausage and biscuits. He didn't feel guilty. He wondered if he should. He had never killed anyone, and he didn't know how to feel about it. He felt justice had been served, for his father and for his brother. Jimmy, who had always believed Ian had been murdered, had been proven right, and he had done what it took to honor their father's memory the best way he knew how. He had made some mistakes, been careless at times, but he got the job done.

William knew there was a chance he could be arrested. Even if the police wrote it off as a suicide, there would be the coroner's report, and that would have to show Nick had been beaten and tied up before he died. It was possible someone had seen William and Jimmy going into the house. Likely, even. Heather could testify to their visit, that they were looking for Nick when they left. They had certainly left DNA somewhere in the house. On the couch. On the chair. If there was a proper investigation, they could be tried for murder. He didn't think he could be

convicted. Not in Osgood. Not by a jury who had
heard that tape. He realized he should have made
copies. The whole business had been messy. He had
let his emotions get the better of him, let himself run
riot when he needed to slow down and make a proper
plan. He could blame Jimmy, but that would be
unfair. William was responsible for his own decisions,
for his own actions. If it came to it, he would suffer the
consequences and not complain. He resolved this in
his own mind that morning at his kitchen table, eating
scrambled eggs and sausage biscuits.

In the meantime, he would put on his uniform
and do his job. He had opened up the cut on his arm
in the excitement the night before, so he cleaned the
wound and added more liquid stitches, thankful
Jimmy had left the tube behind. He showered,
dressed, and packed like any other morning, drinking
coffee from his insulated mug on the walk to his
office. He arrived almost an hour early and sat behind
his Resolute desk to do the class preparation he had
neglected the night before.

His composition students were scheduled to
finish their group papers, and the Major Authors
section would continue dissecting "The Cask of
Amontillado." He had prepared a list of discussion
questions over the summer when he developed the
course. He read over them and wondered what class
would be like without Nick. Would the other students
sense his lack of surprise when Nick didn't turn up?
Would he give himself away somehow?

He wondered how long it would take for the news
to get around. Logan would have found the body when
he got home from work. The police would have come
and kept him busy with questions for quite a while,
but he would have had the chance to call someone or
send a text. Someone would post the news online. Of

course, Logan might not have realized Nick was dead. He might have gone to bed thinking Nick was asleep at the desk, and the whole process wouldn't start until morning.

"I'll find out soon enough," William said, not intending to speak out loud.

There would be some kind of memorial service. William might be asked to speak. He would have to write his speech carefully and practice it in the mirror, make certain he gave the right impression, that neither his voice nor his face betrayed him. There would be a lot of work in the coming days.

"In early, I see," Danny said, appearing in the office doorway. "Are you feeling better?"

"Much," William said. "I think the worst has passed."

"Let's hope so. If it took you down, I don't want any of it. Glad you're on the mend."

"Thanks."

Danny walked away, and William listened to his footsteps, his keys in his door, the creak of the hinges. William would miss Samuels if he had to go away – to prison or on the run. He wasn't sure how he would handle it if he were convicted. He could get a lot of reading done in prison. It might not be that bad. He decided he would weigh the pros and cons later, if it became necessary. He needed to focus on his classes. He was down to thirty minutes to prepare.

The questions for "The Cask of Amontillado" were sufficient, but he might need to lecture a bit, to fill in the gaps where Nick would normally be speaking. He hadn't realized until that moment how much he had come to expect Nick's voice in his classes, how much he had accommodated. He wondered if Nick's choice of courses had been about the guilt over killing Ian. William wished he had been able to ask such questions, that he had been clear-minded enough to consider all the ramifications, all the repercussions.

Someone knocked on his door, and he looked up to find Jimmy, smiling, wearing a Hawaiian shirt. "Morning, little brother." He didn't wait for an invitation, just came in and took a seat.

"Going to a pawn shop today?"

"Yeah. I still haven't found a ring."

"What brings you here?" William was surprised by the visit, and even more surprised to find himself glad to see his brother. He smiled.

"Two things, actually," Jimmy said. "I was wondering if you'd come down to Augusta tomorrow evening and have dinner with me and Wendy. She'd really love to meet you. I meant to ask you last night, but in all the excitement, it just slipped my mind."

William laughed. "I can understand that."

"So what do you say?"

"Sure. I can do that. I'd like to actually."

"I'm glad to hear that, Billy. Really glad. William, I mean."

"What's she like?"

"Well, she's a nurse, of course. I told you that, didn't I?"

"Yes."

"She's real pretty. You know, for her age, but still." William nodded.

"She was locked up for a couple years when she's a teenager, so she understands. Knifed her stepfather for trying to take advantage. They wouldn't lock you up for that nowadays, but they did then."

"Dr. Baker, I can't believe you're here." Matthew Gibbard was at the door. "You're never here."

"I'm here during scheduled office hours," William said. "I've missed them only once this year. Only once in the last five years, as a matter of fact."

"Anyway," Gibbard said, "I really need to talk to you about that paper. I was going to let it go, but my girlfriend did the math last night, and if that paper stays a zero, the best I can do in your class is a C, and I have to have a B in your class because I'm on academic probation, and I have to have a C average, and I know I'm going to get a D in Dr. Ingraham's class." He finally took a breath and added, "That jerk," in a whisper.

Prison sounds very good just now, William thought. Of course, it would likely be full of guys like Matthew Gibbard.

"You, son, are a tact-free zone," Jimmy said.

"Tax free?"

"Tact, boy. You have none."

Gibbard looked to William, to Jimmy, and back to William.

"Look it up," William said.

Jimmy spelled it for him.

"We're having a conversation," William said. "If you want to discuss your zero for plagiarism, schedule an appointment with the dean. I'm sure she'll be happy to educate you on university policy. You're dismissed." William gave him the backhanded wave.

"No, Dr. Baker. That's not good enough. That grade is unacceptable. You have to change it." Gibbard's face had gone red, and he clenched his fists.

"Careful, boy," Jimmy said. "You have no idea who you're dealing with."

"The grade is final," William said. "The dean will tell you the same thing." He stood and went around his desk, getting almost nose-to-nose with Gibbard. "And don't even think of keying my car like you did Dr. Ingraham's."

Gibbard went white and stepped back outside the office.

"There'll be consequences for that," William said.

Gibbard didn't reply, just turned and left, walking as fast as he could, all but breaking into a run. William went back to his desk, sat, and looked to Jimmy, who was grinning.

"You said there were two things?"

"Yeah," Jimmy said. "I came to watch the show."

William shook his head.

"I have a small confession. Last night, I was not entirely honest about the contents of that cup."

"What was in it?"

"Ruffie, couple of sleeping pills, and a few laxatives."

"Nothing fatal?"

"Not in that dose. He woke up this morning with a headache, sitting in a pile of his own shit. How do you like that metaphor, professor? He probably won't remember what happened. We were just a bad dream."

"You had the drugs with you?"

"In case it was her."

William's mind raced. He was confused and angry and relieved, all at the same time. "Why?" He lowered his voice. "Why didn't you let me kill him?"

"When I went through his front door," Jimmy said, "I had an epiphany. That's the right word, ain't it? A flash of insight?"

William nodded.

"When you get like that, you never remember what happened. I couldn't deprive you of the satisfaction. I also thought it might keep us out of prison."

"I'm missing something."

Jimmy smiled. "That's 'cause I haven't told you the good part." He put his hand in his shirt pocket and pulled out a microcassette, tossed it on William's desk. William pointed at it, silently asking. "That's a copy. While you was looking for a vacuum, I took the tape. After I left you last night, I bought a couple of those recorders, hooked them up and made copies. There was a fella at Radio Shack who could not have been more helpful."

"Copies? How many? Where are the others?"

"Well, that one's yours. I have one." He patted his shirt pocket. "And I left the original in a recorder on the front seat of the lovely Dr. Rodgers' car."

"No." William hated to think how she would feel, hearing Nick's confession, finally learning what had happened to Eliza. She would come undone.

"Oh, yes," Jimmy said, "and that's not even the best part. I left Dad's gun, too. Loaded and ready."

"Why would you do that?"

"She's crazy. Any fool can see that. Her creepy house and her floppy-haired boy-toy. When she finds out what he did, she'll kill him. Probably right here this morning. We get revenge, and she gets the blame. Nice and clean."

"Jimmy, did you even consider who else might get shot? This is a school, with thousands of people wandering around."

Jimmy smiled. "I trust Dr. Rodgers to be precise."

"She's a friend of mine. I can't let her do that." William stood, heading for the lobby, heading toward her office, not sure she would be there, not sure where to look.

"Billy, wait." Jimmy grabbed his brother's arm. "It's her choice. Let her make it."

William shook him off and headed down the hall. Students stood in clumps, chatting. A few others sat on the couches, some studying, some talking. Nick was there, looking hungover and confused, a small bandage on his neck, moving his hands much slower than usual, elaborating on something to Charlotte Clements. His eyes widened at the sight of William.

"You will not believe..." Nick said, but the rest of the sentence was lost among screams.

William turned and saw students scattering, clearing the landing between the stairs and the lobby. Then he saw the cause: Heather walking fast, a microcassette recorder in one hand, Ian Baker's .45 in the other. She raised the gun and fired, aiming for Nick, William thought, but she was still too far away to be accurate with a handgun. She wasn't trained for that. There were more screams, people dashing down the hall and into the nearby classrooms. Office doors opened and quickly slammed shut.

Jimmy pulled William backward, dragging him down behind a couch. He wrestled free and stood, looking to see if anyone had been hit. The shot had missed high and put a hole in a poster for the study abroad program. Nick and Charlotte were huddled in front of the couch where they had been sitting. A couple of other students curled in the fetal position on the floor against the wall. William couldn't see their faces, couldn't be sure who they were. He raised his hands, half surrender, half a call for calm.

"Heather," he said, "you don't need to do this."

"He killed her," Heather said. "He killed my Eliza."

"No, he didn't."

"He did," she said, waving the recorder. "He admitted it."

"I didn't kill her," Nick shouted, not moving from his place behind the couch.

Charlotte pulled back, putting as much distance between her and Nick as possible without leaving the cover of the couch. She looked scared, but angry, too. Disgusted.

Heather pointed the gun at the couch.

"No," William shouted.

"He deserves it. He killed your dad, Will. It was him. That's on here, too."

"Charlotte's down there with him," William said. He pointed at the other students. "You'll hit the wrong person. You don't want that."

"Charlotte?" Heather called.

"Please don't shoot me," Charlotte said.

"Charlotte, honey, you can go. The rest of you, too." No one moved. "It's okay. I'm only going to shoot Nick. I promise." William walked over to them. "Don't you try to help him, Will. Don't you dare. What would your daddy think?"

William took Charlotte's hand and tried to pull her up, but she wouldn't budge. He let go and bent down, picked her up and started to walk away.

Nick grabbed his foot. "Help me," Nick said.

William couldn't be sure if Nick had forgotten the night before or if he was just panicked, asking for whatever help he could get. William jerked his leg free and kicked out, catching Nick's ear, just a glancing blow. He carried Charlotte to the edge of the hallway and set her on her feet. "Run," he said. He hadn't noticed Jimmy's movement, hadn't realized he was behind him. Jimmy sat Regina Seymour on her feet, told her to run, too. William looked over and saw the lobby was clear. The other student had gone down the hallway under his own power, whoever he had been. William looked to Heather, and she fired a shot into the couch.

"Stop," he shouted, but she didn't.

She took two quick steps toward the couch and fired another round, aimed low and into the base of the couch. That one found its mark, and Nick screamed. William couldn't see the wound. For a moment, he wasn't even sure there was one. Then the blood began to soak Nick's shirt.

"You got him, Heather," William said. "That's enough." He walked toward her, rounding the couch.

"No," she said. "I want to see him." She dropped the recorder on the floor and went to the couch. She grabbed the back and spun it around, exposing Nick, curled in a ball and bleeding. She stepped closer, stood right over him, and fired another round into his back.

"Heather," William said, "it's over. Give me the gun." He stepped closer still, putting out his hand.

She looked down at Nick, bleeding but still moving, writhing on the floor. She put the gun to his head and fired. The gore of the wound made William nauseous. He choked back bile and took another step toward Heather, his hand still out.

"No," she said, raising the gun to her own head.

William grabbed for the gun and caught the barrel. She jerked back, surprisingly strong, and he lost his grip. They both fell back a step, and she fired. The impact of the bullet took his right leg out from under him, and he went sideways, landing on his shoulder. It didn't feel the way he imagined it would, like a BB magnified some exponential amount, like an impact and radiation, an earthquake in his flesh. Instead, it was like a needle, huge and fast, sticking right through his thigh. Then the hot flow of blood. He looked at Heather, not sure what would happen next.

"Will, I'm sorry. I'm so sorry." She put the gun to her temple and pulled the trigger.

William closed his eyes and let himself roll over onto his back. He could hear Jimmy's voice, could tell he was moving, touching him, something.

CHAPTER 26

W illiam woke up in a hospital bed. He was groggy and couldn't make his eyes focus, but he was sure of that much. Jimmy was in a chair by the bed. He closed his eyes and woke up sometime later. He had no idea how long, but Jimmy was gone, and a woman he didn't know was in the chair. She was reading a book, but he couldn't focus long enough to read the title. She looked up at him.

"Jimmy had a work thing," she said. "He'll be back tomorrow. Next day at the latest."

William wanted to ask who she was, but he couldn't make his mouth work properly. His throat felt dry and cracked. The woman stood and took a cup with a straw in it from the bedside table, held it up to his lips. He took a small sip and then another.

~ ~ ~

He woke up again, not realizing he had fallen asleep. His head was clearer now. He could focus his eyes properly. Officer Phillips stood outside the open door of William's room. He could hear whispers, Phillips talking to someone William couldn't see. He thought he heard the low rumble of Kelvin's voice. The window blinds were open, and he could see it was day. He wasn't sure which day. It felt like Friday must have been a long time earlier, but it couldn't be later than Saturday or Sunday, could it?

He remembered being shot in the leg. It didn't seem that bad at the time. He was thirsty and found the water cup still on the bedside table, the straw still standing in it. He reached for it, but his arm shot through with pins and needles. He had to put it back down and wait for the feeling to pass. His other hand

had an IV in it. Something clear, which told him
nothing. They had stitched up the gash Martin had
given him. *Questions*, he thought, shaking his head.
There'll be questions. He tested his left arm again, and
it worked, still stiff and tingly. The water was too cold
and gave him a brain freeze. He had read about what
causes that, but he couldn't remember. Something to
do with the connections between nerve centers, he
thought. Maybe not. He let it pass and sipped more
slowly.

~ ~ ~

When he woke again, Officer Phillips still
whispered outside. William wanted to call out, to get
whatever would come next under way as soon as
possible. He tried to speak, but all that came out was a
garbled mutter. He drank more water. Phillips had
heard him, though, and turned to look. He seemed
pleased, happy even. William wondered if that would
be good news or bad, wondered what Phillips'
perspective was.

"Dr. Baker, you're awake. I thought I was going to
miss you again."

"Again?"

The woman from before, the one who had given
him the water, came in behind Phillips. She took the
chair, and Phillips stood at the foot of the bed. "He's
been checking in every few hours," the woman said.
She didn't seem to think this was a good thing.
William wasn't sure if she didn't like cops, didn't like
Phillips personally, or didn't like anyone bothering
him. She didn't like something; that much was clear.
She must have read William's confusion. "I'm
Wendy," she said. "Jimmy wanted me to look after
you till he gets back. You're friends have been by a few
times, asking after you. They'll be back tonight, I
expect."

Now that William's eyes were clear, he could see what Jimmy had meant. She had the shape of a middle-aged mother, but her face was still striking. He thought she must have been a knockout twenty years ago.

"Nice to finally meet you," he said.

"Likewise." She smiled, a genuine smile, but it flicked off as soon as she turned her gaze back to Phillips.

"How much do you remember?" Phillips asked.

"About being shot?"

"Yes."

William considered this, let that morning play back in his mind. "I remember it pretty well, I think. Time will tell. Some of it I probably won't be able to forget."

Phillips nodded. "I wanted to be the first to talk to you. We don't know each other very well, but I thought it would be easier if you had fair warning from someone you know."

"Fair warning?"

"There's a whole line of folks who want to talk to you. Ask questions. People above me at Osgood PD. SLED. FBI. Reporters. The shooting got a lot of attention. Word got around pretty fast. People know what you did."

William felt a wave of panic start in his stomach and roll in both directions. He took a deep breath and tried to cut it off.

"You and Jimmy are big heroes," Wendy said.

William turned to her, confused, and she looked back to Phillips. William looked at Phillips and shook his head.

"You don't remember?" Phillips asked. "You got in her way. Dr. Rodgers. Got those kids out of that lobby."

William covered his face with his hands, hoping he wouldn't give himself away. "Didn't seem heroic at the time," he said.

"The students tell it differently," Phillips said. "The other professors, too."

"How long have I been out?" William asked, trying to change the subject. "What day is it?"

"Sunday," Wendy said. "You were in surgery, and you've been fading in and out since yesterday."

William wondered if he'd been awake more than the two or three times he could remember. He hoped he didn't talk in his sleep.

"Your brother saved your life," Phillips said. "You took a bullet in the femoral artery. He put a tourniquet on the leg. Kept you from bleeding out before the paramedics could get in. They were a little slower than usual with the active shooter protocols. We had to declare the scene safe before they could come in."

William had a terrible flash of fear and lifted the sheet to make sure his leg was all there.

"You were lucky," Wendy said, smiling again. "The bullet missed the bone. A couple months of rehab is all."

"For a second there, I thought I'd be racing Mr. Berry down the greenway in matching scooters." He breathed a genuine sigh of relief.

Phillips laughed. "We're all real pleased you're okay, Dr. Baker."

"Thanks."

"I do have some difficult news, though." Phillips picked at his thumbnail, looked at the floor. "It seems your father's accident wasn't an accident." William tried to look surprised and confused. "Nicholas Fuller confessed to running him off the road on a tape that was found at the scene. It appears to be the thing that set her off. Dr. Rodgers, I mean. We're not sure why he made the tape or how it got to her. That's what the others will want to ask you. If you know anything about that."

William shook his head. "I'm afraid I can't help you there."

"Don't know how you could. I don't imagine you'd have been trying to stop her if you had known."

William shook his head again. "It's a lot to process."

"I'm sure."

Wendy cleared her throat. She was not subtle.

"Well," Phillips said, "I guess I should let you rest."

"Yes, you should," Wendy said.

"Just know we're all behind you. The whole force. Want to see you up and walking that greenway again real soon."

William nodded.

Phillips gave a small wave, something between a salute and a tip of the hat, and walked out.

"I hate cops," Wendy said.

"I hadn't noticed."

She laughed. "Jimmy said you were a smart ass."

"He would say that."

"You want some coffee, smart ass?"

"A Coke, actually, if you can get that in here."

"I'll see what I can do." She stood, patted him gently on the arm, and left.

William closed his eyes, tried to lie back and relax. He didn't know how to feel. He really would need some time to process, to come to terms with what he had seen and learned and done. There would be lies to tell. A necessary evil. He would have to tell the same ones over and over – to the police, to the reporters, to his students, to his friends. It would be the price of having revenge and getting away with it. He didn't like the idea much, but it was the cost of doing business, part of the job. He could handle it. He would put on his uniform and go to work.

Thank you for reading.
Please review this book. Reviews help others find New Pulp Press and inspire us to keep providing these marvelous tales.

If you would like to be put on our email list to receive updates on new releases, contests, and promotions, please go to NewPulpPress.com and sign up.

Thanks to...

My parents, who have always acted like my dreams were perfectly reasonable notions.

Jeff Allen, whose insight greatly improved this book.

Bess Park, whose faith in my work kept me on this path.

Jared Yates Sexton, whose counsel made the publishing process a lot less daunting.

CJ Wilson, who allowed his M1911A1 to grace the cover of this book.

The casts and crews of *Ask Me Anything*, *Stitches*, and *Some Other Context*, who gave my words hands and feet.

David Young, Jason Nanz, Kathryn Grayson, Merrimon Avenue Baptist Church, and Fusion, who have sustained me in innumerable ways.

Jesus, who daily saves me from myself.

ABOUT THE AUTHOR

Israel Allen is the son of a minister and an educator. He had lived in seven different towns by the time he was seven years old and has since resided in more than a dozen cities. Home is where his stuff is. He skipped his senior year at Giles County High School for the sole purpose of getting out of Pulaski, Tennessee, while he still could and entered Union University's Religion program at the age of seventeen. He completed his BA in 1995 and continued his education at Union, earning a Master of Education in 1997. He went on to cover education and politics for the *Citizen-Tribune,* pursue the ministry, serve in various public relations capacities for the governor of Tennessee, earn a Master of Fine Arts in Creative Writing at Southern Illinois University, taught at Piedmont Technical College and Lander University, then turned to playwriting and acting. Allen's short fiction has appeared in *The Wanderlust Review* and *The Bastille* (Paris).

NewPulpPress.com

www.ingramcontent.com/pod-product-compliance
Lightning Source LLC
Chambersburg PA
CBHW070550260626
47161CB00002B/563